COLLAPSE
DEPTH

TODD TUCKER

OTHER BOOKS BY TODD TUCKER

NON-FICTION

NOTRE DAME VS THE KLAN:
How the Fighting Irish Defeated the Ku Klux Klan

THE GREAT STARVATION EXPERIMENT:
The Heroic Men who Starved so that Millions Could Live

ATOMIC AMERICA:
*How a Deadly Explosion and a Feared Admiral
Changed the Course of Nuclear History*

FICTION

OVER AND UNDER

GHOST SUB

POLARIS

SHOOTING A MAMMOTH

"Oh God, thy sea is so great, and my boat is so small."

PRAYER OF BRETON FISHERMEN.
GIVEN ON A PLAQUE TO EVERY SUBMARINE
COMMANDING OFFICER BY ADMIRAL HYMAN RICKOVER,
THE FATHER OF THE NUCLEAR NAVY.

GLOSSARY OF ACRONYMS

1MC	An announcing circuit heard by the entire ship
2MC	An announcing circuit heard in the engine room
4MC	An announcing circuit used exclusively to announce serious casualties
7MC	An announcing circuit for communications between the EOOW and the OOD.
AC	Alternating Current
ASR	Submarine Rescue Ship
BCLU	Battery Charging Line Up
BRI	Bearing Repeater Indicator
BST Buoy	"Beast" Buoys, an emergency communications beacon
CAMS	Computerized Atmospheric Monitoring System
CNO	Chief of Naval Operations, the highest ranking officer in the Navy
CO	Commanding Officer
COD	Carrier Onboard Delivery
CODC	Commanding Officer's Display Console
COW	Chief of the Watch
DC	Damage Control or Direct Current
DCA	Damage Control Assistant, the junior officer in charge of the boat's damage control gear and Auxiliary Division.
DOD	Department of Defense
DR	Dead Reckoning, an estimate of position based on course, speed, and time
DSRV	Deep Submergence Rescue Vehicle

EAB	Emergency Air Breathing, a system of breathing masks that plug into fixed manifolds throughout the ship.
E Club	Enlisted Club
EDO	Engineering Duty Officer
EOOW	Engineering Officer of the Watch, the highest-ranking watchstander, and the only commissioned officer, in the engine room of a nuclear submarine.
ESM	Electronic Support Measures
ET	Electronics Technician, an enlisted rating
EWS	Engineering Watch Supervisor, the senior enlisted man in an operating engine room.
Fitrep	Fitness Report
GPS	Global Positioning System
Hipac	High Pressure Air Compressor
JO	Junior Officer, an officer on his first sea tour
LET	Logistics Escape Trunk
MBT	Main Ballast Tank
MCC	Missile Control Central
Medevac	Medical Evacuation
MM1	Machinist's Mate, First Class
MS1	Mess Specialist First Class, a head cook
NATO	North Atlantic Treaty Organization
Nav ET	Navigation Electronic Technician, enlisted men in charge of the ship's numerous electronic systems for navigation.
Navsea	Naval Sea Systems Command
Navsea-08	The title given both to the office in charge of Naval Nuclear Power, and the admiral at its head.
NIS	Naval Investigative Service

NOAA	National Oceanic and Atmospheric Administration
NTM	Notice to Mariners
ODAS	Ocean Data Acquisition System
O-5	An officer's rank: A commander in the navy, a Lieutenant Colonel in the Air Force, Army, or Marine Corps
O-6	An Officer's rank: a captain in the Navy, a Colonel in the Air Force, Army, or Marine Corps
OOD	Officer of the Deck, the top watch officer on a submarine at sea.
OS	Officers' Study
PD	Periscope Depth
POTUS	President of the United States
PRC	People's Republic of China, the Communist Nation of China
PSI	Pounds per Square Inch, a unit of pressure
QM1	Quartermaster First Class
RM1	Radioman, First Class
ROC	Republic of China, Taiwan
ROTC	Reserve Officer Training Corps, a source of commissioned officers consisting of training units at colleges and universities
RPM	Revolutions per Minute
S1-C	One of a series of prototype nuclear power plants used for testing and training naval operators. S1-C was located in Windsor, Connecticut.
SAS	Sealed Authentication System, used to validated launch coded for nuclear weapons
SGWL	Steam Generator Water Level, pronounced "Squiggle."
SOA	Speed of Advance
SRDRS	Submarine Rescue Diving and Recompression System
SSN	A nuclear-powered attack submarine

SSBN	A nuclear-powered ballistic missile submarine
Subpac	Commander of the Submarine Forces of the Pacific
TDU	Trash Disposal Unit
TEU	Twenty-foot Equivalent Unit, a measure of a cargo unit on a container ship.
TMA	Target Motion Analysis
USNA	United States Naval Academy
USNS	United States Naval Ship, a non-commissioned ship that is property of the US Navy.
USS	United States Ship, a designation given to commissioned ships in the United States Navy
VA	Veteran's Administration
VHF	Very High Frequency
X1J	A phone circuit connecting the captain to the officer of the deck.
XO	Executive Officer, the second-highest raking officer onboard

COLLAPSE DEPTH

PROLOGUE
EAST CHINA SEA

For three days, as the big container ship *Ever Able* steamed northward from Singapore, Captain Colin Wright listened to the Chinese military circuit. The Chinese had appropriated a radio frequency along with a huge rectangle of ocean, declaring to the seafaring world that both were off limits indefinitely. The Captain didn't understand a word of Chinese, although he could foresee a day when fluency in Chinese would be required in his profession. But, sensing that it was somehow important, he listened anyway.

He eavesdropped on their chatter in the mess hall while he ate, on the bridge while he stood watch, and in his stateroom as he slept. When he toured the vast cargo areas of the ship, he took with him a handheld radio so he wouldn't miss a second of the unintelligible conversations that had become his constant companion. He tried to decipher what he could from their tone, which sounded in turn bored, aggressive, frantic, and even taunting. The crew became used to the sound of static and Chinese voices that surrounded their brooding captain like a cloud.

On the third day, as he napped at his desk, he jerked awake. The fragments of a sad dream evaporated as he roused himself. He shook his head, trying to discern the reason for his waking.

All the chatter on the radio had stopped. The Chinese had gone silent.

He hurried to the bridge.

·   ·   ·

The bridge was atop the seven-story "house" that contained all their quarters, their mess hall, and hospital. Once underway, it was where the twenty-two man crew spent the vast majority of their time, even though it occupied but a small portion of the ship's massive volume. Almost all the other space was taken up by containers, the metal boxes designed to be lifted directly from the ship and placed onto either train cars or trucks. The ship was near its capacity of 1,164 TEUs, or Twenty-foot Equivalent Units, an unscientific measure of how many containers it could hold. For this leg of their journey they were carrying plastic pellets, Reebok shoes, tires, a variety of car parts from factories throughout Asia, and, he'd been proud to learn, five tons of food for the World Food Programme, destined for Cambodia.

He quietly stepped onto the bridge, where his third mate and a cadet were reliving their adventures in Singapore. They'd visited Orchard Towers, a legendary Singapore brothel that was a veritable shopping mall of the sex trade. It was known affectionately to sailors around the world as "four floors of whores."

"Captain," they both said, acknowledging him as he walked in.

"Reviewing my night orders?" he snapped.

"Captain..." stammered the third mate, surprised by the harshness of the Captain's tone and his gaze.

"Bullshit on B Deck, after watch," he said. "Right now I need you to mind my ship."

"Yes sir," they both said at once.

He stepped up to the radar screen, a plasma monitor with symbols for every ship in the tracking system. By scrolling the cursor over each, he could see their present course, speed, and the closest they would approach *Ever Able*. He noticed a cluster of ships in red near the coast of Taiwan, and scrolled over them.

"Are those the same warships we've been tracking?"

"Yes sir. They've pulled out of the restricted area...I wonder if the exercise is over."

"Interesting," said the captain. He hoped the Chinese were done with their games. It would explain the sudden radio silence as well. "But we'll continue staying out of their way."

He checked the ship's speed: near its maximum of 18 knots. He walked over to a chart table where the second mate had drawn out their course. Their track would take them closer for a few more hours, then, finally, they would start to open distance to the Chinese fleet. A rectangle made of bright red tape marked the off-limits area. The resulting detour would add a full day to their voyage to Shanghai. It galled Captain Wright both as a shareholder of the Evergreen Marine Corporation, and as a man who believed in the freedom of the seas with religious fervor.

The rise of Chinese commerce had been the great change of Wright's twenty-three year career at sea. Chinese ports were now the busiest in the world, and almost all his containers were either bound for China, or, in much greater numbers, contained the products of Chinese factories. But as China's industrial power grew, so too had its military. Once barely a force on the world's sea lanes, they were now flexing their muscle, and not just in Asian waters. They seemed unconcerned about the gentlemen's agreements that the world's merchant fleets had used to coexist with each other for centuries.

There were accents on the VHF radio that reassured him when he heard them, the voices he identified with traditional seafaring nations: Sweden, Ireland, Australia, and, of course, England. For much of his career, he'd known that his American voice on the airwaves had sometimes discomfited other seafarers: his accent marked him, to many, as potentially aggressive, arrogant, and even dangerous. There was a sense that the Americans had more power than they deserved or could safely wield. Now at the pinnacle of his career, when hearing those frenetic Chinese voices day and night, he understood that feeling. He walked to the far corner of the bridge, fiddled with the controls, verified again that the Chinese radio circuit had gone quiet.

"About time they shut up," said the third mate, trying vainly to defuse the tension.

They listened to the static for a few minutes together, when suddenly a few words broke through, a rapid burst of chatter that got their attention. The captain turned up the volume as they went quiet again. Then, from a single speaker came short words spoken at a regular, even pace.

Shi...jyo...bah...

Stepping away from the radio, Captain Wright looked ahead, seeing nothing but ocean as the words continued. The bridge was like a greenhouse, nothing but glass on all sides, and it was the kind of day that sailors lived for: clear, bright, and calm with smooth open water in all directions, nothing to hamper their journey forward. Even though he knew from his review of the radar screen that they were far out of visual range, he lifted his binoculars and stared in the direction of the Chinese fleet. The voice continued on the radio behind him, almost like a chant. Although he didn't recognize any of the words, there was something familiar about it that unnerved him.

Chee...lyo...woo...ssuh...

"Something wrong, captain?" His men stared, perplexed. The captain knew, somehow, that the chant was nearing its conclusion.

Sahn...urr...yee...QIDONG!

With that final, emphatic word, he realized what he was listening to: a countdown.

"*Right full rudder*!" he ordered. The third mate jumped to comply. Wright knew from looking at the chart that a turn to starboard was the quickest way to open distance from the exercise area. The giant container ship began to respond slowly. A shrill alarm sounded on the radar console.

The captain stepped to the screen: a red arrow with an open circle around it had appeared between them and the Chinese fleet. Under it were the words *unidentified contact*.

"What is it?"

It disappeared briefly from the screen, and then reappeared, having closed half the distance to *Ever Able* in seconds.

"She can't be moving that fast," said the third mate, looking at the approaching blip in disbelief, fooled into thinking that the new radar contact was a ship, because the computer had, by default, assigned it that symbol.

Captain Wright ran out the door the starboard bridge wing, binoculars still in hand.

Spotting a small, fast-moving object on the ocean was extremely difficult, but Wright had good eyes and a lifetime of experience staring across the waves in search of peril. He saw the exhaust first, a triangle of intense yellow light behind the missile that was moving directly toward them. A finally honed instinct told them that they were on a collision course.

"All stop!" he yelled, a last desperate attempt to save the ship.

But *Ever Able* was doomed. The missile slammed into the hull amidships, just above the waterline.

λ

BOOK ONE
UNDERWAY

Ensign Brendan Duggan stood at the opening to the massive diesel fuel oil tank, located near the center of the big submarine. The tank was empty, for the moment, except for a lone, unseen enlisted man whose rhythmic banging with a rubber mallet sounded like a mournful gong. When the petty officer was done, Duggan would climb in. It was his second day on the boat.

He had been invited to enter the empty tank by Lieutenant Danny Jabo, who stood there waiting with him, casually fingering one of the twelve large bolts that had been removed to give them access through a twenty-two inch hole. There was a folder of miscellaneous paperwork on the deck: the certification that the tank's air was safe to breathe, a form for Jabo to sign upon completion of their inspection, and a copy of the danger tags that would (theoretically) keep shut all the valves that, if opened, would flood the tank with either seawater or diesel fuel. While they waited, Duggan read through it all earnestly, more eager to make a good impression on the lieutenant than he was to actually study the information.

In the strictest legal sense, Jabo barely outranked Duggan. They were both junior officers on their first sea tour: Jabo near the end of his, Duggan at the very beginning. While Duggan still held the rank of Ensign, the rank given to him along with his diploma at the Academy, Jabo had been promoted twice, first to lieutenant j.g. (junior grade), and then to full lieutenant. So Jabo had been in the Navy just a few years longer than Duggan, but those years were, importantly, sea time: five long patrols on a nuclear submarine. Duggan had exactly zero days underway. But the most important difference between them was something unquantifiable, something not easily reduced to pay grade or days at sea. Jabo was hot shit. He was the Junior Officer all the enlisted men wanted to work for, the one the department heads wanted to mentor, the one the other JOs wanted to emulate.

"You ready?" said Jabo with his mild Tennessee twang.

"I think so," he said, trying to sound somewhere between too nervous and too confident.

"You know the only requirement is that an officer close it out—you don't need your dolphins. So you can go in alone if you want."

Duggan hesitated for a minute, saw that Jabo was joking, and exhaled nervously.

"You're lucky we're doing this," said Jabo. "This is a tough evolution to see. Impossible to get underway."

"Yes," said Duggan, squelching the urge to say, "Yes sir." Even though Jabo did outrank him slightly, junior officers didn't talk to each other that way. But Jabo had that kind of aura. It made Duggan mildly jealous, as the new guy, months away from having anybody respect him for anything. He also fought down the impulse to resent the fact that an ROTC guy like Jabo could rise to the top—he felt like four years of celibacy and eating shit at Annapolis should entitle an Academy guy to hold that role. That had been the promise, that the ROTC guys were barely competent part-timers, while their years of toil at Annapolis would make them military superstars. But despite getting his degree at a school with frat parties and pompon girls, Jabo was clearly an outstanding officer. And Duggan had seen Jabo's wife, Angi, at the farewell party the night before, a redheaded, athletic knockout, the kind of girl he imagined would turn heads even at a school full of southern beauties. Another reason to resent his monastic life at the academy, another reason to be jealous. But, in spite of all that…Jabo was just impossible to dislike.

"He's comin'," said Jabo. Duggan heard it too. The gonging had stopped, replaced by footsteps on the iron rungs of the ladder that were bolted to the inside of the tank. Light from a flashlight grew in intensity as the petty officer neared, until his head popped out of the manway.

There was no graceful way to exit the tank. The petty officer handed Jabo his flashlight and rubber mallet, which Jabo placed on the deck before grabbing his outstretched arms and pulling him through. He got to his feet, took a deep breath, put his hands on his hips, and looked Duggan up and down.

"You the new guy? Sir?"

"That's me," said Duggan, trying again to strike a balance between confidence and modesty. He got the distinct impression that the enlisted man...Renfro, that was his name...was waiting for him to say or do something stupid that he could report back to an amused crew. Renfro had a pencil thin mustache and that muscular, small build that seemed characteristic of so many submariners, standard issue along with the hard, challenging stare. All three of them were wearing identical, insignia-free green coveralls for the occasion, not even a nametag among them. But no one observing the scene would have had any trouble picking out who among them was the respected lieutenant, who was the experienced petty officer, and who was the boot ensign.

"You an Academy guy?"

"That's right."

"Hmm," said Renfro, nodding his head with disapproval. Renfro was "qualified," a wearer (when in a normal uniform) of the coveted silver dolphins. This meant that despite the difference in their nominative ranks, Renfro outranked Duggan in an unofficial, but very important way. It would be months of non-stop work, study, and endless on-the-job training before the captain pinned dolphins on Duggan's chest. (Closing out a tank was one of about two hundred "practical factors" he had to complete along the way.) Furthermore, Renfro was an "A Ganger," a member of Auxiliary Division, the men in charge of the dirtiest, most important equipment on the boat: the diesel engine, the oxygen generators, all the ship's damage control equipment. They made the claim, with much justification, that they were the Navy's truest submariners.

"You ready?" said Jabo.

"Yes," said Duggan. The dark tank didn't seem all that inviting, but he suddenly wanted to get out from under Renfro's hard gaze.

Jabo went in first, somehow effortlessly squeezing his considerable frame through the manway. Duggan followed him, while Renfro stood watch at the entrance.

"Don't worry sir," said Renfro as they descended. "I won't let them start filling it up 'til you're half way up the ladder."

"We appreciate it," said Jabo.

Duggan climbed down the iron rungs, which were welded directly to the side of the tank. The side of the tank was also the concave side of the ship, making it tricky to reach the next slippery step as they curved outward, away in the darkness, most of his weight hanging from his hands rather than supported by his feet, until he was halfway down and the hull curved back.

The darkness of the tank and the geometry of the ladder made it impossible to see how far he had to go; it was deeper than he imagined. He felt himself growing tense as he went further, thought about the single valve handle and the listless watchstanders that were the only things standing between him and thousands of gallons of diesel fuel. As he got deeper, the air in the tank grew thicker, harder to breathe, the smell a combination of diesel fuel and the sea, a more concentrated version of what permeated the entire ship. He kept his eyes on the manway above him, his only escape. It got smaller as he descended, like a full moon in a black sky.

Jabo had navigated the steps deftly and waited at the bottom, swinging the flashlight on its lanyard, making the shiny walls of the tank seem to sway.

"Okay, you know why we're here?" said Jabo. His voice echoed metallically. Duggan realized that he still clung on to the bottom rung, afraid to lose contact with it in case Jabo dropped his light, or the batteries died. He forced himself to let go.

"Duggan? Why are we here?"

"To close out the tank."

"You know what that means?"

"Make sure there's nothing left down here?"

"Like tools and stuff? Sure. Good answer. And?" He held up the mallet.

"Sound shorts?"

"Sound shorts, anything loose. We'll bang on everything, make sure it's all squared away. Because if there's something rat-tlin' around down here, it will be impossible to fix at sea. And remember, we're a submarine...we don't like making noise. Any time we empty a tank like this and do work, before we're done, a qualified enlisted man closes it out, then an officer verifies. Do you know why this tank is empty?"

"We did some maintenance, right?"

Jabo nodded, and pointed his flashlight to a corner of the tank, where a pipe rose like a stalagmite, extending the full height of the space. The walls of the tank gleamed like glass in the beam, the steel preserved pristinely by the blanket of fuel that normally covered it. "We had to fix that: the level detector. You know how that works?"

Duggan nodded. "No...sorry."

"That's okay...hell, you just got here. The tank is always full. As we burn diesel fuel, we let in water. The fuel, being about fif-teen percent less dense, floats atop the water. The sensor floats atop the water-fuel interface. So as the tank empties of fuel oil, the sen-sor actually rises. Keeps the tank full of something all the time, which helps shield the people tank from the reactor." He knocked his flashlight against the aft wall of the tank.

"Cool," said Duggan.

"Yeah, those fuckers think of everything. One more question: how much fuel does this tank hold?"

"Thirty-five thousand gallons," said Duggan, proud of himself for knowing the answer. Right before coming down, he'd seen the tanker truck on the pier, the hoses already extended, ready to send the cargo gushing into the tank where he stood.

"Good job. You have any idea why we carry that much diesel fuel?"

The question surprised Duggan. He hadn't thought it was based on anything…it was just how much the tank held. He was struck by how many things there were to know inside an empty tank…and they weren't trivial, either, they were actually important, capacities and specs developed by some of the finest engineers in the world. He contemplated how many hours he would have to spend at sea before he knew everything he was supposed to know about this giant boat.

"I'll give you a hint," said Jabo. "It's based on a theoretical casualty in which we lose all power except the diesel engine, and this much fuel would allow us to steam for a certain number of hours at a certain number of knots, enough hours to get us out of harm's way. The theory goes."

"I'll look it up."

"Then get back with me and I'll sign your book. Will that be your first signature?"

Duggan nodded.

"Holy shit! What an honor. You owe me a beer when we get back."

Far above them, Renfro stuck his head through the hatch and yelled down. "Hey, topside wants to know what's taking so long. Are you guys blowing each other?"

"Yeah," said Jabo. "But we're almost done."

He handed Duggan the mallet. "Here, start banging on shit."

·   ·   ·

The navigator sat huddled over a chart in a darkened corner of the submarine's control room, frantically making revisions during the last few hours of the *USS Alabama's* refit. He was a small man burdened with many secrets.

For example: he knew the combination of the inner SAS safe, the safe-within-a-safe that held the sealed authentication codes that would allow the launch of a nuclear missile. That series of four double-digit numbers was so secret that he was not allowed to write it down, and he had nightmares about being summoned to radio at the start of World War III and being unable to remember it, his faulty memory removing *Alabama* from strategic service as surely as an enemy torpedo. And, as navigator, he knew the exact locations of their patrol areas, the vast swaths of ocean where Ohio-class submarines maintained their vigils, within missile range of their targets in China and eastern Russia. That kind of targeting information was so secret, classified beyond Top Secret, that even the name of the classification was unutterable to the vast majority of the ship's 154 man crew.

He knew the ship's top speed: not as fast as many novelists speculated, slower than a good speed boat, but impressive enough to those who understood how quietly their 18,000 ton warship could move beneath the ocean at that speed. And he knew the ship's test depth, the deepest at which they ever operated, the depth at which their systems were tested against the maximum sea pressure they should ever face. More secret still, he knew the ship's collapse depth, the depth at which engineers estimated that the hull would finally succumb to the pressure of the millions of tons of water that surrounded them. It was striking what sea pressure could do to the works of man at those depths, the way water could turn into a force as solid and destructive as any weapon. Their XO had a standard lecture he liked to give about the nature of submarining, how seawater was their only real enemy. Torpedoes and depth charges just allowed the enemy inside.

Unlike the ship's relatively unimpressive top speed, its maximum depth would be striking to anyone knowledgeable about diving and submersibles, a very large number that was a monument to the engineering marvel that was a Trident Submarine. But, as the navigator knew and was reminded of every time he so much as glanced at the small, italic numbers that dotted every one of his charts: even that large number was very much smaller than the depth of the ocean almost everywhere that they operated. Another favorite monologue of the XO's: he would hold his hand out at waist-height, the distance to the deck representing the depth of the Pacific. Test depth is here, he would say, pointing to a spot about four inches below his palm. The submarine could travel deep, but the Pacific was very much deeper, a kind of biblical abyss that was difficult for the mind to grasp, even the minds of men who'd spent their whole lives at sea.

But the navigator had another, even darker secret, one more frightening than a forgotten safe combination or the depth at which a submarine becomes destroyed by a heartless ocean, a secret that tortured him as he tried to stay focused on the charts: he knew the ship's mission. Along with the captain and the XO, he'd seen the new orders that he feared would doom them. Doom *humanity*. As navigator he not only knew about it: he had to help plan it, and plot their course right into the belly of the beast. He envied the rest of the crew in their ignorance, their hectic, boisterous preparations for patrol.

"Nav, are you alright?"

The navigator looked up, startled. The Duty Officer, Lieutenant Maple, was staring at him from the conn. He'd stopped signing the thick stack of red DANGER tags in front of him and stared with concern.

"Yes. I'm fine."

"You're bleeding."

The navigator looked where Maple was pointing. He'd been jamming the point of his dividers into his knee. He'd stabbed right through the fabric of his khakis, into his flesh. Blood ran down his leg into a dark red puddle on the deck.

.   .   .

The next morning, Jabo waited outside the Captain's stateroom with his single-page letter of resignation in hand. He hadn't wanted it to be this way, wanted a few more days to warm up to the task, but as with so many of his plans over the last nine years, this had been preempted by the needs of the navy. They'd been ordered to sea early for reasons that had not yet been revealed, and he had to get this letter in the captain's hands before the final mail call, if he actually expected to get out of the Navy at the earliest opportunity: five years to the day after he received his commission from the ROTC unit at Vanderbilt. The ship was still on the surface and rolled gently in the five foot swell that was following them out to deep water. After three years at sea, Jabo knew intuitively that if the rolling was bad inside the protected waters of the sound, they were in for a rough transit to Point Juliet, the earliest they could submerge. The XO walked out of the Captain's stateroom, a wry smile on his face, paused at the sight of him. Like Jabo, he had a letter in his hand, but his was printed on fine official stationary.

"Danny have you heard anything about this girl baby shit?" he asked, waving the letter. The XO was short. But he was solid and spry, with a boxer's build and attitude. His shaved, gleaming head enhanced his tough guy look. There were legends in the submarine fleet about his physical strength, tales of bar fights he'd broken up in Subic Bay and boxing matches he'd won at the Academy. He was a submarine officer of the oldest school, fluent in profanity, torpedo targeting, and dismissive of protocol. Jabo agreed with the consensus that they were lucky to have him.

Jabo was startled by the question. "Sir?"

"The rumor-of-the-month: that radiation on a nuclear submarine means you'll only have girl babies. Have you ever heard this?"

Jabo nodded. "Actually I have, sir. Last patrol in maneuvering they were talking about it, after Chief Palko had his third kid."

The XO furrowed his brow. "Yeah, that dickhead does have three girls, doesn't he? I'll have to get on his ass about that...it's starting to be a problem. Somebody just wrote their congressman asking off the boat because of this bullshit."

"Palko's not the only one," said Jabo. "I remember them going through the numbers...something like eight out of the last nine babies born to crew members have been girls."

The XO grinned and stepped in closer. "So you believe this shit too Jabo? Think neutrons are doing something to kill off all your boy sperm?"

"I'm just saying..."

"You know Jabo, one of the things we ask of our junior officers is to not be stupid. So if you hear anybody contributing to this bullshit...help me put a stop to it."

"Aye, aye sir."

"What the fuck is that?" he said, suddenly turning his attention to the letter in Jabo's hand.

"Sir, if you don't mind, I'd like to show it to the captain first."

"Just what I was afraid of: a resignation letter. Another JO heading for the fuckin' beach. I take it Microsoft was impressed with your resume?" He nodded his head toward the Captain's stateroom. "Go on in, Jabo." He stomped down the passageway, whistling loudly and cheerfully.

Jabo knocked on the open door. "Captain?"

"Come in Danny." A captain could call a junior officer by his first name, but the reverse was never true. The fatherly Captain Shields was calming contrast to the XO, the two complementing each other as they led *Alabama* to its place at the top of all the squadron's rankings. He had salt and pepper hair and a perpetual twinkle in his eye. Unlike the XO, he'd acquired no legends about his physical strength, although he had been an All-America swimmer at the Academy. But he had built a rock-solid career, culminating with his command of *Alabama*, on steady leadership and his almost freakishly comprehensive knowledge of submarine nuclear power. While sailors told stories about a push up contest the XO had won against a Marine Corps General, the captain was of a different caste. He looked like a man who not only could solve quadratic equations in his head; he looked like he was doing it all the time, effortlessly.

Jabo shuffled in and sat on the only other chair in the stateroom. "Captain, I've decided to resign my commission."

The captain nodded thoughtfully, waited a beat, and then took the letter from his hands. He took his time reading it, and then handed it back. "I refuse to accept this."

Danny waited, not knowing what to do, hoping the captain was joking.

"Sir?"

"I don't understand Danny—you've always seemed like you enjoy your job to me."

"I do like my job. And I love this ship."

"So why get out? You can keep the fun going for twenty years or more, just like me."

"I'm not sure it's as much fun if I stay in. I like standing watch and driving the boat. Not writing training plans and filling in spreadsheets."

"You think that's what I do all day, Danny?"

"Not you, sir—but the department heads, frankly, yes. And that's what I'd be doing next if I stayed in."

"Believe it or not, Danny, being a department head can be fun too."

"Like the navigator?"

The captain grimaced. "Come on, Danny. The nav isn't a particularly good example. He's at the end of a very demanding tour, five patrols as a navigator is a very long time."

"It's just..."

"So you're afraid you won't have as much fun as a department head? That's the reason?"

"Captain, if you'll read my letter, you'll see that it's not. I also wonder sometimes what we're doing out here."

"You don't think what we do is important?"

"That's right, captain." Jabo felt ashamed to say it, but it was true. "We're still running a platform that was originally designed to lob missiles at a nation that no longer exists. I feel like we're just shadow boxing out here."

"Listen carefully, Danny. Driving this boat and keeping it safe is important—maybe the most important thing you'll ever do, certainly more important than chasing the next bonus at Microsoft." The boat had lost their last two junior officers to Microsoft and it clearly irked the command. "And, if you don't like our mission, get on an attack boat for your next tour—they're in the fight."

"Not really. I mean, I know they may get to go more places than us, support battle groups and ops like that, but it's no different. Our enemies use box cutters now—you can't really fight them with a nuclear submarine."

Shields sat back in his chair and looked Jabo over. He was smiling. "Are you sure there's nothing else going on here?"

The junior officer and his Captain looked at each other for a minute. Unlike the navigator, Jabo often felt like he had no secrets—it was something about the tight-knit community of shipboard life that he had never quite gotten used to. And, for the past six weeks, he'd had a big secret: his wife, Angi, was pregnant. If the captain had somehow intuited that pregnancy, than perhaps he had also intuited Jabo's strong desire to not have a Navy family, to have his child be a Navy brat. He'd seen far too many screwed up families in the Navy, and no matter what he said in his letter of resignation, that was one of the best reasons he could think of for getting out. His wife was just starting to show the pregnancy on her slender frame, and she'd already entered the Byzantine world of military medicine, Champus, Tri-Care, and the navy hospital. Jabo wondered, as he looked at the Captain, if the secret was out.

"Captain, I've explained myself as best I can in my letter."

"Okay. But I wasn't kidding. I'm not going to accept your letter."

"But—"

"I know, you're worried about missing your twelve-month window. You won't. I can't tell you all the details right now, but we're going to pull into port in a couple of weeks. If you still want to get out, I'll endorse your letter then. But I think in the meantime you may see that it's still possible to do some vitally important missions on a nuclear submarine. If I'm wrong, then I'll endorse your letter and this will be your last patrol. Okay?"

Jabo nodded. He actually felt a sense of relief about not yet having his letter in, as well as a sense of excitement about learning whatever awaited them in their patrol orders. There'd been rumors, of course, especially with the sudden departure. "Okay, Captain. Thank you."

"Thank you Danny—thanks for giving the Navy another two weeks."

They looked at each other for another moment, Jabo waiting to be dismissed.

"You know, Danny, it is possible to raise a good family, to be a good family man,

and be in the Navy."

Jabo nodded without saying anything. It was a discussion he didn't want to have. The captain had a wife, and two daughters, and Danny couldn't tell him that he thought they all suffered because of the captain's chosen career. But moreover: *he* couldn't do it. I can't spend another sea tour away from Angi, he thought, another year where I see her more in my dreams than in real life. And if the captain asked him in response, don't you think I love my wife? Jabo would have had to answer: I must love my wife more. It was the one vanity he allowed himself.

There was a firm rap on the door and the XO let himself in. He was agitated, and not in the bemused way he had reacted to the rumor about girl babies. Jabo wondered briefly if his resignation had bothered him that much. He dismissed that idea as the XO stepped back out and waved impatiently at Jabo to exit.

As they traded places in the captain's stateroom, the XO said something about the Nav. He shut the stateroom door behind him.

Jabo walked to his stateroom, grateful for several things. He was grateful that his beautiful wife was pregnant with their child. He was grateful that, as hard as it was, he'd told Captain Shields of his plans to leave the Navy. And, as he walked up the ladder to the control room to take the watch, he was grateful that he'd been able to have that talk with the understanding Captain Shields, and not his predecessor, Captain Mario Soldato. That guy was an asshole.

.   .   .

"What's up?" said the captain.

The XO remained standing, running his hand across his smooth bald scalp. "It's the navigator. He's gone and done something weird."

Captain Shields leaned back and laced his fingers across his stomach, his face grim, awaiting details.

"Lieutenant Maple said that yesterday in control he stabbed himself in his leg with his dividers. Repeatedly. Got blood everywhere. Apparently Maple took a day to think this over before telling me."

The Captain raised an eyebrow. "What did you say?"

"I told him to shut the fuck up about it."

"Have you talked to the nav?"

"No sir, not yet. I wanted to talk to you first, because I know we don't have much time."

The captain paused. "Time for what?"

"To get him off the boat! Let's get him off with the fucking mail."

The captain waited before responding. He knew the XO had never liked the navigator. In fact, the navigator was a tough man to like. But part of it was that each man was, in his way, a perfect representation of the two different tribes of submarine officers. One was a torpedo-hurling warrior who trusted his instincts. The other, a highly-schooled, bookish, technical expert. The tension between them was as old as the *Nautilus*, the Navy's first nuclear submarine, and the captain realized that he was probably closer to the nav's end of the spectrum than the XO's. "Mike, do you think they have a spare navigator waiting for us on that tug?"

"Fuck sir, I don't know. I'll do it, I'll be the goddamn navigator. Or let's give Jabo a battlefield promotion. I trust him more than I trust that crazy fucking Mark Taylor."

"That's enough," said the captain sternly.

"Yes sir."

They both paused long enough to let some of the pressure out of the room.

"You really think it's that bad?" said the captain. "Bad enough to kick the guy off the boat? Scuttle his career?"

"I really don't know, captain. Maybe this whole thing just confirms a feeling I've always had about the Nav—I don't know."

"I think if you'll really ask yourself—this isn't the craziest thing either one of us has ever seen a man do at sea. Not even close."

"Very true, Captain. But this is our *navigator*. And with so much at stake this patrol…"

"Exactly. And it's already too late for us to turn around, to ask for a new navigator. He's done a stellar job for five previous patrols, and I'm confident he will this time too, before he goes on a well-earned shore tour."

The XO sensed that the decision had been made. "Aye, aye, captain." He turned to leave.

"XO?"

"Yes sir?"

"Pay a visit to Maple. Tell him there's no point in spreading this around. We don't need stories like this getting around with the crew, undermining their confidence in their leadership."

"Aye, aye sir," said the XO. But he knew the story had proba-bly already circled the boat twice. They both knew.

.   .   .

Seaman Hallorann was nineteen years old, just two weeks out of boot camp. He learned quickly that his most urgent priority on-board *Alabama* was to "qualify," to complete all the requirements of a yellow booklet that took him through every compartment of the ship, after which he would receive the coveted silver dolphins to wear upon his uniform. With that goal in mind, as the ship pitched and rolled its way to sea, he found his way to Maneuvering, a tiny box of a room in the upper level of the engineroom. A line in his yellow book read: *identify and observe Maneuvering watchstand-ers.* Sounded easy enough.

"Request permission to enter?" he asked, mimicking a chief he'd observed entering and leaving maneuvering before him.

An officer looked up at him from a thick black book, slightly surprised, slightly amused. His name tag said *Hein*. Hallorann knew he was the Engineering Officer of the Watch, or EOOW, pronounced to rhyme like the sound that a cat makes. He sat be-hind a small raised desk, looking at the backs of three enlisted watchstanders.

"Reason?"

Hallorann held up his yellow book. "Qualifications, sir?"

"Name?"

"Seaman Hallorann, sir."

Hein turned to his watch team. "Should we let him in?"

"Sure," said the one closest to him, without turning around. "This watch is in danger of becoming boring."

"Enter maneuvering, Hallorann."

It was a perfect cube of a room covered on all sides by lights and dials. Beneath the small desk of the EOOW were two rows of thick, black books like the one the lieutenant was reading. Hallorann considered himself a smart guy, had been told that by others: it was one of the reasons the Navy wanted him on a submarine. But he wondered how anyone could ever master all the information available in that small room.

"So, Hallorann, what are we doing out here?"

Hallorann knew he was being fucked with—and that being fucked with would be one of his primary duties until he pinned on his dolphins. Still, he preferred to give an answer that didn't make him sound like a complete shit head. "Strategic deterrence?" he said.

A couple of the watchstanders actually glanced away from their panels at that, impressed.

"Wow, pretty good," said the one on the right, who looked to be running the ships electrical system, a control panel that contained dials marked in units familiar to Hallorann: volts, amps, and kilowatts. "Officer material."

"That is good," said Lieutenant Hein. "And that would normally be correct. But that doesn't seem to be the answer this patrol. Any idea what we're doing here this patrol?"

"It's a trick question," said the one of the left, the steel wheel of the throttles in his hand. He seemed to be concentrating harder than the rest, and Hallorann got the feeling that the ship's rolling motion was making his job harder, as he constantly adjusted the position of the wheel in his hands with each pitch and roll.

The movement seemed to be intensifying. "No one knows what the fuck we're doing out here on this patrol."

"We're going somewhere, that's all I care about," said the watchstander in the middle.

"You're a lucky fuck, Hallorann," said the electrical operator. "I made four patrols before I went anywhere. And that was just Pearl. God only knows where we're gonna end up on this run."

"I'll bet the lieutenant knows," said the thottleman.

"You bet wrong," said Hein. "I'm a mushroom too right now."

"You know why we're mushrooms?" asked the Electrical Operator.

Hallorann nodded.

"Because they keep us in the dark and feed us shit."

"It's something different this patrol, that's for sure," said Hein. "Maybe we'll end up with some kind of unit citation."

"I'll just be happy if I just get one day in a liberty port," said the electrical operator. "Not all that concerned about the implications for my career."

They plunged dramatically. Hallorann barely stopped himself from falling into the back of the electrical operator. An alarm sounded on the far left panel. "Watch it!" said Lieutenant Hein, and the throttleman spun the throttles to the right as all the others made adjustments.

"Screw came out of the water," said the throttleman, as things settled back down.

"Steam flow hit 80 percent," said the middle watchstander. "It was WAY out of the water." Outside maneuvering, something crashed loudly to the deck.

Hein looked a little flustered. He spoke into the microphone on his desk, the words echoing outside maneuvering. "Engineering Watch Supervisor, verify stow for sea." A few seconds later, the chief acknowledged the order into a mike.

"Shit falling all over the place out there," said the electrical operator.

"Fuck, I can't wait till we submerge," said Hein.

It went silent for a minute as things got back to normal. Hallorann felt Hein looking past him, a little blankly. He wondered if he had been in there long enough to get the signature in his yellow book; he felt the need to speak.

"It's pretty rough, isn't it?"

All three enlisted watchstanders turned with raised eyebrows, and Hein grinned.

"This your first time at sea?" asked the throttleman.

"Yeah—how about you?"

The throttleman, without turning, pulled a ballpoint pen from his shirt pocket. "Hey, shit stain, see this pen? It has more sea time than you do."

The reactor operator, in the center, chimed in. "I've got more time eating ice cream at test depth than you've got underway, nub."

Hallorann laughed at that.

"Is the motion getting to you, Hallorann?" Lieutenant Hein asked, still grinning. "All this rocking and rolling?"

Hallorann nodded. "Not really."

"It's okay....everybody feels seasick once in a while."

"Yeah," said the electrical operator. "There was like three inches of puke in the aft head this morning. Mostly looked like scrambled eggs, but I saw some McDonald's fries floating around in there, too, that one last meal on the beach."

The reactor operator spoke up. "There was a line down there at both heads this morning, so Leer had to puke in his hat. It's the only one he's got so he was washing it out in the sink so he could keep wearing it."

"Is that the same hat he shit in?" asked Hein. He turned to Hallorann. "He kept his hat tucked into his back pocket, and once last patrol he sat down to take a shit and the hat fell in the commode without him realizing it, and he took a big dump in it. Couldn't flush it like that, had to pull it out, dump the shit in the bowl, and carry on."

Hein waited for him to react. Hallorann suddenly realized what was happening. They were trying to make him sick...it was a game to play with the new guy. But he still wasn't feeling seasick in the least, he appeared to be one of those guys immune to the ailment, despite a life spent landlocked. And if they thought they could make him sick merely by telling gross stories...Hallorann had spent every summer of high school working at a chicken slaughterhouse outside of Fort Dodge, Iowa. He had a pretty high tolerance.

The throttleman remained focused on his panel, but he seemed like he'd been saving something. "What's your name again, nub?"

"Hallorann."

"Hallorann. Right. Don't listen to these guys, honestly. But if you ever start to feel a little queasy, I know a cure."

Hallorann didn't say anything. The motion of the ship had changed, from kind of a violent pitching up and down, to a roll that seemed to move them in every direction, like a rock tumbling in space.

"OK, take it easy. Mind your panels," said Hein. He was again staring past Hallorann, tiny beads of sweat forming on his upper lip.

"One second, sir, I just want to help the new guy out with my seasickness cure. Wanna hear it Hallorann?"

"Sure."

"Just go to the mess decks, okay, and get one of those ice cream bowls."

"Okay."

"Fill it all the way to the top with mayonnaise..."

"Okay."

"And then microwave it until the mayo is just steaming hot. Then eat the whole thing, every spoonful."

Suddenly Lieutenant Hein pushed Hallorann away from his desk. He stuck his head down into a tiny trashcan that was lashed to the side of it, and began puking dramatically. The three enlisted watchstanders in maneuvering cheered like it was New Year's Day.

. . .

Hallorann excused himself from maneuvering, thinking it wasn't a good idea to participate in the mocking of the young officer. He considered going back forward, but he found himself interested in the engine room, and wanted to explore it further. He'd overheard another enlisted man say that you could actually see the main shaft where it penetrated the hull, and watch it turn, the very thing that propelled them through the water. That was intriguing enough to seek out. It had to be aft, the most aft thing on the boat, he assumed, and he resolved to walk that direction until he found the shaft or until someone told him to leave. He retrieved some foam earplugs from his pocket and shoved them back into his ears.

He passed maneuvering into a space that opened up, a place of large machines and bright fluorescent light. A mechanic was on watch, taking a reading and recording it on a clipboard. His sleeves were rolled up, revealing large, ornate tattoos with Japanese characters adorning images of dragons. He looked up from his clipboard and nodded with a smile. Hallorann began to walk toward him, to ensure his presence there was okay, and to accept help if it was offered.

Two steps later, however, Hallorann was almost leveled by a noise so loud that it had a physical force; he could feel it impacting and deforming his ear drums right through the foam plugs. The noise was so loud that it was meaningless to try to determine what direction it came from, it was everywhere, filling the space, pressurizing it. He fought the strong urge to run in fear. He watched the reaction of the watchstander with the clipboard, to see if what he was hearing was normal. He could see in the startled expression that it was not. The watchstander seemed almost as confused as Hallorann. An announcement came through the speakers, but was unintelligible over the roar. For a moment, it seemed like the sound would consume them all as they stood there, paralyzed by its force.

Then through the tunnel marched an officer Hallorann had not seen before. He was putting on heavy-duty ear protection as he strode aft, and actually had a smile on his face. He brushed by Hallorann without a glance, walking directly toward the roar, which seemed to Hallorann to be one of the braver things he'd ever witnessed. He glanced at the gold dolphins and his nametag as he passed: *Jabo*.

And even though he was walking toward the noise, Hallorann decided that Jabo was the kind of person he wanted to be next to in a crisis. He followed him.

He walked down a short ladder into the middle level of the engine room. Hallorann had to stop finally, even with the foam earplugs and his hands pushed firmly over his ears, he literally couldn't take another step toward the noise, it felt as though it would split his skull in half. Jabo kept walking, armed with both superior ear protection and a supreme sense of confidence. At the front of the space Jabo arrived at a row of three identical machines. He walked right up the center one, assessed it briefly, and then threw over the handle of a valve at the top of it. Instantly the roar stopped.

Hallorann felt himself breathe, and reluctantly pulled his hands from his ears just as an announcement came from maneuvering, Hein's voice: "Number three high pressure air bank is isolated! Engineering Watch Supervisor investigate!" Hallorann could hear in Hein's voice that he didn't understand, even as Hallorann understood, that with Jabo's action the noise and the crisis were over. A chief brushed by Hallorann, the same chief who'd preceded him in maneuvering, walking briskly toward Jabo with a book open. Jabo smiled at him and pointed toward the valve that he'd just shut.

The chief handed Jabo the book and began banging on an adjacent valve, first with his fist, and then with a rubber mallet that another watchstander had appeared with in hand. There were several watchstanders who'd gathered around now, all of whom had been invisible when Jabo first approached the roaring machine. The chief seemed to hear something, stopped banging, and then gestured toward Jabo. The lieutenant slowly opened the valve that he'd shut, braced, Hallorann could tell, to shut it if the roar to began again. When it didn't, he removed his ear protection and put them down around his neck.

"Number three high pressure air bank is restored," came another announcement. Hallorann made his way toward the cluster of men near the machinery. A few cast disapproving glances at him, but Jabo smiled. "Hey, a nub!" he said. "Here to learn something?"

"Yes, sir."

"These are High Pressure Air Compressors," said the lieutenant. "Or 'hipacs.' They compress air into our air banks at three thousand PSI. That sound you heard," he said, pointing to the top of the middle compressor, "was this relief valve lifting. And it wouldn't re-seat. Pretty loud, wasn't it?"

"Yes sir," said Hallorann, moving closer. "It was just air?" That seemed incredible to him.

Jabo nodded. "Yes, but anything at that kind of pressure has to be treated with respect." Hallorann noticed for the first time that the piping immediately around the relief valve was caked in a thick, knobby, coating of white ice. Jabo touched it. "Besides being loud, a stream of fluid at that pressure could put a hole right through you. Or cut your arm clean off. Like a scalpel."

"Really?"

"I'm not shittin' you," said Jabo.

"So what did you do, sir?" said Hallorann.

"I isolated the relief by closing this valve," said Jabo. "That's why you heard that announcement…because that's not a normal configuration, obviously, the hipac isolated from its relief. Then the chief here came down and fixed our sticky relief valve according to the casualty procedure."

"It's called 'mechanical agitation,'" said the chief, tapping the mallet to the palm of his hand.

"That caused the valve to re-seat, so we were able to un-isolate the air bank and get on with our day."

Hallorann nodded. He was so impressed he didn't know what to say.

"Is there anything in your little yellow book about relief valves?" said Jabo.

Hallorann hesitated. "I'm not really sure, sir."

"Well, take a look," said Jabo. "And come get me to sign it if there is." He slapped the chief on his back, and then departed the engine room while they all watched.

.   .   .

Angi Jabo waited only a moment outside Captain Soldato's office before she was called in. Soldato looked slightly lost behind the enormous wooden desk that befitted his status as the new Commodore of Submarine Squadron 17. A television behind him showed CNN with the sound down; Angi knew it was a story about the latest breakdown in negotiations between the US and China, some scrap about a Taiwanese merchant ship. When the story broke, Danny pointed out how many American wars had begun with an attack on a ship: the *Maine*, the *Arizona*, the Gulf of Tonkin. It was something Danny clearly took pride in. It made her feel a little nauseous; she'd been avoiding the news ever since. Captain Soldato shut off the TV, stepped quickly around his desk, and hugged her tightly.

"Angi! Congratulations. Congratulations to you both!"

He stepped back, and Angi found herself surprisingly touched. So far, other than Danny, who'd been a nervous witness to the pregnancy test, she'd told only two people, both of them on the phone: her mother, back in Tennessee, the moment she knew for sure. And Cindy Soldato, the captain's wife. Mario was the first person other than Danny to congratulate her in person, and his enthusiasm for her pregnancy felt downright great.

"Thanks, Mario."

"How do you feel?" he said, a huge grin still plastered across his face.

She shrugged. "Better, now. I was pretty sick for a couple of weeks. How about you? How do you like being Commodore?"

He offered her a chair and sat down on another one, beside her, not behind his desk. "It's depressing as hell. I've been on seven submarines, Angi, punched a lot of holes in the ocean. Now I'm 'one of them,' just another air breather who they'll scrub the decks for once a month when I show up at the end of a patrol."

"I'm sure it's not that bad," she said, laughing at his theatrical self-pity. "Can't you boss them all around now?"

"When you're an officer in the navy, your entire career, you strive to be the commanding officer of a warship. There's no higher calling. Everything after that, no matter what rank they give you, is just bullshit. Excuse my language."

"Well, at least you've got this beautiful office," she said. She could tell he hadn't completely unpacked, but he did have the plaques from seven submarines in a line on the wall behind his desk: *Sunfish*, *Skipjack*, *Baton Rouge*, *Jacksonville*, *Archerfish*, *Omaha*, and the last one from SSBN731, *USS Alabama*.

"I'd rather be driving ships and leading men," he said. "You'll see what I mean someday, when Danny takes command of a boat."

She froze her smile at that, and looked down at the polished surface of his desk.

"Isn't that the plan?" he said.

She cleared her throat. "It seems I can't keep any secrets from you, Mario."

He patted her hand. "Has he turned his letter in yet?"

"I think so—needs to do it soon, before he hits the four-year point."

"Are you doing it because of the baby?"

"No! I mean—I hope not. Lots of reasons. Danny just wants to do something different."

The captain looked genuinely stricken, and Angi noted again the difference between how Captain Soldato seemed to feel about Danny in her presence, and how her husband perceived it. Danny would come home and relay the tirades he'd endured from Soldato, sometimes alone and sometimes as part of a group. On Mario's last patrol, during a botched firing of an exercise torpedo, he'd said, "Jabo, how do you keep the ants off your candy ass?"

But whenever Mario mentioned Danny in front of her, he was like this: pure paternal concern and professional admiration. She thought it a shame that the captain could never show this side of himself to Danny, but after three patrols together, she'd assumed it was impossible, because of some combination of nautical tradition and masculine inhibition.

"Well, Angi, take comfort in this: whatever Danny decides to do, you're going to have this child in a Navy hospital. And Cindy and I are here to help in every way possible. Now that they've taken me away from the boat, I've got plenty of time on my hands."

"Thanks Mario, I really do appreciate it. I do feel sometimes like I need someone to help guide me through the insurance process..."

He waved his hand. "Consider it done. I know all the people at Group Nine who manage this stuff, and I went to the Academy with the CO of the hospital in Bremerton. Everything will be fine."

"I know it will, but thanks for the offer. There's a chance, depending on how long this patrol is, that Danny may be home before my due date..." The Captain immediately shook his head, and she knew with sudden certainty that he would not.

"We're going to take care of you Angi," he said. "You and your baby."

To Angi's complete and utter surprise, she began to cry.

.   .   .

At home that night, Angi got on their computer and studied Taiwan and China. She had been avoiding the news up to that point, afraid to learn what was going on, but she suddenly wanted to know as much as she could, no matter how unsettling. It had seemed odd to her all along that the tensions between these two distant countries would so urgently involve the United States. And it seemed downright bizarre that it might affect her, and her nascent family. Now she wanted to know why.

She had to scan several historical overviews before she found one that seemed relatively untainted by politics. She learned that that China had been fighting for the island of Taiwan for five centuries, and that this tortured history was impossible to separate from the current crisis.

In 1662, the Chinese went to Taiwan and expelled the Dutch, its first European colonial masters. The Dutch treasured the island they named Formosa, for its rice, its large native deer population, but mostly for its commanding position on the Asian sea lanes it contested with Spain and Portugal. Not only Europeans coveted Taiwan, however, and in 1895 the Japanese defeated the Great Qin in the first Sino-Japanese war, leading to a long Japanese occupation. Japanese rule of the island lasted until their 1945 defeat in World War II, when the victorious allies deeded the island back to the Chinese.

Clarity was avoided, however, by the Chinese Civil War. That conflict pitted the Communist Peoples Republic of China, led by Mao Zedong, against the Republic of China, led by Chiang Kai-Shek. The war had raged since 1927, stalling briefly during World War II. As soon as World War II ended the Civil War resumed, until the 1949 defeat of Chiang Kai-Shek. With about two million of his supporters, he retreated to Taiwan, where the ROC declared itself to be the sole, legitimate government of China.

This declaration put the United States in an awkward position. For one thing, it was so obviously untrue. And no one really believed that the ROC, with its corrupt leaders and inept military, would ever pose a legitimate threat to the ruthlessly effective communists of Mao and the PRC. On the other hand, the ROC were fierce-anticommunists, and some of the US's only allies in Asia at a time when the US badly needed allies in that part of the world. So the US began a long, awkward advocacy of the status quo. The unstable arrangement resulted in periodic, predictable crises, many of which metastasized into military action, sometimes on a massive scale. In 1958, China fired so much artillery at the ROC controlled island of Quemoy that the high-quality steel shells became an un-natural resource for more than a generation of island blacksmiths, who became renowned for the meat cleavers they could fashion from the shells that had been intended to kill them. A skillful black-smith could to this day, Angi learned, make sixty cleavers from a single shell.

After spending an hour on Taiwan's history, Angi began to get into Taiwan's recent past and its unique relationship to the US… from Wikipedia she linked to the Taiwan section of globalsecurity.

org. She learned that the US policy had evolved into this: if the Republic of China was not actually China, neither was it a "rebel province" as declared by the real Chinese government, one that could be crushed by a PRC police action. The US, under Richard Nixon, finally acknowledged the obvious when it recognized the PRC as the legitimate government of China in 1979. The US embassy in Taipei, Taiwan was closed, renamed the American Institute in Taiwan. (The Taiwanese equivalent in Washington is the Taipei Economic and Cultural Representative Office.) The US, through a series of presidents, maintained the deliberately ambiguous "One China" policy, without ever specifying what that one China consisted of, or who was in charge of it. The US tacitly agreed to never hint that Taiwan was entitled to the independence that it actually had—by 1990 it was a thriving, prosperous democracy. In return, China tacitly agreed not to invade Taiwan and enforce the sovereignty that it insisted it had over the island.

The current crisis began less than six months before, when Qian Chen, the President of Taiwan, was granted a visa to speak at the University of Notre Dame, his alma mater. This visa represented a reversal of US policy, which had for forty years not allowed top Taiwanese officials to visit the United States—in 1994, Lee Teng-Hui, then president of Taiwan, was not even allowed off his plane in Hawaii while it refueled, lest his presence on American soil antagonize the Chinese. At Notre Dame, President Chen barely deviated from the carefully evolved phrases that characterized Taiwan's odd status, but his mere presence there was enough to aggravate Beijing. In response, they immediately announced a series of surface-to-surface missile tests in waters less than twenty miles from Taiwan's northern port city of Keelung—a distance that an M-9 Dongfeng missile travels in 9.5 seconds. Commercial air traffic was diverted and the Taiwanese stock market crashed as the latest crisis unfolded.

Angi learned what happened next on sinodefence.org, a British website operated by volunteers that called itself, "the most comprehensive and trusted online source of information on the Chinese military." On a beautiful Fall morning, a specially trained brigade of the Peoples Liberation Army drove an 8 x 8 launching vehicle from the province of Jiangxi to a position about sixty miles away in the Fujian Province. Two missiles were fired and landed in the ocean, a vivid but harmless assertion of China's anger and their national sovereignty.

A third missile was launched twenty-two minutes later from the same vehicle: China had announced this in advance, as a demonstration of their rapid reloading capability. This missile followed the same course as the first two initially, and then veered north approximately eight degrees. The missile traveled 576 nautical miles, close to its maximum range, and then slammed into a 170,000 ton cargo ship, the *Ever Able*. The ship was flagged in Panama, but owned by a Taiwanese company, and was bound for Shanghai. The reasons for the missile strike were immediately and hotly debated, the conversation inevitably colored by the politics of the speaker. China claimed the *Ever Able* had sailed into the publicized target area, and, in any case, the Dongfeng missile was not a heat-seeking anti-ship missile: it was a ballistic missile fired to a specific geographic coordinate, one that would be almost impossible to use deliberately against a moving vessel. China's opponents in Taiwan and the United States argued that it was naked act of aggression, and that the time had come at last to defend America's democratic ally against the Godless Communists of the PRC. The president of the United States, a liberal recently elected, was under enormous pressure to act, having just been seen as weak while negotiating trade regulations with China, who made thinly veiled threats about what havoc they could wreak on the US economy should they decide to divest themselves of their vast holdings of US government debt.

While the world nervously waited to see what the long-term consequences would be, there was no doubt about the immediate effects of that errant missile. While it carried no warhead, the sheer weight and kinetic energy of a 13,000 pound object flying at ten times the speed of sound broke *Ever Able* in half. It sunk almost instantly, along with its crew of twenty-two men.

It was almost one o'clock in the morning when Angi stared at the image on her computer screen, remnants of the *Ever Able's* cargo floating on a calm sea. The bow of a rescue ship jutted into the bottom of the frame, but there was no one to save.

.   .   .

The first days at sea were always hectic, exhausting, but there was something of a relief to it as well: both the ship and the crew were meant to be underway. *Alabama's* numerous and complicated systems were designed to operate ideally while in motion, relying on seawater to cool the steam flowing through condensers, shield radiation, and to insulate them from the world of commodores and admirals. The crew was also designed to operate optimally inside a ship at motion, with each division manned to operate a three-section watchbill of six hours on watch, twelve hours off, with plenty of maintenance and training for all hands to do in those off hours, into which also had to be squeezed showering, shitting, shaving, eating, and occasionally sleeping. So while bitching about sea time was an ancient and valued tradition of any maritime force, there was something pleasing about throwing off all lines and getting underway. For almost thirty six-hours, the ship steamed on the surface, each hour rougher then the last, until the ship had finally reached Point Juliet, marking water deep for them to submerge.

Lieutenant Hein, like many men, had rebounded from his seasickness after the initial episode of vomiting. He was standing watch in the control room as the officer of the deck, and he carefully verified their position on a familiar chart of Puget Sound. He then verified that the ship was rigged for dive, and looked to the captain who was standing at his side on the conn. He awaited his order.

Captain Shields nodded his head. "Submerge the ship."

"Submerge the ship, aye sir. Chief of the watch—submerge the ship."

The chief of the watch picked up the 1MC microphone and announced to the crew: "Dive! Dive!" He sounded the klaxon alarm, *Ahh-OOO-Gah*, twice. Modern submarines had, tragically, replaced the traditional klaxon alarm with a poor electronic fac-simile, but *Alabama*, like many boats, had taken an old iron klaxon from a decommissioned boat in the shipyard. The large, gray cast iron alarm was bolted to the deck at the chief of the watch's feet in a completely unauthorized modification to the ship's plans.

After sounding the klaxon again, the chief of the watch threw the switches that opened the vents to the six main ballast tanks, the giant tanks of air at each end of the submarine that kept her afloat. Salty spray shot fifty feet into the air through the open vents, as seawater flooded into the tanks through grates in the bottom. Lieu-tenant Hein watched the controlled sinking of the ship through the periscope and gave a running update to the men in control.

"Forward tanks venting…" He turned the periscope one hun-dred and eighty degrees. "Aft tanks venting….decks awash…" It was always a strange sight to see the dry deck become covered in swirling green water, where just minutes before crewmen had scurried to make the ship ready for sea. Then the scope was at sea level, water splashing over the optics, then it was under. "Scope is submerged. Lowering number two scope." He backed away from the scope and turned the orange ring that brought the scope down. Every part of the ship was under water. Their patrol as a submarine had begun.

.   .   .

The navigator excused himself from the control room without a word, and quickly locked himself into the watchstander's head at the bottom of the control room ladder. He grabbed each side of the small steel sink, and looked straight down at the drain to avoid looking at himself in the mirror. He throat constricted as he thought of the sea surrounding them, just inches away on the other side of the bulkhead, endless, dark, and merciless.

.   .   .

In his stateroom, Jabo felt the rolls ease, without completely stop-ping, as the ship paused at an intermediate depth to get its initial 1/3 trim. The chief of the watch and the dive were working to-gether, moving water from tank to tank, making fine adjustments, until the ship was at a perfect, level angle, and a slow speed, with all the control surfaces at a zero angle. It took time and skill to get it exactly right. Then the ship increased speed, which he could not feel. But it went deeper, which made the rolls completely melt away, and Jabo almost sighed at the sheer pleasure of the moment. Jabo didn't quite feel any kind of supernatural, physical connection to his ship. Maybe that came after a lifetime of sea tours, maybe the XO and captain felt that way. But Jabo was profoundly in tune with the machinery that surrounded him, and it was a special kind of relief he felt as the ship went deep. It was like driving a truck on rutted dirt roads for two days, then finally pulling onto the smooth asphalt of a new highway.

"So you turned in your letter?" asked Hayes Kincaid, his roommate in Stateroom 3. Their third roommate, Hein, was on the conn. At the moment the diving alarm sounded, the earliest moment allowed, they both changed from their khaki uniforms into their blue coveralls, or "poopie suits," and tennis shoes. The poopie suit was one of the great perks of submarine life, and Jabo had trouble imagining how his comrades-in-arms in the surface navy managed to strap themselves into khakis, blues, and shined leather shoes every day.

Kincaid was not only his roommate, he was his best friend on the boat. He was the only black officer onboard, and the only one who'd been enlisted prior to receiving his commission. Kincaid had done a full sea-tour on a submarine as a nuclear electronics technician before being awarded an ROTC scholarship and attending Hampton College in Virginia, where he got a mechanical engineering degree and an Ensign's shoulder boards. Then he went right back to nuclear power school, then right back to sea.

"Well sort of. Not really. The captain refused to accept it."

Kincaid laughed loudly. "Can he do that? Didn't you need to get that in this last mail call?"

Jabo shrugged. "He was a little mysterious about it. Said we'd have another mail call in a couple of weeks, and that the reason we were having the mail call would convince me I want to stay in the navy."

Kincaid laughed again. "*Fuck…that*. You want to come back to one of these? Be a *department head?*"

"That's what I said—I mentioned the navigator —said he doesn't look like he enjoys life all that much."

"What did the captain say to that?"

"Said the nav was a bad example."

"Fuck that! He's a perfect example. That department head tour is when they *get* you. JO tours, XO tours, what are they, three years? Because JOs, like you, they're trying to trick you into staying in. And XOs, they only need one per boat. And the CO tour is down to what, eighteen months? But the departments heads, the Navy knows they've got those guys, they've already decided to stay in—so they keep them out here like five years, wring every last drop of sweat out of them. And then what do they do? Promote half of them to XO and tell the rest to fuck off. No pension, no nothing to show for their trouble."

"What the fuck, Hayes, aren't you a lifer?"

"I've got twelve years in, my friend, 'cause of my enlisted time, and all my time in college counted too. I'll do my shore tour after this, then my department head tour, and then I'll have my twenty. The Navy can do whatever it wants to me after that. I don't give a shit if I don't screen for XO." But Jabo knew Kincaid would—he was an outstanding officer and, despite everything he ever said aloud: he loved the navy.

The rough voice of their Executive Officer on the 1MC: *All officers report to the wardroom.*

"Are we finally going to find out what the hell is going on this patrol?"

Kincaid shrugged. "I already told you the plan. We're going to go to sea, we're going to screw around for three, four, five or six months, and then were going to come back. In a year, we'll do it again."

Jabo laughed. "Maybe you're right." Kincaid worked hard to always be the least impressed person about any event of shipboard life, whether it was a fire in the engine room or the new ice cream maker in the Crew's Mess.

"Let me ask you something, Hayes. Was life on submarines really that much more exciting twelve years ago? Is it that much more boring now?"

"Let me tell you a secret," he said leaning in and whispering. "Life on submarines has always been boring."

"Fuck you, I don't believe it," said Jabo, laughing. "I've heard the stories. Plus, why would you stay in all this time?"

"I like the food."

They stepped out of their stateroom and walked down the short ladder that took them to the wardroom.

·   ·   ·

The Captain was at his traditional spot, at the head of the table, while the XO sat literally at his right hand. The navigator, small and exhausted looking as always, was standing up in front with a tripod that held a chart, a chart hidden by a standard issue navy bed sheet. That was unusual—everyone in the wardroom had at least a top secret clearance, and Jabo felt again that maybe Kincaid was wrong about their patrol being boring. Jabo also sensed some tension in the silent room.

They were all three in their khakis, and Jabo felt a little underdressed in his poopie. Soon the other junior officers in poopie suits piled in, though, all of them just as eager as he had been to get comfortable. The noise level rose. They waited for Hein to arrive, who was being relieved on the conn by the engineer himself, at the XO's insistence…whatever was going on they wanted Hein to hear firsthand. Hein finally arrived, looking slightly befuddled, and sat next to Jabo without saying a word.

The XO convened the meeting. "Everybody shut the fuck up." They all quickly complied. The XO's muscular arms bulged inside his khaki sleeves, and his bald head gleamed in the fluorescent lights. MS1 Straub, the head cook, stuck his head in from the galley door, doing his job and seeing if anything was needed. The XO nodded at him, and he got the message, retreating. The XO locked the door behind him when it shut—another unusual precaution.

"Before we get started," said the Captain. "I'm tempted to ask what the craziest rumor each of you has heard. About our patrol orders, not about girl babies." There was nervous laughter around the table. "Whatever you've heard," said the captain, "I can assure you it's complete bullshit. The XO and I were briefed the morning of our departure by the Admiral, and the navigator found out shortly after." Jabo looked at the nav, whose face was impassive, haunted, exhausted.

"So here's what we're really going to do," said the captain. "We're taking this ship to Taiwan."

There was some muttering around the table, and Jabo watched for just a moment as even Kincaid was unable to hide his surprise, before he slipped back into his mask of practiced nonchalance. But it was truly remarkable news. Because of the nature of their normal mission, they almost never went anywhere exciting. Unlike their brothers on attack submarines who deployed all over the globe with battle groups, Trident Submarines generally followed a fairly predictable schedule of leaving Bangor, Washington, going to sea for a few hundred days, and returning. If they were lucky, every other patrol or so, they might pull into Pearl Harbor. Once, on Jabo's first patrol, they had to surface off of Kodiak Island, Alaska, to medevac a shipmate who'd suffered a heart attack. But foreign ports were just never part of the deal—their deployment schedule didn't allow for it and most foreign nations were hesitant to allow twenty-four nuclear missiles into one of their harbors, with all the protests and controversy it would inevitably cause.

"The United States has a fundamental commitment to the nation of Taiwan," said the Captain. "The nature of which, frankly, is too complicated to explain here. But, in short, we will surface two weeks from now one hundred nautical miles east of the island, we will pull into the Taiwanese navy base at Suao, and then we are going to remove sixteen warheads from one of our missiles, and give the government of Taiwan temporary custody of them. It's all top secret, beyond top secret, until we pull into the harbor, and then the news media of the world will be invited to take pictures. You'll probably all end up on the Nightly News."

"Isn't that a violation of the non-proliferation treaty?" said Hein. Hein had gone to MIT and was one of the smartest guys that Jabo had ever met. It didn't surprise him that he would throw out a question like that.

"That's a good question Jay. I asked the same thing of the admiral. The official line is that we're not proliferating because we're not giving them the warheads—we're allowing them to store them on our behalf. Or something like that. But your intuition is sound—I have no doubt that this will stir up a shitload of controversy, at home and abroad, and will antagonize the Chinese beyond belief. But I believe, as everyone at this table should, that our national leadership has thought this through completely and that they've decided the benefits are worth the risks."

"What do we tell the crew?" asked Kincaid.

"Nothing," snapped the XO. "No one knows where we are going or why. We'll tell them the day before we pull in that we are going to Taiwan, but not why. This is all 'need to know,' and you guys need to know, since you're going to be looking at the chart every night and making sure we're headed in the right direction. You, you, and you," he said, pointing in turn at Kincaid, Jabo, and Jay Hein, "will be straight up three-section OOD starting with the next hour. Get to know and love those charts. Outside this room, only quartermasters and a handful of Nav ETs will know. And I guess we'll have to tell the engineer sooner or later." Everyone chuckled.

"You, you, and you," said the XO, pointing to Morgan, Morrissey, and Retzner, "are our three-section EOOWs." They all happened to be sitting next to each other on one side of the table, all friends and roommates on their second patrol. They nodded in unison. "And you," he said, pointing to Duggan, "Your job is to qualify EOOW, get on the watchbill, and make life a little easier for your six shipmates here."

"Aye, aye sir," said Duggan. Jabo heard the urgent sincerity in his voice. It was a shitty feeling to be the only one in the room without a real role to play.

The XO continued. "All of you can regard any information about our mission just like targeting information— no one else needs to know."

"The rumor mill is already running like crazy…" said Hein.

"Then let it run. I frankly don't give a shit," said the XO. "This is a vitally important, vitally secret mission, one that will have historic consequences. I am honored that they've chosen us to carry this out, and woe to the sailor or officer who fucks it up. Understood?"

Everyone nodded. The XO had made it clear that the question and answer period was over.

"Ok," he said, waving a hand toward the nav. "Let's get on with it. The navigator, as we mentioned, just found all this out. After spending the better part of the last week getting our charts in order for a patrol of the northern pacific, he's got to revise everything. But show them what you've got."

The Navigator pulled down the sheet to reveal a small-scale chart of the entire Pacific Ocean. On it, he'd penciled in a great-circle route all the way to Taiwan. While it looked curved on the flat chart, the course was actually a straight-line across the curved surface of the earth. A large red dot, on the far right hand side of the chart was labeled PA: Papa Alpha. The track connected it to a point on the other side of the Pacific: PZ, Papa Zulu. Point A to Point Z. "This is all I've got so far," he said meekly.

Jabo noticed for the first time behind the nav a small pyramid of tightly rolled up charts that looked freshly-delivered from Group Nine. They must have come over in the last mail bag off the tug. Every one would need to be reviewed by the nav, updated, and approved. And every chart he'd already done this for in their normal patrol areas, working day and night for weeks, was now useless. The captain had delivered on his promise in one way, Jabo thought, in revealing to him orders that were spectacularly different from anything they'd done before, an exciting unforeseen mission for them and their boat. But he'd also confirmed that the navigator's life was pretty fucking miserable.

"We're going to have to really burn it up," said the Navigator. "To make it there in time, across the operating areas they've given us, we're going to have to have a speed of advance of twenty knots the entire time, day and night."

"This is going to preclude a lot," said the XO. "Our sonar will be degraded, we'll be limited in the drills we can run. And we're going to have to keep our heads up. That means you, OODs. You're going to be covering a lot more ground each watch than you're used to—keep an eye on the chart, on the fathometer, all that good shit. Make sure we are where we are supposed to be. You hear me?"

"Yes sir," they all said in unison.

"What's after Taiwan, sir?" asked Jabo.

The XO looked at the captain, who nodded. "After we complete this mission, we'll make another two-week transit, assume a target package, and begin a normal strategic deterrence patrol."

No one said what everybody was thinking: they were going to be at sea for a very, very long time.

"Ok, everybody get the fuck out of here and get some rest," said the XO. "You're going to need it."

.   .   .

The three roommates crowded into the stateroom: Kincaid, Jabo, and Hein. Hein was dogging it a bit, giving the engineer a few minutes more on the conn. They all wanted to talk it over.

"Ever been to Taiwan?" Jabo asked Kincaid.

"Never. Never heard of a boat that has."

"Of course not," said Hein. "It is going to cause a complete shit storm. This is huge!"

Jabo nodded grimly.

"What, aren't you pumped about this? God knows what kind of attention we're going to get…this could be great for our careers."

Kincaid laughed. "You're the only one here all that worried about that, my friend." He nodded at Jabo.

It took Hein a second to process. "Really? You turned your letter in?"

"Not exactly," said Jabo. "Captain's going to endorse it when we get to Taiwan."

"If we make it!" said Hein, grinning. "We'll have to evade the entire Chinese Navy."

Jabo nodded, lost in thought. He was excited, like Hein, like the captain had promised. They were doing something extraordinary. But he was also going to be at sea months longer than he'd expected. With the changes to their orders, he'd originally thought that an early departure might mean an early return; in time for his child's birth.

But the opposite was true. They were going to be at sea longer than normal, and he would almost certainly miss everything. He wondered when and how Angi would learn the news.

．　　　　．　　　　．

The Navigator sat alone in the Officer's Study at 2:00 am, a huge, unblemished chart of the Pacific Ocean in front of him. There was a repeater in the study and the navigator registered subconsciously that they were on course and on track, 280, twenty-two knots, 650 feet. At that depth, they were well-insulated from the upheaval on the ocean surface. They were so seemingly motionless that the five sharpened pencils he had laying on the table only moved when he picked them up. He liked being busy. It seemed to quiet the nervous buzz in his head. If he focused intensely and worked himself into exhaustion, he hoped, he could stop thinking about all the things that worried him.

Counting his years at the Naval Academy, Mark Taylor had been in the Navy thirteen years. For that entire time, he'd been nervous, fearful that he would somehow fuck things up. At times his anxiety was nearly debilitating. During his Plebe year at the Academy, he once dreamed that he was being strangled, and awoke swinging his arms, fending off his attacker. But Plebe Year was *designed* to drive people crazy, as the upperclassmen, with their ritualized hazing, attempted to ferret out any weakness among the newest members of the Battalion. While Mark worried about his sanity, he took comfort in the fact that he seemed to be holding up better than many of his classmates. During Hell Week, another fourth class Mid from his company stood on his desk in his second floor room in Bancroft Hall and jumped, intentionally landing on his knees, shattering them, sending himself away from Annapolis with a debilitating injury. He recuperated for a month and then enrolled at Ohio State University on crutches. It was a measure of how miserable Plebe year was that most of the other mids spoke of his experience with envy. Mark worked hard to cope, and hoped that after his Plebe Year things would get better.

And...they did. For a while. He realized that frenzied hard work seemed to keep his bad thoughts at bay, so he pushed himself ruthlessly in the library and classroom, and chose to study electrical engineering, by consensus the hardest degree at the Academy. His stellar grades soon attracted the interest of the nuclear power program's recruiters who were always looking for motivated young engineers with a high tolerance for abuse. His senior year, he sat for interviews with a couple of psychologists who screened all candidates for the nuclear submarine program. One shrink handed him a piece of paper and a pencil and asked him to draw a picture of himself. Mark drew a stick figure that he hoped looked normal and happy, then worried that the smile looked maniacally toothy and large.

The second psychologist presented him with two columns of activities; in each case he was supposed to circle the one activity of the pair he would rather do. One instance asked if he would rather "peel potatoes," or "kill people." Although his final years at the Academy had been relatively happy, he approached the tests with the attitude that he did have something to hide, and to him, the tests seemed superficial and easy to fool. Some aspiring nukes got called back for a third psychological interview, but Mark didn't even have to do that: the shrinks gave him a clean bill of health, which Mark, with his great faith in the Navy's institutional wisdom, took as vindication. When he left Annapolis with an Ensign's stripes and orders for nuclear power school, Mark began to feel confident that his fears and insecurities had been outgrown, part of the residue of Plebe Year that he'd left behind on the banks of the Severn.

Nuclear Power School and prototype training brought with them a new kind of pressure, and with it, a few worrisome episodes. Once, while at nuclear power school in Orlando, he'd slept an entire weekend. Went to bed on Friday night, and didn't wake up until Sunday afternoon. He awoke to a bed that he'd soaked through with urine. He had to drag his mattress and sheets to the apartment complex's dumpster without his roommate seeing, and slept in a sleeping bag on the floor of his room for the rest of the term.

The second episode was worse. It happened at the S1-C prototype in Connecticut, an operating nuclear reactor that was the capstone of their engineering training. The plant was built to operate exactly like a submarine plant, and even turned a shaft. Since there was no ocean, however, to absorb the energy, the screw turned a generator which dissipated the plant's energy into electrical resistors, which turned it into heat, which dissipated over the Connecticut countryside. When the plant was running, the resistors were hot—it was their job to be hot. They were surrounded by a high fence designed mainly to keep out the raccoons who were attracted to the warmth, but who would sometimes get trapped between resistors and cook, making a god awful mess.

One frigid February night, Mark wandered outside the plant trying to clear his head after a marathon studying session. The next morning he was to be observed as Engineering Officer of the Watch conducting casualty drills. If he performed well, his nuclear power training would be successfully completed. If he failed, his nuclear aspirations would be ended. He hadn't left the site in twenty-four hours, and planned on studying through the night, right up until the moment he took the watch in maneuvering. He was stressed, exhausted, and fairly certain that some of the mumbling he heard inside the large, common study area was audible only to him.

He paused at the high fence that surrounded the resistor bank. He could see where the insulated cables came out of the fake hull, channeling electricity into the resistors. I=V/R, Ohm's Law, flashed into his head, the cornerstone of electrical theory. Like all the other ensigns at the site, he could rapidly and accurately calculate in his head what current would flow through the resistors at a given power level, how many shaft horsepower that translated to, and how much heat would be generated by the resistors as it absorbed that power. Because it was so cold, he could actually feel the heat coming off of the resistors; it felt good on his face as his back turned cold in the chilly night; it even smelled pleasantly warm, like a campfire, something Mark had never noticed before during midnight walks around the installation.

That's when Mark noticed that a long, thin oak branch had fallen from the surrounding trees and landed atop the resistors; what he smelled was the unmistakable aroma of wood being heated to its burning point. There were no trees directly over the resistor bank, but the branch was covered in dried, curly leaves. It must have snapped off in the cold and glided over from the surrounding woods like a paper airplane, landing exactly where it would do the most harm. Mark couldn't do anything himself because of the fence; the branch was unreachable. He immediately turned, intending to run to the nearest phone and alert the Engineering Officer of the Watch. .

But...he stopped.

He watched the branch in a kind of trance, thinking that it was not unlike an experiment Naval Reactors might conjure up, to see what the consequences of a branch falling on the resistor bank might be. He pictured a chart in a Reactor Plant Manual charting the temperature of a wooden branch versus time on a logarithmic graph, a bold horizontal line indicating the auto-ignition temperature of dried leaves. For a few minutes, he thought maybe nothing would happen. But then white smoke began to curl away from some of the leaves, and he smiled as the nostalgic, pungent aroma wafted over him. Then a few of them burst into flame, then, almost simultaneously, all of them were on fire.

The branch burned quickly, and settled into the resistor bank as it fell apart and turned to ash; the crevices between resistors and wires showed vividly in the orange flames. Soon Mark began to smell the sour, acrid smell of an electrical fire, and a few pops came from the resistors as wiring melted and shorted out. Resin inside the resistors melted and dribbled down the side, like gore from a wounded animal. A minute more, and he heard the *KA CHUNK* of large circuit breakers tripping, one right by his feet, that made him jump, and one just inside the hull. A bleating alarm sounded inside the hull, and he heard a muted, concerned announcement of the casualty from inside. He wandered away from the resistor bank, and took the long way back to the classroom where he'd been studying.

The next morning, crews were cutting down every tree within five feet of the outer fence line, and the plant was shut down while they all had training on the incident, and discussed the seriousness of what had happened: a reactor that is creating energy and then suddenly has no place for that energy to go. It could lead, they all reviewed, to soaring temperatures, protective actions, damaged fuel. They all worked through equations to calculate the rate and the extent of the potential damage.

Mark had to wait two days for repairs to the resistor bank to have his observed watch; he combated simulated flooding and recovered from an actual scram. He passed with solid marks. He didn't let the branch incident bother him for more than a few days. After all, it wasn't like he'd thrown the branch onto the resistors, there would have been a fire even if he'd never gotten near it: his presence there was a coincidence. And all the reactor's protective mechanisms had worked properly, protecting it from any damage. He graduated third in his class and received orders to the USS *City of Corpus Christi*. On his way to the west coast, he stopped in his hometown of Lansing, Michigan to marry Muriel, his high school sweetheart.

Mark loved Muriel, but he told her nothing about the fears he had for his own sanity. It was easy to keep from her at first. When they'd dated in high school and during trips home from the Academy, he'd been fine. Muriel was a tough woman, a realist, and Mark knew if he told her, she would immediately seek help, help that would result inevitably in the end of his career. And, in a way, keeping Muriel in the dark made him feel better, just as fooling the Navy shrinks had. Muriel was smart, and perceptive. If she couldn't tell that Mark was crazy...well then, he must not be that crazy. Of course, when she finally realized everything, he had to leave her. A wife telling the Navy that her husband was crazy was one thing. But a spurned wife telling the Navy that her ex-husband was a nut...the Navy would have to shut down if it listened to every allegation hurled by an ex-wife.

Everyone told junior officers that as demanding as the nuclear power training was, going to sea was harder. When he arrived on his first boat, the USS *City of Corpus Christi*, it had just begun a refueling overhaul in the Puget Sound Naval Shipyard. For his entire tour, the boat never left drydock; he had to be loaned out to other ships around Puget Sound to complete his at-sea qualifications.

He completed them with aplomb, pinned on his gold dolphins, received top marks on his fitness reports, and screened for department head with flying colors. The overhaul was demanding and stressful, but Mark got through the entire tour without an episode. He began to think again that he had healed. He did a leisurely shore tour at the ROTC unit at Creighton, then was ordered to report to the USS *Alabama*, where his optimism disappeared on the first day of his first patrol.

It was after the two-day transit to Point Juliet, two days in which he'd spent all but a few moments in the control room staring at charts. The ship had completed its preparations to submerge, and they'd just taken a sounding, confirming that the water beneath them was as deep as expected. After two nauseating days rolling on the surface, everyone was eager to submerge, so the XO was encouraging the OOD, Lieutenant Kaiser, to hurriedly shift the watch to the control room and get down from the bridge.

The last lookout dropped down from the ladder, directly in front of the conn, and Kaiser came soon after. The Nav noticed that there was only one "Open" indication left on the Chief of the Watch's panel, a single green "O" in a row of amber lines; the indicator for the lower hatch to the bridge. As Kaiser spun the ring that sealed the hatch, the nav watched the light turn from a green

"O" into an amber-colored straight line, a line that continued the length of the COW's panel. It was an elegant representation of their status: the ship was completely sealed.

Suddenly, his own throat began to tighten, as if the wheel that Kaiser spun also controlled the flow of oxygen into his lungs.

"The ship is rigged for dive," announced the OOD.

The navigator realized with sudden, overwhelming panic that he was locked in a steel tube driving through the ocean, and would remain so for more than one hundred days. He felt the ship running out of air, his lungs constricting, starving. There was a chorus of voices in control then, the usual yammer of everyone doing their part to get the ship submerged safely. But Mark knew at least a few of those voices muttering in the background were voices in his head, warning him about the danger only he could see.

He stumbled out of control into the watchstander's head at the bottom of the ladder; one of very few places you could be truly alone on the boat. Everyone noticed him stagger out, of course, but the same people had seen him virtually live in control for two exhausting days. And this was his first patrol, before there'd been even a whisper about his odd behavior amongst the crew or the wardroom. Most of the men assumed he'd just done an admirable job of controlling his bladder until an opportune time, or perhaps had finally succumbed to sea sickness. Mark splashed water on his face from the head's tiny steel sink, and tried to pull himself together. Gradually he began to control his breathing enough to return to the control room, where an endless series of charts awaited his review.

Ever since then, he'd recognized that the first day at sea was the hardest, that moment when the ship became a submarine. It was a moment he dreaded, but one he was prepared for. He knew that after that first day submerged, all patrol, every patrol, he'd have trouble separating what really happened to him with what was going on in his mind, the voices of the crew from the voices in his head. The problem, he knew, was getting worse. Stabbing himself in the leg was bad; Maple hadn't been able to make eye-contact with him since. But he knew it was Jabo he had to be careful around, the smartest junior officer on the boat. The rest of the officers might think the Nav was just a little odd, a little stressed out. But he had a feeling he wouldn't be able to fool Jabo for long.

Now it was the start of his fifth patrol. He had thought that he would just tough it out, his last patrol before rotating to shore duty, and then he'd vowed to himself to get help. He'd find a civilian doctor who would treat him in secret, away from the Navy's watchful eyes. Maybe it was as simple as a pill he could take, he'd read about things like that. A good prescription and a shore tour were just what he needed. Maybe he and Muriel would even patch things up. Of course, that had all been wishful thinking before the patrol began and their orders changed.

Now he knew he would never see land again.

.   .   .

The nav realized his eyes were shut, and snapped awake. The bright, fluorescent box of the Officer's Study was empty except for him and his charts. He had a splitting headache, and the color scheme of the OS did nothing to relieve it, everything in the room was painted a different shade of orange, with the exception of the brass clock, the only nautical touch in that sterile space. The Nav noticed with a sigh that the clock had stopped; keeping those old-fashioned clocks wound, six of them placed throughout the ship, was yet another responsibility of the navigator's. He turned back to the clean chart in front of him.

In the case of nautical charts, unblemished was not a desirable thing. It meant the charts had never been used, and hence never been updated with the frequent changes and revisions that they received from a variety of sources, including the NOAA. Their home charts, the ones near Puget Sound, were smeared and smudged with notes and numbers that had been added as more detailed depth surveys were taken, sand banks shifted, and, occasionally, ancient shipwrecks were identified beneath the waves. When planning the ship's track with those charts he could be confident that while there were many hazards, every hazard had been identified. But now, they were not only steaming through an area that the *Alabama* had never been through, it was an area far from the traditional shipping lanes to and from Asia. The new charts he'd received from Group Nine were pristine, with vast swaths of light blue that, the navigator knew, did not indicate a lack of hazards, but a lack of information. With a stack of bulletins and messages, he was adding what few updates he had, but the charts were still dominated by unmarked stretches marred only by the dark pencil line of the ship's track that the navigator had laid out. The ship was travelling so fast, it was all he could do to keep up with their track, getting a chart updated and approved by the captain and XO just in time to hand it to the OOD as they raced westward. He involuntarily glanced at the stopped clock again; he didn't know what time it was, and he didn't how long it had been since he'd slept. He glanced at the edge of the chart, the small island of Taiwan, the looming mass of China.

His hands started shaking at the magnitude of what they were doing, at the magnitude of his role in it.

The end of the world, he heard, in a voice that was not quite his.

You have to stop this submarine.

. . .

Danny Jabo was not born to be a naval officer. There was nothing remotely nautical in his family heritage, nor was there anything suggesting he was destined to wear the gold braid of an officer, which even in the navy of the world's greatest democracy carried the faint whiff of aristocracy. His father was the son of a farmer who'd learned to repair air conditioners at the county's vocational school. He'd passed on to Danny a keen mechanical aptitude, which helped him in the Navy, and an uncomplaining, tireless attitude about hard work, which helped him more. His life had not been without drama or tragedy—he had a little brother die in the crib when he was just five, a loss from which his sad-eyed mother never completely recovered. But it was a solid, good upraising in Morristown, Tennessee, forty miles east of Knoxville, at the edge of the Appalachians. There was an old joke that navy chiefs told when asked where they would go upon finally retiring. *I'm going to strap an anchor to my back,* they said, *and start walking inland. When someone points to me and says, "hey, what's that thing on your back," that's where I am going to live.* His hometown, Jabo thought, when he first heard that joke, is that place.

He'd learned about ROTC scholarships from his high school guidance counselor, and applied to both the air force and the navy, mainly because both services, on their brochures, seemed to offer something that was more technically alluring than the Army's marketing literature. One part of the process required him to go to Fort Knox, Kentucky, home of the nearest available military hospital, and get a physical, an event that marked the first time he'd ever set foot on a military installation of any kind. Both services, impressed by his grades, his test scores, and his glowing recommendations, offered him full scholarships. The deal both services offered was this: they would pay for 100% of his tuition to any school that he could get into that offered their particular flavor of ROTC. Danny and his father researched the issue carefully, and after a flurry of applications to southern schools, Vanderbilt was the most expensive school with ROTC that he could get into, and thus, they figured, the best deal. Vandy offered Navy ROTC but not Air Force. So before he even entered the Navy, Danny became a Commodore.

And eight years later, after three summers at sea, a college degree, and a year of the navy's exhaustive nuclear power training, he found himself wandering the passageways of a Trident submarine. It was sometimes dizzying to think about, like he had just awoken one day and discovered that he was one of twelve officers on a nuclear warship. But at the same time, he knew he'd made the right choice, because he loved his job, and couldn't imagine serving on a carrier, one of hundreds of officers and thousands of men, or on some supply ship or auxiliary, no matter how necessary those support ships were. He loved being part of an elite group at the tip of the spear, and he knew that he would miss that prideful feeling most of all when he resigned his commission.

He was looking for Hayes Kincaid. They were about to watch *Enter the Dragon* in the wardroom, and he knew Kincaid would want in. Soon, after the rigors of the three-section watchbill fully set in, he knew they wouldn't be able to burn a flick together like that. Whenever one of them was off watch, the other would either be on the conn or in the rack, getting what sleep he could. So he thought they should enjoy it while they were able.

He suspected Kincaid was exercising in Missile Compartment Lower Level so he headed that direction. Kincaid was a dedicated athlete, and one of few men to return from a patrol in better shape than when he left. Their workout gear was limited, but Kincaid made the most of it with every spare moment, putting himself through punishing workouts. The centerpiece of his routine was the treadmill, on which Kincaid attempted to run five hundred miles every patrol, tracking each run on a sheet of graph paper.

As Jabo walked by the Officer's Study, he saw that the door was closed, and wondered if Kincaid might be in there, perhaps reviewing some charts or writing a letter home for the impending mail call. He put his ear to the door before knocking; the way things were going he didn't want to interrupt some high-level discussion between the XO and CO, afraid they might drag him into the conversation. He heard something, muted talking, muttering on the other side. He lightly knocked on the door with one knuckle and the talking stopped. He knocked again, and opened it.

The navigator sat alone at the table, a pristine chart in front of him.

"Oh, hey Nav. Just looking for Kincaid."

The navigator didn't say a word, didn't nod or respond at all.

"You okay, nav?"

Still without saying a word, the navigator bent back down over the chart and resumed making corrections. Jabo watched him for just a second, and then closed the study's door.

Well, he thought. That was fucking weird.

.   .   .

Angi took the Kingston to Edmonds ferry, on her way to Muriel Taylor's condo. She was able to walk onto the ferry, leaving her car behind in Kingston and saving five dollars, as the Taylors lived within walking distance of the other ferry terminal. She'd decided to make the short, pleasant trip across Puget Sound to tell her friend about the baby.

The cat was not quite out of the bag, but it soon would be. Cindy Soldato, for all her good qualities, was not discreet, and besides, Angi was showing to the point that her pregnancy would soon be undeniable. She and Muriel had drifted apart in the last two patrols, but they had been close friends at one time, and Angi would always be grateful to her for showing her the ropes when she first arrived, all the things a clueless new navy wife needed help with, from getting a military ID card to how to shop in the Navy Exchange. Back in those days, they both often talked about how they wanted to have a child when the time was right—and how the time seemed like it would never be right. Muriel had withdrawn since then, and rarely attended any of the social functions that brought the wardroom wives together, so they rarely spoke anymore. Muriel's absence was accompanied by the predictable rumors of trouble in their marriage. But Angi decided she still wanted Muriel to be one of the first people to know about her baby, and that she would tell her in person.

She called ahead but Muriel hadn't answered, so she took a chance and hopped on the ferry anyway. Even after three years, the Washington State Ferries had not lost their novelty, and she loved drinking her latte (decaf now) and watching the scenery from a window seat, hard to believe the ride you could get for a six bucks. There were days, and especially nights, when the thought of pregnancy scared Angi very much, most often in the form of her wondering if she was up to the task. But there were more days like this, when she was excited beyond words, happy to be pregnant, happy that she and Danny were doing this. She felt the ferry rumble as the big engines reversed; they were pulling into Edmonds.

She disembarked and made the quick walk through the ferry terminal into the cute streets of Edmonds. Coffee shops, crafty boutiques, a music store that was somehow surviving the age of digital music. A few nice restaurants that were still closed because of the early hour. She thought with a brief pang of loneliness how nice it would be to eat dinner there with Danny, watching the ferries come and go.

Soon she was at the door to Muriel's condo; she could feel the effect of the pregnancy in the short walk, she felt more winded than she should have been. Just as she was getting ready to knock on the door, it flew open, and she saw Muriel, looking completely shocked and exhausted, standing in the doorway, the room behind her filled with cardboard boxes.

"Muriel?"

"Angi? Oh my God…" She put her hands over her mouth.

"Are you moving?" she asked, stating the obvious.

Muriel shook her head, and started to motion her in. "What am I thinking…there's no where to sit. Let's go get some coffee. Or maybe some wine."

I can't have either, thought Angi, but she decided to wait. It seemed they both had big news to share.

.   .   .

They went to Waterfront Coffee Company, an old hangout, and it made Angi remember how much time the two of them used to spend together, and how long it had been. At the counter, Muriel ordered a double shot of espresso, and Angi ordered a decaf latte.

"Decaf?" Muriel said. "It's only ten o'clock."

Angi smiled, and pulled her hands down to her hips, pulling her oversized windbreaker tight across her belly.

"Oh my God!" said Muriel, and her face finally brightened, looking something like the Muriel she used to know, optimistic and always enthusiastic. "How long?"

"Almost three months," she said. "You're almost the first person here I've told. I had to talk to Cindy to get the ball rolling on some of the insurance stuff."

"Well if Cindy knows, I'm surprised I haven't heard yet." The heavily pierced employee handed them their coffees across the counter, and they found an isolated table in the back.

They spoke at length about the pregnancy: the due date, the morning sickness, the odds (unlikely) that Danny would be by her side at the birth. Finally the conversation hesitated and Angi decided to ask.

"So...moving?"

Muriel looked down at the scratched table and nodded.

"Are you guys going to your next duty station? Does Mark have orders for shore duty yet?"

"He might," she said. "I have no idea. But I'm going home."

Angi hesitated, knowing the rest of the story would come out. It certainly wasn't uncommon—every patrol, a certain number of wives would just decide they couldn't take it anymore, and head back to wherever they'd come from. Being a Navy Wife was hardest during deployment, and that's also when leaving was the easiest. But it was still shocking, and sad, to see it happen to a good friend.

"Can I ask why?"

Muriel took a deep breath. "Honestly Angi...I think Mark is going crazy."

"What do you mean?"

"There'd been little things, of course, but I just wrote it off to the stress. I mean, don't they all have to be a little crazy to do what they do? But I really started to worry after his third patrol, Mario's last. Mark had just completed all his command qualifications, and Mario had given him a stellar fitrep. Everybody is telling us he's going to screen early for XO. And then—he doesn't."

"Oh no!"

"So he starts working even harder than normal, round the clock, all the time wondering how he failed the Navy. He's pouring over old fitreps, looking for faint praise, anything that might have stopped him from screening early. Now keep in mind, it's not like he's been passed over— he just hasn't screened early. But there's no telling him that."

"I know it's a really tough jump, from department head to XO."

"Even tougher now because they've gotten rid of so many boats—Mark's year group has just been decimated. I understand all that. But I start to see changes in him. He stops eating, for one thing. He's losing weight like crazy, and he didn't have that much to begin with. And then the nightmares start."

"Nightmares?"

"He starts moaning in his sleep, every couple of nights, really tortured sounds, sometimes bordering on yelling. I tell him to get to a doctor, you know, a psychiatrist, but he won't hear of it, says that will be the end of it, that he'll never screen if the Navy thinks he's crazy."

Angi nodded, and didn't say what she was thinking: that Mark was right. Nothing would end a career faster.

"Here, look at this," said Muriel, digging something out of her gigantic purse. She handed Angi a small black book.

"A bible?"

"Right about the time he doesn't screen early, he starts reading two books constantly. Whenever he's home, which is not that often, he's sitting there reading either the bible, or *Rig for Dive*."

"*Rig for Dive*?"

"Some old World War II submarine book. He'd sit there with both books, at the kitchen table with a highlighter in his hand, like he was studying them. Goes from one to the other…*Rig for Dive* to the Bible and back. This is a guy, keep in mind, who didn't spend a Sunday in church the whole time he was growing up. Didn't even want to get married in a church, I had to insist on it. Now he's studying the bible like his life depends on it. Look inside."

Angi flipped it open. There were passages highlighted in a rainbow of colors. Muriel had been right; the density of highlighting increased rapidly near the back of the book, where nearly every word was highlighted. There were also densely written notes in the margins. Angi looked close. "What does this say?"

Muriel nodded. "That took me a while to figure out too. They're equations. Engineering equations. He'd write them all over the freaking bible while he was reading about Armageddon."

"Do you have the other one? The submarine book?"

"No, I looked. I think he took that one with him. I guess he gave up on the bible."

Angi felt a deep sense of unease as she paged through it; it did look crazy. The juxtaposition of all the mathematical symbols against the numbered, columned pages of the King James Bible was positively creepy. But still...

"They're all nerds," she said. "One time I caught Danny writing on a notepad as he watched football—he said he was 'keeping score in hex.'"

Muriel nodded vigorously. "I know what you mean, but I'm his wife. Something is definitely wrong with him. So finally, after he refuses to listen to me about seeing someone, I invite over my neighbor one night to meet him. A neighbor who happens to be a psychologist."

"Oh Muriel..."

"That's pretty much what Mark says as soon as he realizes who he's talking to. Asks the guy to leave, very politely, and then tells me that I am trying to ruin his career. No I'm not, I said, I'm trying to help you!"

She started crying then and Angi reached out to touch her hand.

"So, he pretty much moves onto the boat at that point. I didn't see him or talk to him for a week before. When they left early—I didn't even know. He didn't even call me. So, I sat around here for a week, and just thought—I guess our marriage is over. So I called the movers and here I am."

"I don't know what to say, Muriel. I'm so sorry."

She looked down at the table. "He was such a sweet guy when we got married. And smart! My God, he was smart, the smartest boy I'd ever met. And now he's a wreck. I swear, Angi—I hate the fucking Navy."

Angi held back on that one—she wasn't about to defend the Navy in this situation.

"The only thing I'm wondering about now…should I tell someone?"

"What do you mean?"

"Should I tell somebody that I think they've got a certifiable nutcase onboard the *Alabama*? Should I give this bible to someone?"

Angi thought that over. "I don't know, Muriel."

"I don't either," she said. "What would I tell them? That my husband has been having bad dreams and reading the bible? They wouldn't believe me, so fuck it. Let the Navy deal with him."

.   .   .

As Angi rode the ferry home, she wondered if *she* should say something. After all, it wasn't just the Navy's problem. Her husband was onboard that boat, the father of her unborn child. And if the navigator was losing his mind, that was probably information she should share with someone. But, she kept coming back to what Muriel had said—she didn't have a lot to go on. Nightmares and bible reading, hardly enough evidence to declare a man insane. And what if Muriel was wrong? What if she was just another disgruntled Navy wife trying to stir up trouble for her husband? A call like that really could spell the end of Mark's career, just the suspicion it might cause, especially as he was on the verge of screening for XO. Danny had certainly never said anything about the Nav going crazy, just that he worked harder than anyone he'd ever met and wasn't particularly fun to hang out with. But certainly, he'd never said anything about the man losing his mind. She looked at the black surface of the water as they sped across the Sound. She remembered the first time she'd ridden the ferry during Danny's first patrol, how while looking out at the water she was almost struck dumb with the thought: Danny's *under* there. As the ferry pulled back into the Kingston terminal, Angi decided just to keep Muriel's conversation to herself. If there was a possibility that the

Navigator was going crazy, she'd just have to add it to the long list of things she worried about while Danny was at sea.

. . .

Kincaid watched as the red digital numbers on the treadmill turned from 4.9 to 5.0. Halfway there. He felt strong. He wasn't breathing too heavy, and the dull pain in his right knee had departed, as it usually did around mile three. He cranked up the speed to 7.0, put the incline up another half percent. He felt his legs respond, a satisfying tightness in the hamstrings, and felt the sweat start to soak through the collar of his T-Shirt.

Kincaid was the only black officer on the boat, and one of just six African-Americans on the entire crew. The Navy was historically the least integrated service, Kincaid well knew, and the nuclear navy was the most lily white part of the whole operation. In addition, Kincaid was the only prior-enlisted officer on the boat. He'd signed up right out of high school, gone to boot camp at Great Lakes Naval Training Center, and completed the whole, grueling, nuclear power training pipeline as an enlisted man. He got halfway through one patrol on the USS Tecumseh, and in looking around at the officers it occurred to him: I'm as smart as those guys. So he applied for a special commissioning program for nuclear-trained enlisted men, got accepted, and attended Hampton College on a full ride courtesy of the US Navy. Then he went through the nuclear training pipeline all over again, this time wearing khaki and an ensign's gold bars.

All that made him a few years older than his JO peers: he was twenty-seven. But Kincaid made sure none of them thought they were in better shape. He devoted every spare minute to working out, using every piece of the paltry exercise equipment the ship stored in Missile Compartment Lower Level: the treadmill, a rowing machine, a stationary bike, and a punching bag. Unfortunately, everything except the treadmill and the punching bag was broken. It had all been scheduled for replacement, but their orders had changed before the new equipment arrived. The broken gear didn't disrupt Kincaid that much; his routine centered on the treadmill.

But it bothered him deeply, as a submariner, to go to sea with shit broken.

Kincaid tried to run five hundred miles every patrol, tracking his progress on a sheet of graph paper taped to the state room wall. Each sheet from each patrol went into green half-inch binder. Whenever possible, he did his run in ten-mile increments, which took him about ninety minutes. It was the longest he could go, especially early in a patrol, without pissing people off for monopolizing the treadmill. Already, though, the competition down there in Missile Compartment Lower Level was starting to wane. People were getting lazy. A new patrol was like the New Year: everybody had resolutions. I'm going to qualify chief of the watch. I'm going to learn to play guitar. I'm going to lose twenty pounds. But usually by the third week, he pretty much had the place to himself.

The thought made him feel stronger, as he listened to the repetitive slapping of his Nikes on the belt beneath his feet. He didn't listen to music when he ran. The treadmill ran on a non-vital electrical bus, the first busses, by design, to start shutting down if things went wrong with the ship's electrical plant. On his first patrol as an officer, he'd been on the bike when the 2MC announced a reactor scram. Another JO was listening to some heavy metal on his head phones, trotting along dumb and happy on the treadmill. Kincaid yelled out to him, but he didn't hear him any more than he heard the announcement. A second later the bus dropped, the treadmill shut off, and the JO ran clear over the rails, flipped over, and broke his collarbone. So Kincaid decided he could live without the music, listening instead for any announcement, bang, or alarm that would make getting off the treadmill a good idea.

He saw Jabo climbing down the ladder at the far forward end of the compartment. He spotted Kincaid and struck a Kung Fu pose. Kincaid jacked up the speed a couple of more tenths, feeling competitive. Jabo was strong, a natural athlete, one of those guys Kincaid would want next to him if he ever needed to be dragged out of a smoke-filled compartment. But he didn't want Jabo to think for a minute that he was in better shape. For a variety of reasons, Kincaid usually had a chip on his shoulder about other junior officers. But liking Jabo was effortless. And in addition to being his best friend, he was a superb naval officer: smart, loyal, and good. He took on every task with a complete devotion to getting it done properly. A word popped in Kincaid' head that he didn't think he had ever used to describe another human being. Jabo was *dutiful*.

Jabo had made his way to his side. "Come on Hayes, let's go."

"Let's go what?"

"We're burning *Enter the Dragon*."

Kincaid looked down at the console. "Two and a half more miles." He consciously made his words sound as easy as he could. "Almost done."

"Thirty minutes on the treadmill," said Jabo, pointing to a laminated sign that hung on the bulkhead. "That's the limit. I'm here to enforce the rule."

"Fuck that. You see anybody else down here?"

"Maybe I want on it."

"When I came down here, it still had my stats from yesterday on it. Ten miles in an hour and twenty-two minutes."

"Maybe it was somebody else."

"No one else on this pig could do that run," he said.

Jabo put his hand over the red emergency stop button.

"Don't you fucking do it!" said Kincaid, laughing now.

Jabo feigned he was hitting the button again. Kincaid was losing his rhythm laughing. He finally dialed down the speed, and brought the treadmill to a stop. "Alright, motherfucker. Seven point five miles. Let me go write it down and I'll meet you in the wardroom."

"An old guy like you shouldn't be running like that anyway," said Jabo. "Gonna fuck up your joints."

"Old guy? Feel like going for a race?"

"I feel like watching a movie," he said. "Eating some shitty food, drinking some watery Coke, and watching a movie while we still can."

•   •   •

The movie ended just in time for Jabo to complete his pre-watch tour prior to relieving Hein on the conn. In missile compartment third level, the level where the majority of the crew slept in nine-man bunkrooms, Jabo stopped at the ship's laundry. Petty Officer Howard was wearing boxers and a t-shirt, doing laundry while reading a well-worn copy of *The Shining*.

"Shouldn't you be studying for your quals?" asked Jabo, pointing at the book. Howard was his favorite kind of sailor—enthusiastic without being a kiss ass, smart, and funny—the kind of guy you didn't mind spending a couple of hundred days a year with sealed in a steel tube. He'd gotten himself in trouble after the last patrol, driving drunk from the E Club on base to the barracks. It was a classic kind of stupid, avoidable, young man's mistake—the distance from the E Club to the barracks was about two hundred yards. Howard had said he wanted to get his car out of the E Club lot because he was worried his stereo would get stolen. Jabo was one of several officers who'd gone to bat for him after the incident.

Howard thumped his chest, where his silver dolphins would have been if he'd been wearing his uniform. "I qualified last patrol, sir! You know that."

"What about Diesel watch? Chief of the Watch? Diving Officer? There's always something to qualify for."

Howard rolled his eyes. "Ok sir, let me get my poopie suits clean and I'll get right on it." He stood and peered into the small glass window on one of the ship's two dryers. "Looks like they're almost done."

"Excellent. You can come up to the conn on the next watch, I think we may be going to periscope depth to get the broadcast, you can sit with the Chief of the Watch."

"Seriously?" Howard was paying attention now. On a normal patrol, trips to PD were rare. Offering a seat like that to Howard was a big deal, giving him a leg up on a big watchstation qualification. "What time?"

"Come up about halfway through the watch," said Jabo. "I'll see what I can do. I'm not even positive we're going, but I know we need the broadcast…if you happen to be in the control room when we do, and you're prepared, I don't see why you can't get the signature."

"Thanks sir, I'll be ready!"

"Good," said Jabo, and he continued his tour.

.   .   .

He finished the tour, as always, in the control room, reading the captain's night orders, checking the deck log, and looking at the CODC display, the Officer of the Deck's view into the ship's sonar suite.

"What's that?" said Jabo, pointing to a contact designated Sierra Nine. They'd been tracking it loosely for the whole watch.

"Not sure," said Hein. "We've been trying to get away...not really doing any good listening at this speed."

"But he keeps hanging on?"

"Still there every time we slow down."

Jabo punched a few buttons on the console, bringing up the contact's estimated course and speed.

"She's following us? That's what you've got in here."

Hein shrugged. "Who knows? We're going so fast, it's hard for us to listen."

"But easy for someone to listen to us."

Hein smirked a little...Jabo could tell he didn't really believe they were being followed. But he knew they should be assuming the worst right now, and he didn't like the complacency he saw from his friend Hein at that moment. It was sloppy thinking for an OOD. It would be hard, but he vowed to learn more about Sierra Nine during the six hours of his watch.

Jabo crossed the control room to finish his pre-watch tour with a check of the ship's position on the chart. Even with all the advanced, electronic navigation at their disposal, the ship's position, marked in pencil on a paper chart, was still a cornerstone of navigation. Jabo took his time as he did it, even though he could tell Hein was eager to get off the conn now that his six hours were nearly up.

"Are these our assigned areas?" Jabo asked QM1 Flather, the assistant navigator, who was standing nearby with a pencil tucked behind his ear. He looked as exhausted as the navigator did, all the last minute changes to their patrol orders had taken a toll on him as well.

"Here, here, and here," said Flather, wearily thumping his thumb on a succession of three blue boxes that progressed westward. "They are changing fast because we're moving so fast."

"Where are the orders?" Flather handed him over a clipboard with their assigned areas from Subpac. Jabo carefully checked all three areas on the chart, verified that all three had been drawn in correctly. It was critically important. Staying inside the proper rectangle at the proper time ensured that they wouldn't collide with any other US submarine, as no two boats would ever be assigned overlapping patrol areas. Conversely, if, while in the assigned areas, they heard another submarine on sonar…it wasn't friendly.

Jabo then looked over the ship's track on the chart. He checked the time of the dead reckoning, followed the track to the left, realizing with shock that Flather had actually plotted their predicted position, three hours into the future, past the left border of the chart, into the margin.

"Where's the next chart?" said Jabo. "Why haven't you changed?"

"Not approved—Nav's still got it," said Flather. "Still going over the updates."

Jabo frowned and Flather shrugged. He looked up at Hein.

"There's no chart."

Hein came over to join them. "I think the Nav's almost done with it, he's finishing up in the officer's study. I've been asking him about it for the last hour, he finally stopped picking up the phone."

Jabo tapped his finger on the table. "I need to see that chart."

"Ah shit, Danny, it's six o'clock already. I'm starving."

"Sorry, Jay, really. I've got to see where we actually are before I take the conn."

"Alright," said Hein, falling wearily into the captain's chair. "Fuck. Go find him. Quickly please."

Jabo slid down the ladder out of the control room and headed for the officer's study where he'd last seen the nav. He felt bad—relieving the watch late was a bad deal, and doing so more than a few times could quickly lead to a reputation that he didn't want. But on the other hand—he didn't feel right about taking the watch without seeing where they were going. Hein should have insisted on getting that chart into the control room. He knew that they were operating under some extraordinary circumstances, but his instincts as an Officer of the Deck, honed over three long years at sea, wouldn't allow him to take the watch when their position was plotted into blank space on the margin of a chart.

He stuck his head in the Officers' Study. The nav wasn't there, but the chart was. He also noticed, to his displeasure, that the coffee pot had been left on, and the space was filled with the bitter smell of the scorched, empty pot. Jabo glanced at the chart. The stamped box at the bottom had not been signed, which was required before he could use it for navigation. *Where the fuck is he?* Thought Jabo, as he rolled up the chart. It irritated him that the Nav would walk away from the chart like that when they had needed it in control for at least an hour. He couldn't imagine what a higher priority would be. He walked down another ladder, to the wardroom, and walked in.

The captain and XO looked up at him over their coffee cups. "Danny, aren't you supposed to be relieving young Jay?" said the Captain.

"Yes sir, just need to get this chart approved by the nav, thought I might find him in here."

The captain and XO looked at each other. "You need that chart for the next watch?" said the XO.

He hesitated for just a second—he knew what he was about to say would put both the Nav and Hein up shit creek. "We need it right now. They've got us plotted in the margin, heading off the edge."

A look passed between the XO and captain. The captain sat back and raised an eyebrow. "No chart at twenty knots. Jesus Christ."

"Give it here," said the XO, pulling a pen from his pocket. "I'll approve the fucking thing."

As he reached for his pen, the 4MC crackled. The 4MC was an amplified phone circuit designated for use in emergencies only. Just the sound of its distinctive static was enough to trigger an adrenalin surge from an experienced submariner.

"*Fire in missile compartment third level!*" came the announcement. "*Fire in the ship's laundry!*"

The chart forgotten, Jabo bolted from the wardroom without a word and headed aft, toward the fire. He heard the XO and CO clamor up the ladder to control behind him. As he ran, he was surprised to see the navigator hurrying forward, donning his flash hood and his firefighting gloves, also moving toward control. The navigator was supposed to be in control during emergencies, so he was going in the right direction. But for all his responsibilities, he didn't have much to do aft of the forward bulkhead, and Jabo wondered what he was doing back there while a needed chart was languishing on the Officers' Study table. All thoughts about the nav disappeared as Jabo smelled smoke and saw an orange glow coming from the laundry where just minutes before he'd been chatting with Petty Officer Howard.

·   ·   ·

There is no such thing as a minor fire on a submarine, a sealed tube containing 154 men and a very finite quantity of breathable air. Fires consume oxygen as they emit toxic fumes, most notably carbon monoxide. Fires threaten electrical systems as wires and breakers melt and scorch. And throughout the ship ran pipes full of high-pressure fluids and gasses, substances that didn't react well to open flame: hydraulic oil, high pressure air, and pure oxygen, a breech in any of which could turn a simple fire into a blowtorch, and a compartment into a furnace. The ship's pure oxygen was manufactured just aft of the laundry, in Machinery Two, and it was the oxygen generators that Jabo thought of as he ran to the scene.

"Lieutenant Jabo is the man charge!" he shouted as he arrived. Men were hustling, several in their underwear, fresh out of the rack. He spotted MM1 Jantzen, who seemed to be the second highest ranking man on the scene, already putting on a sound powered phone head set. He relayed to control that Jabo was in charge. Both Jabo and Jantzen pulled their EABs, or emergency air breathing masks, over their heads. He breathed in to pull the mask against his face, verifying the seal of the rubber, then plugged into the manifold over their heads. He took a deep breath of the cool, oily-smelling air.

The navigator's voice on the 1MC announced, "Fire in the Ship's Laundry, Lieutenant Jabo is the man in charge. The fire main is pressurized."

Jabo turned; there were fire hoses located throughout the ship, twenty-two in all at every level and compartment, and memorizing their locations was one of the first things a new man did when he reported to the boat. There was one directly behind the laundry, and he was surprised that there wasn't already a hose team at the scene ready to unleash, they were trained to put water on a fire in seconds.

But there was a problem; he saw a group of men frantically pawing at the hose. He leaned over, then detached from his EAB manifold, took two long steps, and moved closer.

"What's wrong?"

Petty Officer Yowler looked up at him, his face red and sweaty behind the mask with frustration. "It's pressurized in the rack!" he said. "We can't get it off!" Jabo saw what he meant. Someone had turned the valve on before the hose had been removed from its rack, engorging it with water and freezing it in place. It was immovable and useless to them. He stopped himself from asking who the fuck did something that stupid—there would be time to worry about that later.

He tapped three men on the shoulder who were standing around the rack, struggling with the hose. They turned, and since they all had EABs on, hiding their faces, Jabo glanced at their chests. One of the three did not have dolphins. "You know what you're doing with that hose?" he asked the nub.

"Yes sir!" he shouted through the mask. It was the new guy, Hallorann. Jabo was pleased to see him rush to a hose and a fire.

"Okay—forget that hose. Go up to Mike Seven, bring that hose down here from second level. String two of them together if you need to." He pointed to three others. "You go get Mike Two, up forward. Get both fucking hoses on this fire now!" The six men ran off without a word.

Behind him, two men had stuck two portable carbon dioxide extinguishers into the laundry and exhausted them with a quick white blast. It didn't slow the fire at all. The lights in the missile compartment suddenly went out, the non-vital electrical bus either being secured as a safety measure or as a side-effect of the fire. Diagrams of the ship's electrical system ran through Jabo's mind like a series of rapidly advancing slides; he thought about the weapon's system 400 Hertz generators one level above them. With the lights out he could see the orange glow of the fire through the billowing gray smoke that was pouring from the laundry.

Jabo had been in fires before on the boat, all the previous ones being electrical, in nature, or "Charlie Class" fires. The biggest had been on his second patrol, when the breaker for a main seawater pump breaker exploded in the engine room. With those types of fires, once the electricity was secured, if it was secured quickly enough, the fire usually diminishing rapidly. But this appeared to be an "alpha" class fire, one feeding on some kind of fuel and leaving ash behind. He heard Jantzen reliably relaying the information about the pressurized hose frozen uselessly in its rack to control, and imagined the XO seething at the news.

Both hose teams arrived almost simultaneously, both nozzlemen jacked up, ready to rumble, one hand on the hose, one hand on the nozzle.

Jabo stepped back, out of their way. "GO!" he shouted.

Both hose teams stepped forward and the nozzlemen threw open their nozzles. High pressure saltwater shot forward in two white, cold torrents. It was the only time you'd ever see submariners enthusiastically bring seawater into their space. Salt water was corrosive and undrinkable. It gathered in their feet in puddles that turned into streams, water that would find its way lower and ruin much of what it touched. The water that hit the fire, in the meantime, turned into clouds of steam and floated upward, filling the missile compartment, and would condense and lead to grounds on electrical systems that would take days to isolate and fix. Seawater was an enemy to a submarine, something they obsessively fought to keep outside the "people space," but here they were shooting it into the boat as fast as they could bring it onboard. They did it because there was nothing, absolutely nothing, that was better for fighting a fire than large volumes of water. Within seconds you could feel the nature of the situation change, as the acrid smell of smoke gave way to the heavy softness of billowing steam, and the orange glow shrunk, then disappeared.

"Stop!" said Jabo. He had to tap both nozzlemen on the shoulders to get them to throw the bales forward and stop the flow of water. He cautiously stuck his head in the laundry, a crowbar in one hand and a battle lantern in the other, shining its beam through the haze.

There were two washers and two dryers. One set looked to be completely ruined; charred and blackened. Jabo hoped that the other set might be saved—otherwise it would be a long, smelly trip to Taiwan. The charred dryer was stuffed with blackened rags—overstuffed, probably the cause of the fire. Using a crowbar, he gently pulled open the sagging door to the dryer to verify that the fire was out. Something caught his eye inside, something foreign atop the rags. He pulled out the smoldering object, and the words on the cover were still recognizable. It was *The Shining*.

He dropped it to the deck and walked out of the laundry where Jantzen was waiting for him. "To control, the fire is out. Sending in an overhaul team and setting the reflash watch."

Jantzen repeated his words into the phone.

.   .   .

Jabo was at the scene for another thirty minutes, overhauling the fire and setting the reflash watch, the whole time sucking air in his EAB as the smoke remained thick and the air unbreathable throughout missile compartment. Finally he was relieved by Lieutenant (j.g) Retzner, who Jabo knew, after his one patrol, was qualified enough to supervise the recovery efforts, even without dolphins on his chest. Once he got through the bulkhead to the forward compartment he was allowed to remove his tightly-fitting EAB, to his profound relief. In Crew's Mess he sat for a moment and drank two glasses of water, parched and exhausted from the fire. He noticed the tips of his shoelaces had burned down to the knots.

MS1 Straub approached him, wiping flour from his hands. He'd already begun to prepare dinner. "Lieutenant? You're wanted in the wardroom."

·   ·   ·

The captain, the XO, and Lieutenant Maple, the Damage Control Assistant, all sat around the table. A large pitcher of ice water sat between them, and they let Jabo drink another glass before they began. The smell of smoke clung heavily to his clothes, and he wondered again if they were going to be without an operational laundry for the next two weeks. The wardroom's bearing repeater showed they were slow at 160 feet, executing a wide turn to the left. Clearing baffles, he knew, preparing to go to periscope depth so they could ventilate the smoke from the ship.

"Good job at the scene, Danny," said the XO. "I'm glad you were there."

"Thank you sir."

"What do we think happened?" asked the captain.

Lieutenant Maple spoke up. "It sounds like a dryer was overloaded with cleaning rags, and then secured without cooling. It got overheated as it sat there. In addition, there was a book inside the dryer. That's probably what caught fire first."

"A book? In the fucking dryer?"

"Yes sir. We'll find out whose book during the investigation."

"I already know," said Jabo with a sigh. All eyes turned to him. "It's Howard's. I saw him reading it on my pre-watch tour. In the laundry."

"And the fucking genius decided to stow it in a clothes dryer," said the XO. "Wonderful. You saw this on your pre-watch tour?"

"That's right."

"Well then, this brings us to our second problem. I guess you didn't notice that Mike Six was pressurized in its rack."

Jabo shook his head. "I thought someone turned it on too early during the firefighting, in the heat of the moment."

Maple shook his head. "We talked to everyone at the scene. They said it was pressurized in the rack when they got there, before the fire even started."

"And I don't suppose you remember looking at the hose during your tour and seeing otherwise?"

Jabo shook his head. Fuck, he thought, he'd been standing right there. "No, I didn't look at it. I like to think I would have noticed if it was pressurized like that, but I can't swear to it. I talked to Howard for a few minutes and moved on."

"Alright then," said the Captain, putting his fists on the table. "Training opportunities for all, officers and crew." The captain's X1J phone, a direct line to the conn, buzzed beneath the table. He spoke briefly to the OOD and hung up. "Looks like we're ready to go to periscope depth and get the smoke off the boat." He left the wardroom with Maple in tow.

When the door shut behind him, the XO smiled. "You fucked up Danny. You should have seen that hose."

"I know sir. I fucked up. It won't happen again."

"And Howard fucked up too."

"Yes sir, it looks that way."

"I'd like to take that fucker to mast right now, but the fact is, we need him on the watchbill. We'd be port and starboard in machinery two without him. So we'll wait, until either we pull in and get a new A Ganger, or until someone else qualifies machinery two. You're going to handle the investigation. Do it during all of your spare time."

"Yes sir."

"No point in telling Howard about this—I don't want him to know helping somebody qualify will get him to mast faster."

"Good idea sir."

The XO leaned back in his chair, sighed, and cracked his knuckles over his head. "You think he pressurized that hose, too?"

Jabo was a little shocked by the question. He'd assumed that someone had thrown open the valve in the excitement of arriving at the scene, a stupid, but somewhat understandable, mistake. But if the hose had been pressurized in the rack before—the XO was asking if Howard had done something much more serious than fuck up a load of laundry. "I don't know...you think he'd fuck around like that?"

"Just asking the question."

"Sir, Howard may be a fuck up. But he's no saboteur."

"Well let's hope that this was just a pure act of stupidity then. And God help the sailor who did it when I find out who he is. Get up there to control and see if you can help, Hein has been on the conn forever. Relieve him at periscope depth"

"Relieve Hein at periscope depth, aye sir."

.   .   .

When Jabo walked out of the wardroom, Howard stepped out from behind the ladder to control, looking worried.

"Howard. We were just talking about you."

"I didn't do anything!"

Jabo grimaced. "Howard, you want to know my personal philosophy in situations like this? Say the following words: 'I fucked up, and it won't happen again.'"

"But I didn't!"

"Howard, they found your book in the dryer. On top of a big pile of rags."

"I know—Yowler told me. I didn't wash any rags. As soon as my poopies were dry, I got out of there—I was going to head to the conn to go to PD, like you said."

"And the book?

"I keep that book in there, shoved between the deck and the hull. I would never put it in the dryer!"

"So what do you think happened?"

Howard shook his head. "I have no idea. But I got my poopies out of the dryer and left. I was changing in my bunkroom when they called away the fire."

Jabo thought it over—it was weird. Howard had just been drying poopies, he'd seen it with his own two eyes. And why would he throw a load of rags in after, along with a book?

"I don't know what to say Howard. I fucked up too—I should have seen that hose pressurized in the rack. And if you did make any mistakes—take responsibility for them, you'll come out better in the end."

Howard shook his head at that, and walked away frustrated, his young man's sense of justice violated. Jabo walked up to control, still reeking of smoke, his feet tired and his head pounding, and took the conn from an equally exhausted Lieutenant Hein.

He pressed his right eye to the periscope and turned slowly around, one complete revolution every minute. It was dusk, and the ocean was like glass, smooth to the horizon where sea and sky met, different shades of the darkest blue. Ship control was easy and the scope stayed a steady three feet out of the water; Jabo calculated that the distance to the horizon was about 2.5 miles. So the Alabama's periscope pointed up in the exact center of a five mile diameter circle, inside of which, Jabo verified with each revolution, there were no other ship was in sight, no running lights of any kind, white, red, or green. He looked west and saw nothing, no running lights of any color. If Sierra Nine was out there, he couldn't see it. *Alabama* was profoundly alone.

.   .   .

The Navigator spread his charts out in the Officer's Study and erased the track that he had carefully laid out in the days before. They hadn't lost much time. The Captain had opted to use the diesel engine rather than the blower to ventilate the ship, which did the job in about half the time. Within two hours at snorkel depth, all atmospheric tests in the missile compartment proved benign so they stopped the rumbling diesel, and descended back to 400 feet. In total they'd lost almost three hours during the fire, almost half a watch. Which meant they were behind, and would have to move even faster to make up their track.

It was so weak, he thought. A fire in the laundry.

Optimism had shot through him when he first heard the alarm, smelled the smoke. And the closest hose made useless! Maybe the fire would cripple the ship, he thought, turn them around, end their disastrous journey to Taiwan.

But that was stupid, he now knew. A mere fire in a clothes dryer wouldn't stop this ship, this mission, not even close. Huge forces were at work, malignant forces. And he was an idiot to think that a few burning rags could stop that. But would what could?

Almost all equipment on the boat, like the washer and dryer, came in pairs. For just this reason: redundancy meant reliability. There was only one reactor, but that sacred machine was incredibly well protected by men and machinery. It was hard to imagine an equipment malfunction that could make them turn around.

But people were different. The submarine had lots of equipment but few people. Already the watchbill was stretched to the limit. If crewmen started dying, then the ship would have no choice but to turn around. Especially if they died in large numbers.

The navigator's tried to stop his hand from shaking by refocusing on the chart. He was running out of time: they were halfway to Taiwan.

.   .   .

Mary Beth Brown picked Angi up at her house in her new Lexus. They took the Kingston Ferry across the sound, and then drove to Bellevue, home of the Bellevue Square Mall. The parking lot looked like a luxury car dealership, and Angi knew it was Microsoft money, perhaps with a sprinkling of Starbucks fortunes interspersed as well. It was much different than the Fords and Chevys that populated the lot at the Silverdale Mall, where she lived, a blue DOD sticker on every windshield. As they walked in,

Angi noticed how the two malls even smelled different, Bellevue smelling like very good coffee, while the mall in Silverdale smelled of burnt popcorn

"So, one more patrol?" Mary Beth asked, as she waited for the Jimmy Chu black pumps in size 8, marked down to a mere $350. Unlike some of the officers' wives, for whom Navy service seemed like a sacrifice, Angi had never had money, and neither had Danny. Danny's dad was a heating and air conditioning repairman, while Angi was raised by a single mom who worked in an ink factory. She never once thought of herself as poor, but, looking back, they certainly never had an excess of money lying around. One of the stranger things she and Danny had in common was that neither one of them, in their entire lives, had ever gone on a family vacation.

So to them, the Navy salary had never seemed like a hardship. In fact, she drove a new car, a Honda Accord, for the first time in her life, and she absolutely loved the house they'd purchased together with a VA loan. But, after spending a few hours with Mary Beth Casazza, whose husband had lined up a job at Microsoft before getting out of the navy the year before, she was starting to become aware of the things she couldn't buy on Danny's lieutenant's salary, even with sea pay, sub pay, and the nuclear power bonus tacked on.

"That's the plan," Angi said, considering trying on a pair of Manolo Blahniks, even though she would never, she vowed, no matter how much money they someday might make, ever spend that much on a pair of shoes. "If I'm not mistaken, I think he's already turned in his letter."

Mary Beth rolled her eyes. "Isn't that amazing, when you think about it? That you don't know? That the Navy can just do whatever they want to him, as long as they want? I'll bet you can't wait to get out."

"I don't know about that," said Angi. "Danny's never hated the Navy, and neither have I."

"But the baby?" she was smiling.

Angi raised an eyebrow.

"Cindy Soldato told me."

Angi nodded. "I guess it's ridiculous to pretend it's a secret any more, now that I've told Cindy. I'm a little over three months."

"You must be so excited!" said Mary Beth. She had the shoes now, was sliding her feet into them. "And Danny will be back... "Angi watched her doing the math in her head.

"Oh no, honey. . ."

She nodded. "Yes...probably not back in time. That's okay. My mom will come in town."

Mary Beth put her hand on her arm. "No, honey, it sucks."

"You're right. It does suck. But we're not the first to go through it."

Mary Beth was shaking her head. "Soon, you won't have to worry about any of this shit. Has Danny applied to Microsoft yet? Larry says they are hiring Navy guys like crazy right now, love the nukes"

"Didn't you say he's working all the time?"

Mary Beth nodded. "In comparison to the real world: yes. But compared to the Navy? He's home every night. He's home for dinner probably three nights a week. And he's home every Saturday and Sunday, just like he's supposed to be. And the money...let me tell you Angi, you'll get used to it in a hurry. We're going to France this summer. After I get that out of my system, maybe I'll talk Larry into getting me pregnant."

At the register, Mary Beth decided at the last minute to get another pair of the same shoes in brown.

·   ·   ·

The submarine was, in many ways, just an arrangement of tubes within tubes. Different tubes contained different fluids: water, air, steam, radioactive coolant, refrigerant, drinking water, pure oxygen and pure hydrogen all coursed through different parts of the ship. Some fluids were at high pressure, like the hydraulic oil kept at a deadly three thousand pounds per square inch: a tiny stream ejected from a pinhole leak in that system could pierce a man's skull. Other systems ran at low pressure but were hazardous in other ways, like the burbling, unending stream of sewage that 154 men created as they lived their daily lives. Most of the tubes ran from fore to aft, the main axis of the submarine, carrying their cargo from its source to its conclusion. Twenty-four of the biggest tubes, however, pointed straight up and down, as they contained Trident nuclear missiles, the submarine's reason for being. The biggest tube of all was the submarine itself, a giant tapered tube of HY-80 steel forty-eight-feet wide at its widest point, and five hundred and forty eight feet long, blunted at the forward end by the sonar dome, and pinched off at the other by the seven-bladed screw that propelled them through the Pacific Ocean.

Being a qualified officer on the submarine meant being able to identify every one of those tubes on sight: what it contained, where it ran, the implications of a breech. To learn it all was daunting, as the pipes ran everywhere, layered on top of each other in every direction, but the patrols were long, diversions were few, and the men had all been screened carefully for their intelligence and their ability to work tirelessly in pursuit of engineering knowledge. Ensign Brendan Duggan was on his first patrol, in the first stage of the process, tracing the pipes and ducts of a few isolated systems at a time, learning how they tied together to make some part of the boat function. By his third patrol, he'd know every pipe of every system, and be able to hand draw most of the systems with every valve in place. Danny Jabo, on his sixth patrol, was in the final stage of the learning process. Having learned the physical composition of every system, he was tasked with learning the philosophy of its design, why it was a certain capacity, why one material had been chosen over another to construct it, the trade offs that the engineers had made in designing it, between safety, efficiency, and silence.

As part of this process, Jabo was walking Ensign Brendan Duggan through the boat, pointing out valves and ducts, attempting to help him qualify Battery Charging Line Up officer. Jabo knew almost nothing about Duggan. He was an academy guy, Jabo remembered, from somewhere in the south. He'd heard that he knew something about bluegrass music, and a rumor that he'd brought to sea a dulcimer, or a mandolin, or something like that. Thank God he'd had the sense to keep the thing stowed thus far: a nub officer couldn't be seen doing something as frivolous as playing music.

Battery Charging Lineup Officer was traditionally the first thing a new officer qualified on board, usually in his first week at sea. The BCLU verified that the ship's ventilation system was operating normally prior to a battery charge, as charging the battery released a number of undesirable elements into the ship's atmosphere: hydrogen being the most dangerous. It was an unavoidable byproduct of the process that crammed electricity into the battery's wet, acid-filled cells. Prior to the charge an enlisted man went through the ship and set everything up, but such was the importance that an officer was required to physically verify the position of every valve and every switch. To learn the battery charging lineup was good for a new officer because it took him through every area of the ship. An officer who knew what he was doing could complete it in under thirty minutes. Like so many things a new officer on a submarine did, it was at once tedious and highly important.

Duggan's qualification was important to Jabo because it would put him one step closer to the watchbill, which might, at some point, result in an extra six hours of sleep for him. Which was why Jabo was willing to take an hour out of his sleep prior to taking the watch to walk through the ship with him, in an attempt to get Duggan to the point where he could withstand an oral examination by the engineer and get qualified, a small step toward becoming useful.

"What's this?" Jabo asked, pointing to a large, humming machine in Auxiliary Machinery Room 2.

"A scrubber," said Duggan confidently. "At least one of them has to be running during a battery charge."

"Correct," said Jabo. "What does it do?"

"Removes carbon dioxide," said Duggan.

"What creates carbon dioxide?"

"I do," said Duggan. "We all do. It's a product of respiration."

"Right," said Jabo. Which is why non-qualified personnel on the boat like Duggan were sometimes called "scrubber loads."

Along with non-qual, nub, dink (short for "delinquent"), and host of other insults. "So how does it remove CO_2?"

Duggan hesitated just a moment, recalling a scrap of information from his memory. "It heats up a catalyst..."

"What catalyst?"

"MEA. It heats up the MEA..."

"How hot?"

Duggan stopped. "I don't know."

"Look that up," Jabo said. Duggan was frustrated, he could tell, thinking this was more information than he needed to know to perform the battery charging line up successfully. "You're going to need to learn it sooner or later," said Jabo. "You might as well learn it now. And it's important—this is actually one of the hottest pieces of machinery on the boat. You should know how hot. Okay?"

"Okay," said Duggan, writing down the "look up" in his little green notebook.

"And what's this?" said Jabo, continuing the tour, laying his hand on a machine on the other side of the space.

"A burner. Removes hydrogen."

"And?"

Duggan hesitated a moment. "It removes something else?"

Jabo laughed. "Now, that's something you really should know. Carbon Monoxide."

"Okay," said Duggan. Jabo noticed that he had brought the battery charging checklist along with him. "Let's go through the whole thing, see if you can actually do the line up. Ready?"

"Sure," said Brendan. He was eager to get started, eager to qualify something, contribute something. That yearning was a good quality, and at this stage in Brendan's career, the only aspect of his personality that Jabo cared about. Jabo was already walking forward, to the battery well, where the procedure would start.

"Danny? Can I ask a stupid question?"

Jabo stopped. "Sure."

"The scrubbers remove carbon monoxide, right? And the burners remove hydrogen and carbon monoxide, right?"

Jabo nodded. He was starting to wonder if they were rushing through this…that was pretty fundamental stuff. "So what's your question?"

"What about everything else?"

"Everything else?"

"Yeah, I mean, that's three things we're actively removing from the atmosphere. All this equipment, all these systems operating, organic compounds breaking down, people living inside here for months at a time, I mean, surely those aren't the only three things building up on the boat, right?"

"Well, we monitor for a bunch of things, as you know. I suppose if anything else built up to a dangerous point, we'd go up to PD and ventilate."

"Sure," said Duggan. "I told you it was a stupid question."

"No," said Jabo. "I'd tell you if it was. Actually it's a pretty good fucking question."

They'd made it to the battery well, in the lower level of Auxiliary Machinery One, right next to the diesel, the ship's two most important back up energy supplies sharing a room at the bottom of the submarine in the forward compartment. Jabo knelt next to the hatch of the well. "Okay, what do we have to do now?"

"Get OOD permission."

"Before that."

"Oh shit." Duggan hesitated a minute, and then stood and removed his belt and pens from his pocket.

"That's right," said Jabo. "Remove all metal." He stood to do the same. He didn't enjoy going in the battery well—one of the reasons he wanted to get Duggan qualified in a hurry. The hundreds of liquid acid cells in that tight compartment emitted a strange, sour smell, and Jabo always left the well feeling itchy for hours. But he couldn't let Duggan go in by himself. "Are we ready?"

Duggan nodded. Jabo pointed to the phone.

Duggan picked it up, and growled control with the phone's tiny lever. Slightly nervously, he said, "Chief of the Watch, Ensign Duggan, request permission to enter the battery well. For training."

He awaited a response. Jabo heard the Chief of the Watch relay a request from the officer of the deck. "I'm with Lieutenant Jabo."

He covered the phone with his hand and looked at Jabo. "He said to wait one."

"That's weird," said Jabo. Surely Hein wanted another officer to qualify for the battery charging line up as much as he did...he started unconsciously reaching for his belt, sensing something was about to happen.

Hein's voice on the 1MC: "All officers report to the wardroom for navigation brief."

That explains it, thought Jabo. "We'll finish this up later," he said to Duggan, who dejectedly put his belt back on.

.   .   .

They were assembled in the wardroom once again, for a navigation brief describing the second half of their journey to Taiwan. The mood was considerably less jovial than it had been during the first brief. After two weeks of straight three section watches they were all tired. The fire had shocked them all out of complacency, and the watch officers had become more demanding of the crew, and the senior officers more demanding of the watch officers. Looking around the wardroom table, Jabo saw a lot of hollow eyes, a lot of men who'd been living on caffeine for too long.

The captain rapped the table with a knuckle. "Alright Nav. Let's get started."

The Navigator propped up the small scale chart on the tripod once again, showing the great circle route to Taiwan. He'd made a red "X" on the their current location. "Here we are," he said, hitting it with a pointer.

"Is that your whole brief, nav?" asked the CO. Everyone but the navigator chuckled.

"No sir," said the Nav. He fumbled to pull another chart down and put it across the easel.

"Just put it on the table, nav," said the XO. "All you JOs get your greasy fucking elbows off, learn some goddamn manners."

Everyone backed off and the nav unrolled a huge white chart of the Pacific Ocean across the table. There were boxes marking their assigned areas, and their track, moving relentlessly westward. "Because of the time we lost during the fire, we've had to increase our SOA to twenty-two knots. And I've built into that going to PD twice a day for the broadcast."

"Just a half hour per trip, gentlemen," said the XO. "So no fucking around up there. Slow down, clear baffles, get up, and get the broadcast. We'll need to shoot trash at the same time, and anything else we need to do slow."

Jabo stared at the chart. Other than the marks made in the navigator's neat pencil, it was almost devoid of information, an unmarked expanse of pale blue. He ran his fingers along the ship's track. "It's so bare," he said. "There aren't even that many soundings."

"These areas are far from the major shipping lanes," said the navigator, looking down at the floor, avoiding eye contact. "And far from the normal Trident operating areas. They don't get updated as frequently, and these areas aren't surveyed like our normal waters."

Jabo nodded; it made sense. Some of their normal operating areas were surveyed so well that they could fix their position within a few feet just by taking a series of soundings, measuring the water's depth, determining the exact contour of the ocean floor and finding a match on the chart. Looking at a chart like the one in front of them could lull a watch officer into a false sense of security, as it appeared to describe a vast area of deep, featureless ocean.

"So at twenty-two knots, how deep do we need to be, Lieutenant Morrissey?" asked the Captain. Morrissey was on his second patrol, trying desperately to qualify OOD. The question the captain asked related to the ship's "submerged operating envelope," part of the bedrock of running the ship safely, and something every OOD was supposed to know so well that it became part of his intuition. Morrissey furrowed his brow in thought.

"Six hundred and eighty feet?" he said.

"Is that an answer or a question?" said the XO. "Grow some balls."

"My answer."

"Well you happen to be right. Now I'll ask one of these smart ass OODs why that is. Lieutenant Kincaid?"

"Two things limit depth at that speed," said Kincaid. "A stuck stern planes incident, and the threshold for cavitation."

"Is that right, Morrissey?" said the XO.

"Yes sir."

"So what's this cavitation that Kincaid is so worried about?"

"The noise made by collapsing bubbles of water vapor in the low pressure area behind the ship's propeller," said Morrissey.

"Good job. At that speed we need to run pretty deep so that we don't pop out of the water in an accident, and so that we don't cavitate and make a lot of fucking noise so the bad guys know we're coming." He paused. "Which brings us to the second reason we are here. Danny, dim the lights."

Suddenly intrigued, Jabo leaned back in his chair to hit the switch. The XO clicked a few keys on his laptop and projected a grainy image onto the movie screen pulled down at the front of the room. It was a black and white satellite photo of a two submarines at a pier, tied along side each other, head to tail. He instantly recognized it as a Soviet design, the long, blunt conning tower being distinctively Russian. It took him just a moment longer to identify the specific class.

"Anybody know what these are?" he asked.

"Russian," said Jabo. "Kilo Class." There was a murmur of admiration among the other JOs at Jabo's acumen. The short squat body of the enemy boats and the somewhat blocky lines of the hull made them look at the same time primitive and yet seaworthy, as indeed they were. Kilos were one of oldest and largest classes of submarines made by the Russians and the Soviets before them.

"You're sorta right, smart ass. They're Soviet Kilos, but these particular boats belong to our friends the Red Chinese. Our friends in intel tell us that these are a particular version of the Kilo called a Project 636 boat. Jabo, do you know what that means?"

"They call it the 'black hole,'" said Jabo. "Because it disappears from sonar."

"Correct again. Running on its battery, it's one of the quietest submarines in the world. We'll have training on it tomorrow night in the wardroom after dinner. Danny, I think you just volunteered to give it. So study up tonight while you're on the midwatch. Teach us what we need to know: max speed, sound signatures, armament, etcetera. Got it?"

"Aye, aye sir."

The XO cleared his throat and turned to the captain. All were silent, waiting to hear why they suddenly needed to understand the specs of this particular Russian submarine.

"On the broadcast, about an hour ago, we received a message from SUBPAC saying that these two boats have departed the Chinese submarine base at Ning-bo. Heading for the open seas. Anybody want to guess what they're doing?"

No one said anything.

"Me neither," said the Captain. "But we've been reminded by SUBPAC, who has been reminded by the national command authority, about how important our mission is. And we've also been reminded that China considers the seas we are entering to be their sovereign, territorial waters. So if they were to identify an unknown submerged contact in those waters…let's just say we're not going to let that happen."

For a moment they all just stared at the screen, absorbing the fact that the boats depicted in the grainy, aerial image were now their adversaries.

The captain continued. "We have to get to Suao in time, and we have to get there undetected. This is the mission we've been handed, and I intend to complete it successfully. So follow the navigator's track, and memorize every angle of the submerged operating envelope. If we stay inside it then the best minds in the

Navy assure us that we'll remain undetected and safe. Be smart. Any questions?"

"No sir," they all said in unison. Jabo glanced at the navigator, the only other man not staring at the movie screen, perhaps lost, he thought, in a mental calculation of how far they'd come, and how far they had yet to go.

·　　　　·　　　　·

Every junior officer on his first tour had two major duties: he was both a watch officer and a division officer. As a watch officer, he would routinely stand six hour watches, either as Officer of the Deck or the Engineering Officer of the Watch. The OOD, in control, was the captain's direct proxy, responsible for everything that happened to the ship during that period. Approximately three hundred feet aft of control, in the small sealed cube inside the engine room that was Maneuvering, resided the EOOW. He reported to the OOD, and was responsible for the numerous complex systems and procedures inside the nuclear propulsion plant. His mission, it was often summarized, was to keep, "the lights burning and the screw turning."

The division officer role was in a sense the junior officer's "day job." He was in charge of a division of enlisted men with specialized training responsible for some specific area of the ship's operations. While officers on the boat were generalists, expected to know everything, enlisted men were specialists. There was a division of men responsible for the sonar system, another for the missiles, yet another for cooking all the crew's meals. These divisions each had a chief or first class petty officer with many years of experience who really ran things. But he reported to a junior officer who generally signed the forms, approved leave, assigned responsibilities, and, when necessary, administered discipline.

Jabo's division was Radio; his title was Communications Officer. He reported to his department head, who happened to be the navigator, one of three department heads. The other two were the engineer and the weapons officer. Department heads, on their second sea tours, would occasionally stand watch, but their lives largely revolved around the department that they ran. Communicator on a Trident Submarine was an especially sensitive role on a normal patrol, because of the strict requirements that the sub had for staying in constant communication while on alert—ready within seconds to receive authorization and launch nuclear missiles should the order be issued.

In one sense, the extraordinary nature of their patrol made Jabo's job as communicator easier: he no longer had the unending stress of worrying about the depth of floating antennas, the vagaries of sunspots on low frequency radio waves, and the fear that a few seconds of lost communications would make for a black mark on an entire patrol. But now, the ship had to download its entire day's message traffic in a single burst, with each trip to periscope depth, so Jabo had to process a great many messages at once, drinking in two giant gulps what he used to drink all day long in sips. As communicator he was expected to read every single message, and then decide who else should read each one. Anything of particular sensitivity would be sent to the captain immediately. The ship had been at periscope depth at midnight when he took over the watch from Hein. As soon as radio reported that the entire broadcast was onboard, Jabo lowered the scope, went deep, and turned the lights back on in control.

"Ahead full," he ordered.

"Ahead full," repeated the helm, and the dinging of the engine order telegraph indicated that maneuvering also acknowledged the order. Jabo watched the ship's speed rise.

"How long were we up there?" he asked the quartermaster.

"Twenty-three minutes," he said, looking at a stop watch. "We're getting better at this. Like an attack boat."

Jabo nodded; it was good. A few weeks ago a thirty minute trip to PD would have been extraordinary; now it was routine. It was also a necessity if they were to get to Taiwan in time. Jabo rubbed his eyes and let them adjust to the lights in control. He wandered over the short distance to Flather and the chart.

"We're right here," said Flather. They'd also gotten a GPS fix while at PD, and Jabo was interested to see two pieces of information revealed by the fix. One, their dead reckoning, even at high speed, had been pretty accurate. The fix was just a few hundred feet off the last triangle that indicated their DR position. Flather had dutifully adjusted the DR track to account for the new fix. Secondly, they were right on track, right on schedule.

"Flather, does it ever bother you how blank these charts are? I wonder how good the data is."

Flather nodded. "Yes sir, it does, sometimes. These areas just aren't surveyed that well, not even by the merchant fleet. So we don't have a lot of information to work with."

"So do these charts ever get updated?"

"Not like our normal charts. We're supposed to go through things like this," said Flather, pulling out a thick, paper-clipped document from the shelf behind him.

"What's that? Notice to Mariners?"

"Yep, NTM. They come out once a week—and this one's fifty-eight pages long. Describes stuff all over the world that you might or might not want to incorporate into a chart. Normally, our charts are so up to date, these don't usually help us all that much, we've already got the information. But in water like this...I'm reading every one of these freaking things."

"You find anything in there that affects us?"

Flather nodded, and pointed to a box he'd drawn on the southwestern edge of the chart and highlighted in yellow. "That's from this NTM. Some surface ship noticed some discolored water right there where the water is supposed to be 8,000 feet deep. Shouldn't be any mud in water that deep. So it may be a sea mount of some kind, who knows. So I put in on the chart, even though it's far from anywhere we'll be. Maybe we'll swing southward on the way home, who knows. But I wanted to get it down."

"And you've got to read through all of these?"

Flather shrugged. "Me and the nav split them up, we're trying to look ahead at the water we're heading into. We're about halfway through all the NTMs for this year, although I'm getting through them faster than the nav…he's just got so much shit on his plate right now."

Jabo flipped through the Notice. Every entry was marked by a latitude and longitude, followed by some piece of information: an ODAS buoy location off the coast of California had changed. A "dangerous wreck" had to be added to a chart in the Gulf of Mexico. The interval of a lighthouse's flashing light in Ireland needed to be altered. Each correction was seemingly minor. But, Jabo knew, given the right circumstances, it was the kind of information that could turn a watch shitty in a hurry.

"Sir?" Jabo looked up to see RM1 Gurno standing at the conn with a clipboard. "The broadcast for your review." It was a bonus for them, the OOD and the communicator being the same person, one less officer to track down or wake up in order to get the broadcast reviewed.

Jabo walked up. "Anything good in there?"

"Nothing you need to wake the captain for. But look at this safety flash." He opened up to it and pointed to a paragraph.

Safety flashes were messages they received when the navy had identified a safety concern that needed immediate attention. They usually resulted from death or serious accidents, and were thus more interesting reading than the normal message traffic about wind warnings off Bremerton and new regulations about the disposal of plastic at sea. Jabo read the paragraph.

"Holy shit…"

"I know!" said Gurno, giggling.

"How do you get a testicle ripped off on a rowing machine?"

"I don't know, but they are now officially banned on Navy ships. We're supposed to put an Out of Commission tag on ours right now. Did you see the boat?"

Jabo looked. It was the USS Michigan, also based out of Bangor. "Oh man…" he said. "I know a ton of guys on that boat. I wonder if it was an officer."

"No way," said Gurno. "The victim had testicles."

The watchsection laughed appreciatively.

The story of the lost testicle and the rowing machine was indeed brief, and lacked the horrifying details that they would have to get the minute they returned to land. His eyes drifted toward the next safety message...something about R-118, the new refrigerant they'd taken on in their refit, some new warning about it. His eyebrow raised when he saw that apparently, this variety of Freon could mutate into Phosgene, a kind nerve gas, when exposed to very high temperatures. Thanks for letting us know, Navsea, he thought to himself, after we're already sealed inside a can with the stuff. He scanned to see the classification of the message, thought it might be interesting to share with his father if he could, the heating and air man. He heard the laughing in the control room stop and looked up to see why. The XO was standing in front of him, a stack of books under his arm.

"Sir."

"Danny. Anything good on the broadcast?"

"Someone lost a nut on the *Michigan*."

"That is good news. Here," he said, handing over the books. "For your training tomorrow...information about Kilo class submarines. Make it good, lots of pictures so the young ones don't let their attention wander."

"Yes sir," said Jabo. He took the stack of books and the XO wandered over to take a quick look at the chart before leaving control for a few hours of sleep. Jabo wondered if the XO actually expected him to read, digest, and then summarize all those pages in one watch. He checked his watch. He had four hours left on the conn and still needed to read through the broadcast. Well, he thought. Giving training on Kilo submarines was a lot more interesting than analyzing the effects of chlorides on the steam generators, or studying the navy's latest personnel policies. Because, in addition to the roles of Watch Officer and Division Officer, every junior officer on the *Alabama* had a third role that was just as mandatory. This fell under the category of, "shit the XO tells you to do."

. . .

At 3:15 in the morning, Hein wandered into control.

"Head break?" he asked Jabo.

"Shit yes," said Jabo. "Thanks." Head breaks were the most needed on the midwatch, because of the vast amounts of coffee consumed, and the hardest to come by, because everyone who could be sleeping was in the rack. They quickly exchanged the keys and Jabo bolted from the Conn as the quartermaster was recording the relief in the deck log.

"This is Lieutenant Hein, I have the Deck and the Conn."

As the helm was acknowledged, Jabo darted back up the ladder and grabbed a few of the books that the XO had left for him.

"Just a head break Jabo!" shouted Hein.

"This will just take me a second..."

He bolted down the ladder into the watchstander's head where he took a fantastically long and satisfying piss. He washed his hands and took the books into the Officers' Study.

The Navigator was there. He looked up from his chart without smiling or speaking, and then went back to work. Jabo edged around the table to the locker in the corner that contained the books he was looking for.

The shelf held their small library of submarine history, all the classics both modern and ancient, novels and nonfiction: *Wake of the Wahoo*, *Hunt for Red October*, *Clear the Bridge*, and *Run Silent, Run Deep*. Jabo was looking for anything that might liven up his lecture on the Kilo.

"Brushing up on your submarine history, Jabo?" said the Nav. There was something snide in his tone.

"Doing some training for the XO..."

"If you're looking for *Rig for Dive*, I've got it."

"I don't think I need it—that's World War II, right?"

The nav chuckled. "Yes. Good guess."

Jabo felt himself getting pissed off at the Nav's smirk. "Crush Martin, right? Lost his boat after that?"

The Nav suddenly turned and swept his hand over the row of history books. "They're all about lost boats. Lost men. All the nonfiction ones, anyway."

"Not all of them…"

"Let's see…" The Nav tapped one of the book's spines. "The *Wrasse* went down somewhere in the Sea of Japan, nobody knows where: ninety-two men." He tapped another. "The *Tang*, sunk by one of her own torpedoes, 74 men lost." He pulled an ancient paperback half way out to read the cover. "The *Wahoo*, gunned down by Japanese planes in the La Perouse Straits, 79 men. Fifty-two submarines this country has lost in all. Three thousand men still onboard." He pulled another book out and threw it on top of his chart: *U-Boat Commander*, by Gunther Prien.

"Our enemies haven't fared any better. The hero of Scapa Flow wrote this right before his boat disappeared. "

"Dangerous work," said Jabo, feeling the need to say something.

"Suicide," said the Nav. "And submarines are built for suicide missions."

"Not anymore…"

The Navy laughed hard at that, almost a bark. "Jesus, Jabo. You really believe that? You think anyone has ever believed that a Trident Submarine would ever come back from a war mission? How loud do you think we'd be during a launch of our twenty-four missiles? How far would that sound carry? How vulnerable would any Trident be during a strategic launch? We'd be lucky to get all twenty-four missiles away before the first torpedo found us."

"I don't know…"

"Take a look, Jabo," said the Nav, pointing to the other side of the room, to the books that contained all their war fighting tactics and procedures. "See if you can find a procedure for reloading a Trident submarine. There isn't one. No one plans on us coming back."

He sighed deeply and slumped back in his chair.

Jabo returned to the conn.

.   .   .

At 0545, just as the scent of frying bacon was beginning to drift into the control room, Kincaid arrived. As they were nearing the end of the formal turnover, Jabo brought up the incident in the Officers Study.

"So he said that we're on a suicide mission?"

"That's right," said Jabo.

Hayes thought it over for a moment. "I've heard that kind of shit before. It's something boomer sailors tell themselves to make it sound like what we do out here is tough."

"I guess," said Jabo. "I guess you had to be there. This didn't seem like some kind of posturing. He seemed…"

"Depressed? Pissed off? He's a department head. He should be depressed and pissed off."

Just then, the navigator started walking up the ladder to control, a bundle of rolled charts under his arm. He walked right by the two friends without saying a word.

Hayes shrugged. "I'm ready to relieve you."

"I'm ready to be relieved. Ship is on course two-seven-five, Ahead Full, depth six-five-zero feet."

"I relieve you."

"I stand relieved."

"This is Lieutenant Kincaid, I have the Deck and the Conn."

The watchstanders acknowledged in succession as Jabo signed the deck log, then walked the short distance into radio. He had a few minor matters he needed to take care of before he could lay down and get a quick nap before the real workday of the ship began. He handed off the previous night's messages to Gurno which he had finally read and reviewed. "Route these to the navigator, please. He's in control."

"Aye, aye, sir," said Gurno, fresh from a shower and breakfast. Jabo could barely keep his eyes open.

He reviewed and signed some planned maintenance charts for the division. Leaving radio, he briefly considered breakfast, but decided he needed sleep more than he needed food. So he stumbled down to his stateroom, shut the lights off, and closed his eyes knowing that soon he'd be awoken as the day's drills began with the general alarm; or the flooding alarm; or, maybe, if the XO was in the mood for something exotic, the rapid, high-pitch beeping of the missile emergency alarm. The ship's tight schedule would somewhat neuter the drills; they would have to simulate emergency blows, snorkeling, and trips to periscope depth, most of the things that made drills fun and interesting. But there would still be drills, and that still required everyone to be awake, no matter if you'd been up all night on the midwatch.

Jabo didn't fall asleep right away. He was still troubled by his conversation with the navigator. But like all submarine officers, he'd learned that when given the opportunity to sleep, you must sleep, no matter how disturbed you were from the last watch, no matter how pissed you were at the XO, and no matter how depressed you were that you had to wake up in a few minutes for the next round of bullshit. You had to fall asleep fast because you didn't know how many hours, or days, might pass before you got another chance. That pressure alone had kept him awake on his first patrol, that feeling of panic that he needed to get to sleep in a hurry, but couldn't. Since then, he'd mastered the art of falling asleep quickly.

Jabo started breathing deeply, pretending to sleep being the important first step. He had a few vivid, happy memories that he retreated into at times like these. All of them were about Angi.

He recalled the time he'd been driving home from the base early one morning, the refit after his second patrol, exhausted after an all-night watch in the engine room during a marathon round of testing on the primary relief valves. As he drove through a pouring rain, the sour smell of the engine room still clinging to his khaki uniform, he was startled to come upon Angi as she ran down Westgate Road. She was running away from him and didn't see him. She seemed oblivious to the rain, even though she was drenched, from her sleeveless Nike running shirt to her Saucony running shoes, the one luxury she allowed herself on their meager budget.

He slowed down so he wouldn't pass her too quickly, not wanting to splash her, but also wanting to watch her a little longer. He was struck, once again, that someone so beautiful could love him. She was athletic, but she didn't like it when Jabo described her that way. She was southern belle enough to think that adjective was an alternative for beautiful, a backhanded compliment in the same way that her grandfather inevitably described bigger girls as "healthy." But that's not how Jabo felt—to him there was no better, no more alluring description of his wife's physical beauty, the way her body was young, strong, and fast. Her shirt clung to her skin in the rain, and water ran down her toned legs, each step sending up a splash that would find its way, eventually, into Puget Sound.

He fell into something that was deeper than sleep, something like an attempt to heal, or hide.

.   .   .

He'd been asleep two and a half hours when the first alarm sounded, about two hours longer than he'd been counting on. There'd been a debate in the wardroom among the drill team about whether or not they might allow a brief period of snorkeling. The captain finally decided they could, as long as they grabbed the broadcast at the same time and only ran the diesel for about fifteen minutes. This took time to work into the drill plan, which allowed Jabo to sleep for those extra minutes, and when he heard the fire alarm sound, and jumped out of bed and into his poopie suit, he felt *good* for the extra sleep, felt like a million bucks, hoped he would be he first officer to the scene so he could take charge, put out the simulated fire with non-simulated enthusiasm. When Kincaid's voice announced after the alarm that the fire was in the Supply Office, Jabo was already sprinting aft, thinking about what hoses were closest, how pissed the Supply Officer was going to be if they moved a single sheet of paper on his desk, and how much fucking fun his job was.

.   .   .

The dinner plates were cleared away and Jabo hurriedly set up the projector and the computer. The first image was an interesting one he'd found of a Kilo actually being delivered to the Chinese atop a cargo ship. It was rare to see a sub completely out of the water like that, and seeing how easily it fit atop the cargo ship highlighted how small it was. It took up barely half of the big ship's top deck.

According to the watchbill, Jabo was supposed to be on the conn; it had been twelve hours since his midwatch ended and it was his turn again. But he'd been assigned to do this training, so the XO had detailed the engineer to relieve Hein for the training period, which pissed the eng off on a number of levels; if a department head needed to be assigned some menial duty on behalf of a junior officer, then philosophically he believed it should never be him, as the head of the most important, most demanding department on the ship. Secondly, the act seemed to imply that the engineer didn't need to know anything about Kilo submarines; he was the engineer after all, concerned about the reactor compartment and aft, and he was always sensitive to being slighted as a kind of support officer, a non-warrior. But someone had to be on the conn during Jabo's training, and the XO, for whatever reason, decided to send the sullen engineer to control, perhaps if for no other reason he thought his three-section junior officers needed a break more than him.

"Danny, let's get started," said the XO. He flipped off the lights.

"This was the first Kilo submarine purchased from Russia by the People's Liberation Army, in 1995," said Jabo. "Now the Chinese own a total of twelve of these boats. Our intel tells us that two are Type 636, the most capable platform, and as the XO mentioned last night, one of the quietest submarines in the world."

"But they're diesel boats, right?" asked Ensign Duggan. "They're only quiet when they're running on their batteries." Fresh out of the navy's nuclear power training, he'd been indoctrinated to believe that nuclear propulsion was the pinnacle of human achievement, and that all other modes of power generation were dirty, noisy, and primitive.

"Don't underestimate this new generation of diesel boats," said the XO. "I'm sure that Danny will get into the specifics, but they can run a long time on their batteries."

"Four hundred miles at three knots," said Jabo.

"There you go."

"But they're on the surface the rest of the time?" said Duggan. "Running the diesel?"

"That's right," said the XO. "And you know what that sounds like to us? When they're running their little diesel?"

Duggan shook his head.

"It sounds like a fucking diesel. Like a fishing boat, or a merchant, or any other fucking thing in this ocean that runs with an engine and a propeller. And then they kill the engine, submerge, and disappear." Jabo felt bad for Duggan. Like every newly reported ensign, he'd been absolutely living in the engine room, trying to qualify Engineering Officer of the Watch. No one really expected him to know about the capabilities of enemy subs, they wanted him to know how to charge the battery, shift the electric plant, and answer a bell: keep the lights burning and the screw turning.

"The 636 boats were improved over older Kilos in a number of ways," said Jabo, after he felt like Duggan had had enough time to squirm. "But especially in sound silencing." He clicked through to a new photo of the Kilo, an aerial shot of a boat on the surface, a puff of white diesel smoke coming from behind the sail. "The main shaft speed has been reduced to lower noise, and the entire hull is covered in sound-absorbing anechoic tiles."

"But they're still pretty crude, right?" asked Duggan.

There was a silence...he'd had a chance to shut up, and had declined, in an effort to look smart. Ensigns were told sometimes in training that their leadership would respect them for speaking up, for being an active part of the conversation in the Wardroom. This, of course, was bullshit.

"You think we don't need to worry about these guys?" said the XO. "Is that what you're saying, Duggan? Think I'm wasting your time here?"

"No sir..."

The XO's forehead vein started to bulge. The Captain sat back and smiled, ready to enjoy the show like the rest of them.

"Okay, Duggan, let's assume for a minute that you're right and the best analysts at NATO are wrong, and that these improved Kilos are pieces of shit."

"That's not…"

"Let's also assume that they aren't very capable operators, that they are not disciplined, because God knows, the Chinese are known for being happy go-lucky dipshits, aren't they Duggan?"

"XO…"

"So, since you're fresh out of Sub School let me ask you a simple question. Duggan, when you are war gaming, and you put three shitty fighter jets against one really good fighter jet, who wins?"

Duggan, Jabo was happy to see, had finally decided to stop talking and take his beating in silence.

"I'll answer: the shitty jets usually win. You might get one, maybe two, but three on one is too much. How about…three shitty tanks against one really kick-ass American tank?"

Duggan was looking at his hands.

"That's right, kids, the shitty tanks win. So, how about…two shitty subs against a one billion dollar US Trident submarine with the best minds in the country aboard? Now, how about two not-so-shitty diesel subs versus one Trident? How about two pretty good diesel boats, perhaps the best, quietest diesel-electric boats in the world, against one Trident submarine manned by junior officers who think because they are nuclear trained college graduates that no fucking Chinese skipper in a diesel boat can ever hurt them?"

Everyone was quiet now. Duggan looked like he wanted to melt away.

"Okay, XO, I think you've made your point," said the captain. "You oncoming guys—go take the watch. I am sure the engineer is breaking out in hives up there."

BOOK TWO

AHEAD FLANK

Angi was drifting off, not quite asleep, when the phone rang. "Hello?"

"Angi, its Karen Duggan."

Angi could hear worry in her voice; it woke her right up. "What's wrong?"

"Have you heard anything about a fire on the boat?"

A chill went through her. Almost every patrol there were rumors like this, and almost every patrol they proved to be baseless. Well, not *baseless*, but usually exaggerated somehow, a grain of truth mutated in the Petri dish of a bunch of wives with too much too worry about and not enough real information. "No I haven't heard anything, Karen."

"Please," she said, "tell me if you know anything. I am really freaking out about this."

Angi sympathized with Karen, who'd moved out west with Brendan, thousands of miles from her family just weeks after getting married—just like she and Danny had. She remembered that hopeless feeling of not knowing anything, the feeling that everyone else somehow knew more. "Karen, I haven't heard anything, I swear, but I'll ask around. Why don't you tell me what you've heard."

"I was talking to one of the chief's wives at the exchange, and she said they had a friend at SUBPAC who said that they had to order some equipment for the boat and rush it to the shipyard in Japan, said that something had been damaged in a fire and had to be replaced. She sounded like she knew what she was talking about, but shit, what do I know?"

Angi thought it over. It sounded ominously specific. And those chiefs' wives always did seem to have access to better information than the wardroom wives...

"Karen, I am going to make some calls, and I'll get right back to you. But I am sure it's nothing. If it was bad, the Navy would have told us something by now."

"Okay, Angi, thanks." Angi could tell that her last statement had made her feel better. Only someone on their first patrol would believe it.

.   .   .

She called Denver Kincaid first.

"Denver, have you heard anything about a fire on the boat?"

"Molly Hein just called and asked me the same thing," she said. "Do you think there's something to this?"

"Molly might have just heard about it from Karen, too...I don't know. I think I'm going to call Cindy," she said.

"Let me know..."

"I will. I'm sure everything is fine."

.   .   .

"Cindy, this is Angi."

"Hello Angi, how are you feeling?"

"Fine, just tired all the time...listen, sorry to bother you, but a couple of us have heard something about a fire on the boat."

She paused to await a response from Cindy. There was none.

"It's just...I thought if there was an announcement getting ready to make the rounds, maybe you could let me know, so I could head off some of the panic with the new wives, you know..."

Still Cindy said nothing.

"Cindy are you there?"

"Yes, Angi, I'm here. No I haven't heard anything about a fire. But I am sure everything is okay. If there was a fire."

For the first time, Angi felt a real stab of dread. Cindy was the absolute worst person in the world at keeping secrets, and everything she said just confirmed to Angi that something had gone wrong. If it was just a normal, baseless, meandering patrol rumor, Cindy would have wanted to dissect every detail, add her own elaborations, usually colored with her multiple decades of experience as a submarine wife. By not saying anything, she was saying everything.

"Cindy, is there anything you can tell me?"

"Angi, I am sure everything is fine."

As Angi hung up the phone and replayed Karen Duggan's phone call in her mind, something else occurred to her. Why in the hell would repair parts for *Alabama* be heading toward a shipyard in Japan?

.   .   .

The wives in port adhered to a hierarchy that roughly mirrored the one their husbands followed at sea—it just made thing easier. The captain's wife was in charge, the XO's wife was second in command, the rest of the officers followed in line, and the enlisted men's wives followed a whole separate organization, one of petty officer's, chiefs, senior chiefs, master chiefs, and the Chief of the Boat, a system of rank and protocol that even after six patrols Angi only vaguely understood. But one rule was crystal clear: the divide between the wives and the men in uniform could never be broached. She could call the captain's wife, but never the captain.

But Angi was on her last patrol, was pregnant, and was pretty sure the navy had something they should be telling her. She felt like the navy owed it to her. She dialed one more number. And after speaking to a yeoman and a civilian secretary, she finally got through.

"Captain Soldato."

"Mario, this is Angi."

"Angi, how are you feeling?"

"Captain, did something happen on the boat?"

He cleared his throat. "Angi, you know I can't talk about stuff like that. If there's word to go out, it will come through the usual channels..."

"Mario, please, I won't tell anybody, I just really need to know…"

"I'm sorry, Angi, I hope you understand…" Angi could hear the regret in his voice, and desperately tried to read his tone for clues…she regretted that she hadn't driven onto base to ask him in person. She had considered it, but thought it might give Cindy Soldato enough time to let him know about the rumor. She felt her head spinning with fear, she couldn't even picture what it would mean to have a fire on a submarine. What was there to burn? What would happen to the air?

"Captain was there a fire?" she could hear the desperation in her voice.

There was a long pause, she could feel in the silence Mario considering telling her the truth, and she could feel him rejecting it.

"Angi, I'm sure everything is fine."

.   .   .

Captain Soldato hung up and felt horrible. It was the plague of ships at sea, the way the wives could seize on any grain of information and work themselves into an absolute frenzy. Cindy had called him earlier this morning and told him about the rumor—Angi had not been the first to call her. He told Cindy pretty much what he'd told Angi—that even if something had happened, everything was okay now. And he couldn't say anymore, which pissed Cindy off. He wished he could just tell her that they'd had a fire in the damn laundry, no one was hurt, and in a couple of weeks even the laundry would be repaired. But to disclose that would disclose that the ship would get a new washing machine in two weeks, which meant it had a port call in two weeks, which would lead to a million other questions, a million other rumors. As much as he hated to leave poor Angi in the dark like that, he had to.

But something he wouldn't tell Angi, or Cindy, and that he even hated to admit to himself: he was worried too. He'd poured over the *Alabama's* message, and was able to piece together from the scant information inside that the fire had been serious, not just a smoldering pile of poopie suits. There'd been water damage on three levels, which indicated several hoses had been brought to bear. The ship had fought electrical grounds for two hours after the fire was extinguished, some of them serious, meaning a lot of water had been discharged from those hoses. And then the ship had to ventilate with the diesel for almost two hours. Meaning there was a lot of smoke. A lot.

But the most disturbing thing in the message was a single line about how the fire hose closest to the scene had been made useless, pressurized and immovable in its rack. It disturbed Soldato because most of his comrades at squadron took it to mean that someone onboard *Alabama* was really fucking stupid—some dumbass had arrived at the scene and flat-out panicked, turned the valve lefty-loosey and taken a fire hose out of service. And he didn't believe that. Some captains he knew liked to look back at their old boats and see how things deteriorated once they stepped away. But Soldato knew too many of the men, respected the captain and the XO too much. The ship, and the crew, were not fuck ups.

Which left a disturbing alternative—someone had done it on purpose. It was the one thing that all the engineering genius in the world couldn't account for. It was the reason they worked so hard to screen the men before they even set foot on the boat, and that in the history of the force, submarines had accepted only volunteers. A saboteur was a nightmare scenario, and the idea of it worried the captain so much that he missed a refit review meeting for the *USS Florida*, as he sat at his desk and brooded.

. . .

Jabo checked the ship's position again on the chart. He had just taken the conn, the officer of the deck on the six-to-midnight evening watch, still pleasantly full after a meal of spaghetti and meatballs. He could still smell the garlic bread, and hear the clatter below decks of the meal being cleaned up.

They were on track...barely. They'd run some drills that afternoon, what few drills they could run without slowing the ship much below the required twenty-two knot SOA: a radioactive spill in the engine room, an electrical grounding isolation exercise, a fire in the engine room. All lame, except for the fire. During that one they'd gone quickly to PD, practiced ventilating, and while they were up acquired the broadcast—Jabo still needed to review those messages. And, in a huge departure from the simulation while at PD, they shot what trash they could. A submarine disposed of trash by compacting it into metal cylinders ten inches in diameter and shooting them from the bottom of the boat in a device that functioned much like a torpedo tube. Getting rid of garbage was turning out to be one of the real limiting factors of their rapid advance across the Pacific. Like going to periscope depth, shooting trash required the ship to slow. But unlike acquiring the broadcast, shooting trash took more than twenty-three minutes, and the metal tubes were starting to pile up. The trash room was at capacity, and the overflow was now stacked in the torpedo room like cordwood. The smell was starting to become an issue, and the crew had taken to marking the ripest cylinders with yellow post-it notes so that, when the opportunity to shoot a few cylinders presented itself, the foulest would be sent to the bottom of the ocean first.

But Jabo's next six hours represented the distillation of their priorities. There would be no going to PD, no shooting trash, and, most importantly, no slowing down. If they kept at twenty-three knots, by the end of his watch, they would have just made their way back to the red dot that marked their required position on the chart. By the end of the midwatch, they would have gotten ahead enough to allow another quick trip to PD, another broadcast, and maybe send a few more cylinders of trash to their watery grave.

He read the deck log entry from the last watch's trip to PD and something caught his eye.

"Did you take this sounding?" he asked Flather.

"Yes sir."

It was 1,850 fathoms. The chart, at the position of their fix, read 2,900 fathoms. "That's a big difference."

Flather shrugged. "Since it was more than ten percent off, we told the navigator and the captain. It's in the standing orders. There's still plenty of water under us." And that was true. A fathom was six feet, so even at their current depth, with the current sounding, they had more than 1,000 fathoms, or six thousand feet, of water between them and the ocean bottom. Still, the discrepancy bugged him.

"Does that bother you?"

Flather shrugged again, this time in a way that said: I've got much bigger shit to worry about. "You know how these charts have been—they're pretty sketchy. So I'm not entirely surprised that some of the soundings are a little off."

"A little? It's over a thousand fathoms off. A fucking mile."

"Maybe it's the fathometer," said Flather. "It's less accurate in very deep water." Jabo could see that Flather was getting his back up, insulted by any implied inaccuracy on the chart or in the sounding.

"True enough," said Jabo. "But let's take another one. It'll make me feel better."

"Captain's permission?"

"Don't need it to use the secure fathometer at this speed."

"Be aware that the secure fathometer is even less accurate, and this speed will degrade the accuracy even more," said Flather. He was being pissy now.

"Noted."

Flather turned to the console on his left, spun a few dials and flipped some switches, in a minute he was ready to go. He turned to Jabo for final confirmation.

"Go ahead."

He pushed the button at the center of the console. A discrete, focused pulse of sound shot from the bottom of the boat to the ocean floor, then bounced back to the sensor on the hull. The fathometer measured exactly how long it took the sound to make its journey. It then corrected the speed of sound for the ocean's temperature, one of the values Flather had entered, added in the depth of the boat, and in less than a second, displayed the depth of the ocean: 1,840 fathoms. Flather noted it in his log, then wrote the number, in his tiny, neat script, next to their estimated position on the broad, featureless chart of the Pacific that was supposed to tell them where on the planet they were. The consistency of the two readings, to Jabo, probably ruled out equipment malfunction. Which meant one of two equally disturbing possibilities: either their chart was inaccurate. Or they weren't where they thought they were.

Someone cleared his throat at the conn and Jabo turned. IC2 Lester stood waiting with his clipboard. Lester absent-mindedly turned and reset the timer for the BST buoys as he waited to get Jabo's attention. The "beast buoys" were distress beacons attached to the side of the boat with explosive bolts, designed to float to the surface and alert the navy that a Trident submarine was in serious trouble. A number of things would cause the buoys to automatically launch: excessive depth, certain conditions inside the hull, and a timer that had to be manually turned at least once every three hours. If no one thought to turn the timer in that amount of time, the logic went, then everyone on the boat must be dead. In one legendary Trident submarine incident, USS Michigan in drydock forgot to secure the buoys, as they are supposed to be in port, and then no one wound the timer. After three hours, just as designed, the explosive bolts fired, the twin buoys rocketed off the side of the boat, crashed into the drydock basin, and began broadcasting their distress signal, a frequency that was continuously monitored around the clock by three dedicated teams of radiomen around the world. According to the legend, the president of the United States was actually awoken before the buoys were shut off, and the captain was relieved of command before the sun came up. Good electricians, like Lester, turned the BST timer habitually, every time they walked by it.

"Yes Lester?"

"Review my logs sir?"

Lester was the Auxiliary Electrician Forward, a roaming watchstander with responsibilities all over the forward section of the ship. The Officer of the Deck was required to review and initial his logs periodically, but a good watchstander, like Lester, would prompt the OOD to take a look when something was wrong. Jabo really wanted to study the chart, puzzle over that inconsistent sounding. But Lester knew what he was doing, he'd spent two years on a fast boat before coming to *Alabama*. Jabo knew he wouldn't be bothering him without reason.

He crossed the conn and took the clipboard. He scanned it quickly, wanting to see if anything jumped out at him before asking Lester what his concerns were. There were only a few red circles on the sheet, from the last watch, when they'd been at PD. They'd ventilated briefly, and the oxygen level in the ship had actually drifted high out of spec, slightly beyond the twenty percent they tried to maintain with their normal underway O_2 bleed. (There was an upper limit for oxygen because too much of it could make fires more likely and intense.) Since going back deep, the crew of *Alabama* had managed to breathe it back down into specification. And for the last two hours, Jabo could see everything was in black. He scanned over the rows that were the normal areas of concern; hydrogen, electrical grounds, the bilges. Everything at first glance looked good. But that's why they put smart guys like Lester on the watchbill: to let them know what was wrong before alarm bells started going off.

"Check out Freon," said Lester.

Jabo scanned the second sheet, where a long list of contaminants were measured by CAMS, the ship's computerized atmospheric monitoring station. Freon was, indeed, drifting higher, especially in Machinery Two.

"That's weird," said Jabo.

"I know," said Lester. "Especially since there's no refrigeration gear back there. And look at this…" Lester flipped ahead a page, to a row in which he checked the temperatures of the two main freezers, which were almost directly below their feet.

"Not out of spec…"

"But getting there," said Lester. "They usually go high before meals, as the cranks are going in and out of there getting food, but usually by now they're going back down. They're still going up."

Jabo sighed. "I'd say we may have a refrigeration problem."

It was one of those things they didn't spend a lot of time teaching you until you actually arrived on a boat: the importance of the ship's numerous refrigeration plants. An ensign was conversant on his first day on the boat in the language and philosophy of nuclear propulsion, thanks to a year of rigorous training, both in the classroom and at a working reactor. He could also fake it reasonably well in a conversation about torpedoes or sonar, or any of a handful of tactical systems that he'd studies at submarine school for three months immediately before reporting to the submarine. But refrigeration was one of those things they were expected to learn at sea, despite the fact that it was a system whose collapse could affect almost every other system on the boat: and it wasn't at all about the food stores. The same plants that cooled the ship's refrigerators and freezers provided cooling water to all the ship's electronics as well.

"Chief of the Watch, get Chief Yaksic to control."

The chief of the watch was already sending the messenger to the goat locker; like any good COW he'd been eavesdropping and anticipating. "He's on his way, sir."

A *whoop* on the panel and a blinking red alarm light caught the COW's eye.

"Number one oxygen generator is shut down on high voltage," he said.

Motherfucker thought Jabo. His blood started pumping and he started running through procedures in his mind, aligning priorities, trying to figure out what the fuck was going to happen next, and what he could do about it.

·   ·   ·

Petty Officer Howard made a slight adjustment to the voltage of the number one oxygen generator, and waited a moment to verify that the individual cell voltage was drifting back down. Since they'd started up the machine that afternoon after the drills, voltage had been edging high again, a tendency that had worsened in recent days. He'd calculated in his head that he had just enough time to complete a round of logs before getting back to the machine and adjusting it, lest its own protective systems shut it down because of the excessive voltage. The machine needed maintenance, real maintenance, with contractors, engineers, and work plans. But that would probably have to wait until they were in port, if not dry dock. In the meantime, it was his job, for six hours at a time, to keep it running.

The oxygen generators were some of the most advanced, most temperamental, and most important machinery on the boat. They manufactured breathable oxygen from the only raw material that the submarine had unlimited access to: water. Using high voltage electricity, the generators ripped the H_2O of water into its constituent parts: hydrogen and oxygen. The hydrogen was pumped overboard and the oxygen was either piped into the boat or stored in banks for later usage. But the net result of this giant exercise in basic water chemistry was a machine that combined high voltage electricity with high pressure cells of two of nature's most explosive gasses. Which is why most men on the boat routinely referred to the oxygen generator as "the bomb," and why almost every oxygen generator in the fleet had hanging somewhere near it a picture of the *Hindenburg*.

It was Howard's skill at running the oxygen generators, he knew, that had kept him away temporarily from the green table—captain's mast—and whatever variety of punishments awaited him for the dryer fire. The captain and XO wanted to take him to mast, which would, at the very least, mean he would have to re-qualify every watch station. And probably worse: he might lose rank, he might lose money, he might even be kicked off the boat. Shit, who knows—they might even send him to the brig. He'd gotten a recent free pass for his DUI, so he was not expecting leniency. Even if he knew that he was not at fault for the fire.

But they had to keep Howard on the watchbill for now because of the oxygen generators. Only two other men were qualified to run them. If they busted him, they'd have to go port and starboard in machinery two, meaning each watchstander would have to stand an exhausting cycle of six hours on watch, six hours off watch, instead of the normal three-section watchbill of six on, twelve off. Apparently, the captain and XO didn't want to have the oxygen generators, along with the other crucial atmosphere control equipment in the space like the burners and the scrubbers, tended by exhausted men. So they'd reluctantly delayed Howard's punishment. Howard knew he was lucky—Captain Shields was a merciful man. Merciful to him, merciful to the men who would stand port and starboard in his absence. Captain Soldato would have done the opposite, would have taken him to mast the night of the fire, busted him, screamed at him, and laughed as they racked his shipmates and gave them the good news that they were six on and six off for the rest of patrol because of Howard's fuck up.

So Howard was determined, absolutely determined, to stand each watch flawlessly. That, combined with the passage of time, might make whatever sentence they eventually passed on him a little more lenient. And his secret hope: if enough time passed, maybe he would find out what actually started the dryer fire. Although, certainly, he was the only person on the boat that thought the crime was unsolved. He'd been working on it, writing down what little information he had, a few thoughts about the possibilities, trying to piece it altogether before they finally got around to hanging him. He kept his notes on two neat sheets of yellow notebook paper, and when he was on watch they were on his clipboard, directly behind his logs, so he could record his ideas as they occurred to him, points of data that, when fully assembled, would prove his innocence.

As he finished tweaking the oxygen generator back into compliance, it was that clipboard he grabbed, ready to take another perfect round of logs in machinery two, a small step on the road toward redemption.

He started on the level he was in, third level, taking logs on all the operating machinery. No burners were running, but, oddly, two scrubbers were. This despite the fact that carbon dioxide was at zero, because of the recent ventilation. He finished his round of logs on both machines, noted the high but appropriate temperature of each: both were running perfectly, if needlessly.

He descended the ladder to Machinery 2 Lower Level. In addition to the machinery that concerned him as a watchstander, it was also home to the ship's modest complement of exercise equipment. But no one was working out—with the tempo they were operating everyone was too tired to exercise. It was too bad, it was nice having the company down there, made the watch go a little faster to watch someone else using the space recreationally, even if he was at work. It depended on the person, of course.

During the first hour of the watch, the navigator had come aft to work out, wearing faded blue USNA gym shorts and a plain white T-shirt stretched across his bony shoulders. Howard caught himself staring at the pink, starburst-shaped scar on the nav's knee, from when he'd stabbed himself with the dividers in control: that story had rapidly become legend with the crew, further evidence that craziness was tolerated among officers. It was another example of Captain Shields's willingness to give second chances; rumor had it that the XO wanted to throw the nav off before his knee had scabbed over. The navigator had caught him staring at the scar and Howard quickly averted his eyes and finished his logs. He made note of the nav's presence in the same section of the logs he would have recorded the smell of smoke, flickering lights, or mysterious rattles that might give away their position to the enemy.

Howard saw gratefully, upon descending to lower level for the second time, that the navigator had already gone. He stood at the bottom of the ladder and took the emptiness in, true solitude being unusual on the boat. He realized he was staring at the deck, zoned out in a way that surprised him: he was actually relatively well-rested. He shook his head to clear the cobwebs, then lifted a deck plate to check the level of water in the bilge, one of the entries on his logs.

He put his pen to the paper and tried to write DRY but couldn't remember how to get the word started. When he remembered, he couldn't get the tip of his pen to the appropriate box, directly below the DRY he'd written an hour before.

Shit. He stood, shook his head again. Something was wrong, he realized, he was suddenly leaning on the aft bulkhead, trying to get his bearings, his back cold against the steel. It was getting harder for him to think, he started to slide down into a seated position.

Even as he faded out, he realized that something was out of place. It was a knack all experienced watchstanders had, the ability to know that something was out of position before they'd actually isolated what it was, an ability they'd gained by staring out at a normal line up for hundreds of hours. Reactor operators in the engine room were known for it, an uncanny way of looking at their panel of over fifty indicators as one giant picture, sensing immediately that some dial had moved from its normal position, even though it would take another half second to figure out which one. Howard experienced the same thing surveying Machinery Two Lower Level.

Part of him knew he needed to climb the ladder; whatever was wrong seemed worse in lower level. But then he isolated exactly what was wrong: a small valve in the very corner of the space, a valve he'd never seen operated, a valve that was always closed, its purple-handled operator perpendicular to the pipe. The handle, Howard realized through a fog, was sticking straight out, parallel to the pipe, and the valve was wide open. This could be it, he thought with his last conscious breath, lunging toward the valve. I'll shut it, save the day, save the crew. The fire will be forgotten. He collapsed with his hand outstretched, the clipboard crashing against the deck.

.   .   .

"Get him yet, chief?"

"No sir," he said, growling machinery 2 even as he spoke. "Howard's not answering."

Jabo's mind raced, electric, in casualty mode, even though no alarm had yet sounded and no urgent words had yet crossed the 4MC. Something was happening—he knew it wouldn't be long.

The oxygen generator was shut down, Freon was creeping up high in machinery two, the ship's freezers a level below him were warming up, and, most ominously, Howard was not communicating with them from the space where two out of three of these events were taking place. It could be that Howard was simply combating the problem, and whatever was going on he deemed more important than answering the COW's calls. That was a real possibility, and it was something Jabo was sensitive to, the fact that sometimes a situation demanded action more urgent than updating control. Not more than a few minutes had passed since the oxygen generator shut down; it was very possible that Howard had his hands on the knobs, trying to make the thing safe, recoverable, and that a report was forthcoming.

"Quit calling him," said Jabo.

"Aye sir."

Jabo saw Lester at the ladder to control, ready to go.

"Yes," said Jabo. "Go down there, see what's going on, see if he needs help."

"Aye sir," said Lester, already running down the ladder, giving the timer of the BST buoy a twist as he passed.

Jabo thought it over, trying to connect all the dots. He thought back to his pre-watch tour, remembered seeing Howard in Machinery Two, dutifully on watch a few minutes early, reviewing his logs, something else out of the ordinary that he couldn't quite remember. The one piece of the puzzle that still didn't fit was the Freon in machinery two, he couldn't figure that one out. How did Freon get down there? Would Freon somehow shut down the oxygen generator? Jabo didn't see how it could, and he remembered that the number one generator was getting a little squirrelly, it had shut down on high cell voltage twice early in the patrol. But somehow the watchstanders had figured out a way to keep it running, some adjustment they could make to it during the watch. Jabo seemed to remember hearing that Howard was the one who'd figured it out, he was always kind of a prodigy with those machines. So why had it shut down? And why did Jabo have a bad feeling that he was missing something, something big?

The 4MC speaker crackled. Jabo knew that whatever was happening was about to start.

"Injured man in Machinery Two!" came Lester's voice across the scratchy speaker. "Petty Officer Howard is unconscious!" He sounded winded, his breathing heavy.

"It's the Freon," said Jabo out loud. He grabbed the 1MC. "Injured man in Machinery two, Petty Officer Howard is unconscious! High Freon levels in Machinery Two, all hands in the missile compartment don EABs."

He hung up the mike. He heard steps running below and around him as the crew responded to the alarm. Some of those footsteps, he knew, were the captain on his way to control. "All ahead one third," he said, and the helm's hand shot to the engine order telegraph, which soon matched the order with a ding of its bell.

"All ahead one third, aye sir. Maneuvering answers ahead one third."

"Dive make your depth one-six-zero feet."

"Make my depth one-six-zero feet aye sir," said the diving officer, and he began giving orders to the helm and lee helm, bringing the ship shallow, ready to clear baffles and go to periscope depth, ready to ventilate. The change in bells and the depth change had already slowed the boat to under fifteen knots. The big rudder as they cleared baffles would slow them more, below ten knots so they could pop up, raise the snorkel mast, and get whatever bad air they needed to off the boat, bring clean air on. Jabo thought about the track on the chart, what this was gong to do to their speed of advance, but he quickly pushed it aside—that was not at all his priority at the moment. Making the ship safe was his duty. And he knew he was missing something…it gnawed at him.

Ensign Duggan stomped into control, started putting on the headphones by the white board on which they tracked casualties. The navigator was right behind him, he would take over making announcements to the ship and run the damage control efforts as Jabo brought the ship to periscope depth.

"Freon?" said Duggan to the navigator as he put his headset on. Jabo was concentrating on the green CODC sonar display, looking for any contacts to come into view that might impede their trip to PD. Things would start materializing now, the sounds of distant ships that had been masked by their own relatively high noise level borne of their high speed. Jabo could feel the up angle in his feet, the dive was aggressively driving up, pleasing him.

"Yes," said the navigator. He spoke into the 1MC, announcing to the entire ship, "Rig for General Emergency."

"Freon's harmless, right?" said Duggan to the nav when he hung up the mike.

"Yes," said the nav. Jabo could hear the annoyance in his voice, and he felt it too. Now was not the time for Duggan to either seek nor display knowledge; they were fighting a real casualty. "It's harmless," continued the nav. "But it's heavy; it displaces air."

Which means at the moment, in machinery two, it's pretty fucking harmful, thought Jabo. He pictured it all pooling back there now as they took the up angle, collecting invisibly against the bulkhead and the wall of the diesel fuel oil tank. The up angle was good, the Freon would roll backwards, away from the berthing areas. Jabo wondered how the berthing check was going, wondered if they would soon hear about any one else unconscious. Depending on how much Freon was back there, it could be above the second level deck plates now, gathering like an invisible pool of water that Howard may have unknowingly descended into. Jabo pictured it, rising like floodwater up to the oxygen generators, the burners, the scrubbers...

That's when it finally clicked.

He grabbed the 1MC, saw the nav raise an eyebrow at that, as did the captain, who was just entering control. Jabo almost shouted into the microphone.

"Secure the scrubbers!" he said. "All hands throughout the ship don EABs. There may be phosgene in the atmosphere!"

Everyone in control reached for an EAB, as did Jabo.

"Both scrubbers are secured," said the navigator sourly, getting the report on the phones. He still didn't have an EAB on, and Jabo fought the urge to snap back at him, order him to put one on. The captain also stared at him a little befuddled, but he pulled an

EAB from the overhead and put it on, and the nav then followed suit.

Jabo stepped down to the CODC display, pulling on his own EAB; the trip to PD was suddenly more urgent. He remembered his pre-watch tour: both scrubbers were running for no apparent reason. There was no doubt that Freon had somehow filled Machinery Two, and with two scrubbers running at temp, it was more than enough to create Phosgene gas, just as the message had warned. It sounded like they had unlimited Freon back there and unlimited heat from the scrubbers; it was like they were running a fucking phosgene factory. They had to get up quickly and get clean air onboard. If the sonar screen was clear when they slowed down, Jabo was going to recommend to the captain that they emergency blow to the surface.

But the screen wasn't clear, not even close. Surface contacts were everywhere. Blowing to the roof might add a collision and flooding to the list of shit going wrong. The captain leaned over his shoulder as he stared at the congested sonar display.

"Phosgene?" His voice sounded distant coming through the built in mouthpiece of the EAB.

"Yes sir, there was just a message about this a few days ago—the new refrigerant can mutate into Phosgene at very high temps, and both scrubbers are running back there." "Both scrubbers are running?" said the captain with a raised eyebrow.

"Not sure why."

"Noise isolation exercises last watch," said the navigator, with his back turned to them. He was somehow eavesdropping even with the headset on and a dozen people jabbering in his ear. "We were determining the TIMS baseline." TIMS was a system of noise meters on virtually every machine on the boat. Originally designed to aid in sound silencing efforts, they'd learned to use it for maintenance. A baseline for every connected machine was established, and if the noise level went up, it could mean something was going wrong with the machine and someone needed to take a look. They periodically had to run equipment to gather baseline data.

"And that might create phosgene?" asked the captain.

"Yes—we received it in a safety flash last week."

"I don't remember that." Jabo saw him file it away. They both were focused on the grainy green sonar display in front of them, where several bright white bands indicated that they were not alone in their patch of ocean.

From sonar: "Conn, Sonar we have six contacts…"

"We see them," said the captain. He was touching them on the screen, he stopped on the brightest one. "What do you hear at two-one-zero, the contact designated Sierra Two?"

There was a pause, and then Petty Officer Leer, the sonar supervisor, appeared at the door to control. What would normally be a five second walk took a minute as he unplugged his EAB, walked to them, and replugged in the manifold by the CODC in control, the look of concern evident even through his plastic mask. "These guys just came out of nowhere when we slowed. We're effectively surrounded by them. Maybe a fishing fleet, maybe squid boats."

"Distance?"

"I'll need a TMA maneuver to be sure, but we can hear the screws turning, clear RPM counts—they're close. Probably within two thousand yards. I thought I could hear chains rattling on one of them."

"So fishing boats. Very close fishing boats."

"That's right."

"Danny, give them a TMA maneuver."

"Helm, right full rudder."

"Right full rudder, aye sir! My rudder is right full."

"Make your course zero-one-zero."

"Make my course zero-one-zero, aye sir." Leer took a deep breath, unplugged his mask, and trotted back to sonar.

The ship began turning immediately, and the white bands shifted radically on the screen. Assuming that the contact's course and speed remained constant, the ship could change course like this and calculate with a fair degree of accuracy the distance and course of the contacts: it was the art of Target Motion Analysis. Performed skillfully, this would allow them to choose a safe place to arise to periscope depth. But turning also unveiled the section of ocean that had been behind the submarine, its acoustic blind spot, or baffles. As they turned, two more white bands emerged.

"Wonderful," said the captain.

Leer was back in sonar and on the mike. "Conn Sonar, two new contacts coming out of the baffles. Eight now in all."

"We see them," said the captain.

"Sonar, conn, we'll take two minutes on this leg and then do another maneuver."

"Aye sir."

Jabo looked away from the console and saw Lieutenant Maple standing there with a green book of all the ship's piping diagrams. He was breathing heavy, the mask of his EAB was fogged from perspiration.

"Are you here to solve the mystery of the Freon?" said the captain.

Maple nodded, and opened the book to the page he'd saved. "Right here," he said. "Freeze seal piping. It's the only Freon pipe anywhere down there. Yaksic went down there and the valve was wide open. He shut it, but it probably dumped the whole system."

"Freeze seal," said Jabo. "Fuck." He cursed himself for not thinking of it. Whenever maintenance was done on a high pressure water system, the water had to be isolated from the work, lest the workers be sprayed by water that was high pressure, high temperature, or, in some cases, radioactive. Good practice required that the work, and the workers, be protected by at least two closed valves. But sometimes, by virtue of the location or other unusual circumstances, two valves weren't available. In these cases, flexible tubes of Freon could actually be wrapped around the pipe, and freeze a slug of water in place, a frozen chunk of ice that could seal a system amazingly well—Jabo had seen them perform hydrostatic pressure tests with 1000 psi against freeze seals. So throughout the ship ran purple pipes linked to the central Freon reservoir, in case this kind of work was necessary.

Yaksic had appeared in control at Maple's side.

"Yaksic, any good reason that valve may have been operated?"

"None sir, not even by accident. It's out of the way, just above the deck plates in lower level."

Jabo's internal clock ticked—enough time had gone by, they needed to make another maneuver, he didn't want to waste a second getting to periscope depth. "Sonar, conn, turning to port for TMA."

"Aye sir."

"Left full rudder, aye sir, my rudder is left full."

"Make your course two-three-zero."

"Make my course two-three-zero, aye sir."

The ship swayed again, and Jabo watched the CODC display. Thankfully, no new contacts appeared, although the eight they had to track now presented a daunting enough challenge. The picture was starting to form in his mind of the ocean over their heads, the relative position and size of the fishing boats. He'd chosen the course two-three-zero because it looked like it might be a safe path to PD, and because it kept them generally on track, although they were so slow he didn't see how they could ever make it up on their voyage to Taiwan. Jabo started thinking about periscope depth, the preparations to ventilate, calculated how long it might take them to replace the ship's bad air with good: fast with the blower, faster with the diesel, fastest with both. Petty Officer Hurd, the fire control operator, had appeared at the side of the conn—it would be his job to plug and unplug Jabo's EAB as he spun around on the scope. There was a lot of chatter in control, rigs being reported, people looking up facts about Freon and Phosgene. Jabo forced himself to focus on the CODC. His job at the moment was to get the ship up to the roof, so they could get the bad air off and the good air on. Everyone else would take care of everything else, but his job was to get the boat up if the course was good.

It was not.

Leer came into control, without his EAB so he could hustle faster.

"Put that fucking thing back on," ordered Jabo.

"Turn right!" said Leer. "We are driving bearing rate on Sierra Six!"

The captain came over to the CODC, he and Jabo both saw that Leer was right. The Sonarmen could actually listen to the contacts with their headphones, didn't have to wait for the data to accumulate in visual form on the screen, and what Leer had heard was very, very close. By "driving bearing rate," Leer meant that the Alabama's own motion was causing the change in bearing rate, as opposed to any motion by the contact—which meant they were dangerously near.

"Right full rudder!" said Jabo.

"Right full Rudder aye sir...my rudder is right full..."

The big ship swung right, and the bright band of Sierra Six's noise bent away from them, but it was so close now...

"We're going right under them," said the captain calmly. "Rig the ship for collision."

"Rig for collision!" said the navigator into the 1MC, and the chief of the watch sounded the collision alarm. Not even the hull of a giant freighter could hit them at a depth of 160 feet—that's exactly why that depth was chosen to prepare for periscope depth. But these were fishing boats, and there were a lot of things they might be dragging: nets, chains, maybe even an anchor. And that's if they'd correctly guessed about the nature of the surface boat. It could be even worse if it was dredging, laying cable, trawling... there were a great many reasons to avoid driving your submarine underneath a surface ship.

"Go deep, captain?"

He shook his head. "No point now. We're already under them."

They continued to swing right, but the noise of sierra six was a bright band that had consumed the display. The captain toggled one of the display's switches, changing the scale so they could see more. Jabo was amazed at his calm.

As they passed under Sierra Six, they could hear a pinging through the hull, a watery, high pitch ping as regular as a metronome.

"Their fathometer," said the captain, still watching the display. Sierra Six was behind them now. The captain waited… "steady here."

"Steady as she goes!" ordered Jabo.

"Steady as she goes, aye sir," said the helm, as he swung the rudder left to steady the ship on the bearing at which the ship was heading at that moment. They were pointing almost due north. "Sir, ship is steady on course zero-zero-five."

"Very well, said Jabo.

"This is it," snapped the Captain. "Let's go up."

Jabo stepped back and put his hands on the orange ring over his head. "Raising number two periscope." He swung the ring to the left and the scope smoothly and quickly rose until the eyepiece came into view. He put his right eye to the scope and was now looking into the ocean.

Still spinning slowly around, searching 360 degrees around them, he twisted the handles toward him so that he was also looking up, looking for anything that was too close. He couldn't see Sierra Six, the visibility underwater was not that far. Had he seen anything, he would have ordered emergency deep without hesitation. But it looked clear after three complete circuits around. Getting up briskly was crucial now, this was when the ship was at its most vulnerable. While no ship on earth could run into them at 160 feet, the same was not true as they ascended to periscope depth. Once they got to PD, they would actually be able to look around with their eyeballs, see the types of ships around them, the course and speeds they were on—it would be easy to make smart decisions. But the journey from 160 feet to PD was fraught.

"Dive make your depth seven-eight feet."

"Make my depth seven-eight feet, aye sir."

As they were trained, the control room instantly went silent with that order. The ship pointed up slightly, and they began to rise, as Jabo spun slowly around, continuing to verify that nothing would obstruct their trip to the surface. A lone fish swam frantically in front of the scope, trying to get out their way, a trail of tiny bubbles in his path. The water lightened as they rose, turning from a dark, almost blackish green to a lighter aquamarine. Jabo could see the sun through the water as they rose; he was somewhat surprised that it was so bright out. They'd kept the boat on Pacific Time, and he'd lost all track of what time it was in the world above them. The scope broke through the water as Jabo continued to spin. The only sound was a slight hiss every time Hurd unplugged and replugged his EAB, which kept him from wrapping the hose around the scope as he spun. It was a sacred rule—between 160 feet and PD, no one but the OOD was allowed to speak, and the entire control room awaited to hear one of two reports from him once the scope was clear: "no close contacts," or "emergency deep!"

"Scope is breaking..." it was momentarily obscured by a splash. Then it was out.

"Scope is clear." Jabo turned three complete times, noted all the contacts right where he thought they should be, but none were on top of him, none had the narrow profile of boats on a collision course. He counted them as he spun, counted nine, one more than they'd seen in sonar. But after three complete revolutions he was certain that they were not going to run into anybody.

"No close contacts!" Jabo said.

The control room watchstanders breathed a collective sigh of relief, and began filling the silence again with their orders, comments and recommendations. Jabo kept his mask pressed to the scope. "Sonar, conn, mark surface contacts on the following bearings..." he pressed the red button the scope handle each time the crosshairs in his scope hit the center of one of the fishing boats. "Mark...mark...mark...mark..." Nine times he marked a contact, and each time Hurd called out the bearing as he pushed the button. After a complete revolution, satisfied he'd marked all the visible contacts, he switched the scope to high power and began a search of a ninety-degree arc of ocean. He let Hurd work on the contacts' solutions in fire control. While satisfied that they were safe at their current course and speed, he was concerned that they had somehow missed one in sonar, one that was close enough to see.

"Sonar conn—which contact is the one we missed?"

There was a pause, the Leer's voice on the mike: "Designate Sierra Nine. About zero-four-five relative."

Jabo swung the scope to the starboard beam and rolled the handles forward to put the magnification in high power. Yes, there it was, another fishing boat. His heart raced for a minute as he discerned a narrow angle on the bow—it was pointing right at them. Then he saw the black ball hanging from the front super structure: the day shape for a boat at anchor. Out of the corner of the control room, by the navigator's chart, he heard an unusual whooping alarm that took him a second to identify: it was the ESM alarm. ET1 Daniels, the ESM operator, spoke up.

"Sir, we have a Siren Echo surface radar, bearing zero-five-zero."

"Siren Echo?"

"Soviet-era military shipboard radar."

"Soviet military?"

"Yes sir."

Jabo stopped rotating a minute, took another long hard look at Sierra Nine. It sure looked like a fishing boat. But he could now hear the rhythmic whine of the radar on their ESM antenna, in time with the rotation of the radar antenna he could see atop the little boat's highest mast.

"Sierra Nine is at anchor."

The captain was in his ear. "See anything to make you think it's not a fishing boat?"

"No sir. Maybe they bought that radar at a salvage auction or something…"

"Or maybe somebody out here is looking for submarines."

The other odd thing about Sierra Nine, other than its high-grade military radar, was that it appeared to be at anchor in what was supposed to be very, very deep water. "Quartermaster, mark charted depth."

Flather took a second to read the chart. "Two thousand fathoms, sir."

"That's really deep for a fishing boat to anchor in, isn't it?"

"Really deep," said the Flather. "I doubt he has that much chain. Maybe it's a sea anchor."

It's possible, thought Jabo. It was curious, for sure. "Take a sounding," he said.

Flather turned to the fathometer, calibrated it, and pushed the button. "Two thousand fathoms," he said. "Just like the chart says. At this depth and speed—that should be a good reading."

At least where we are, thought, Jabo. But that fishing boat appeared to be holding fast, like a boat would at anchor. He considered giving a slight right rudder, so they could edge closer, take a look. As he stared out at the boat, a dozen other tasks popped into his mind, things he'd pushed out of the way for the harrowing trip to periscope depth. They'd need to transmit another casualty report. That message would go, to among others, Captain Soldato, the commodore, who would probably start to wonder what the hell was going on inside the boat he had just recently left in good working order. But there was something weird about Sierra Nine, anchored there in the middle of a fishing fleet, her high-quality military radar spinning away. And no one topside hauling nets or traps. If he were just a little closer, he could maybe see inside, see what was on the deck…

He heard hard, determined footsteps on the control room ladder, and recognized them as the XO's. Jabo heard him plug into the EAB manifold at the top of the ladder, and take a deep breath, then another, he was winded, as if he had made the trip from Machinery Two to control without stopping to breathe. Jabo listened to the hiss of twenty pound air being forced into the mask and taken into the XO's lungs and waited for him to make his report to the captain. Finally he spoke.

. "Howard's dead."

•   •   •

Angi drove the short distance from their house to the Trigger Gate. They lived off base in a small house on a circle of small houses surrounded by towering Douglas Firs, every home inhabited by a family, civilian or military, whose livelihood depended on the fleet of eight Trident submarines that called Bangor, Washington, home: *Ohio, Michigan, Florida, Georgia, Alabama, Alaska, Nevada,* and *Henry M. Jackson.* And while Angi and Danny lived off base, they were barely off base, just a few hundred yards from the gate, and within earshot of the enormous cranes of the distant Delta Pier, whose endless beeping they heard day and night as they rolled back and forth on their railroad tracks, preparing boats for their next patrol. As she pulled up to the gate, the young sailor in dress whites saw the gold bar of her windshield's sticker that denoted an officer, snapped to, and saluted her as she passed.

She was to meet the Soldatos at 48 North, the base's all hands restaurant. It was part of the "upper base," a complex that included the exchange, the commissary, the chapel, and the gym: almost every place that Angi ever needed to go. Not only were the submarines invisible from the upper base—you couldn't even see the water, separated as it was by most of the base's 7,000 heavily wooded acres. The piers were a much different, grittier world, wet and slightly dangerous, guarded by men in fatigues with guns, populated by workers with hardhats and tattoos. Crewmen weren't even allowed to wear their working uniforms, their cotton khakis and dungarees, on the upper base, which looked more like a community college campus than it did a port for eight ships of war. Some of the old salts, in the most derisive words they could muster, accused it of looking like an Air Force base.

It was a lunch she'd put off as long as possible. Cindy Soldato had been calling with increasing frequency, her heart (perhaps) in the right place, but her attention could be suffocating. Angi was the only pregnant wife in the wardroom at the moment, and Cindy could focus her considerable energy upon her, generous with her advice about everything from filing military health insurance claims to breast feeding. In one week, her own mom would arrive from Knoxville, and Angi wondered if she would be able to survive all the mothering she was about to endure.

When she walked into the restaurant Cindy and Mario were deep in conversation, always a funny contrast to see them together. Mario was small, dark, highly animated, his hands moving with every phrase, leaning forward toward her. Cindy on the other hand was a fair Southern belle with perfect posture, her hands folded neatly in her lap as she listened with a look of rapt attention that looked like it might have been practiced in front of a mirror. Cindy had met Mario when he was one of a group of midshipmen at the Academy drafted to escort Virginia debs to some kind of cotillion. Early in Danny's tour, at a wardroom party, Angi made the mistake of mentioning they were both from the South. Cindy's smile had tightened and she didn't respond: the old prejudice of the plantation south against those from the mountains endured, even in a Navy town along the Pacific Coast, even with a woman who'd scandalized her family, she liked to boast, when she married an Italian Catholic from Cleveland. Mario saw Angi walking toward them and stood.

"Angi!" He looked down at her belly unabashedly.

"Angi, please sit down," said Cindy, actually pulling a chair out for her. "How are you?"

"Fine, fine," she said. "I feel really good. I was sick a few days last week, but thankfully that phase appears to be over."

"Good!" said Cindy and Mario together.

"About the worst side effect I have now is really weird dreams. And I'm tired— but that may just be laziness."

They laughed. A waiter came by and took their orders: they all ordered chef salads. Mario's phone was sitting on the table, every few seconds it would emit a short staccato buzz. He glanced down at it every time, but it never seemed worthy of much attention, he didn't even pick it up.

"It never stops," he said, noticing her interest. "They code the messages: a short little buzz like that means I need to see it but it's not a crisis. Anything really important gets the 'danger signal': five short, rapid blasts."

"You must come to resent that little thing."

"Not at all," said Cindy. "It's because of that phone he can pay for our lunch!"

"It's true," he said. "In the bad old days, I would have been afraid to leave the pier, afraid something would happen and they wouldn't be able to find me." The phone buzzed once on cue, and they laughed again. He read the screen. "The Seattle Seahawk cheerleaders are going on base for a fundraiser...they want me to set up a tour of a boat for them."

"Don't give the tour yourself, Mario."

"Why not?" he said, indignant.

"You're an old man. Let some poor JO do it."

"I am pretty old, it's true. Most of the submarines were still diesel boats when I first went to sea," he said to Angi. "Some of the old timers were World War II guys back then...I wish I would have gone to sea with some of them, heard their stories."

That prompted Angi. "Captain, have you ever heard of a book called *Rig for Dive*?"

"Sure...it's a classic. Written by Crush Martin, captain of the *USS Wrasse* in World War II. In his first two patrols he sunk something like eighteen Japanese ships. Became a war hero and wrote that book."

"Did you ever meet him?"

He shook his head. "No...he wrote that book, left for his next patrol, and never came back. They think the Japanese got him somewhere in the Yellow Sea, but we'll never know. It happed to a lot of those guys...it was unbelievably dangerous. But Crush Martin is kind of a patron saint of the sub force...a real warrior."

"Wasn't he controversial somehow?" said Cindy.

Mario nodded, impressed with her knowledge of submarine history. "Yes...in his first patrol, he sunk a Japanese troop carrier with a torpedo. Then they surfaced, and a bunch of the crew were floating around, clinging to wreckage and lifeboats. Martin ordered his men to machine gun the survivors."

"Oh my..." said Angi.

Soldato shrugged. "They say that's why he didn't get the Medal of Honor—that incident. Because by any measure, tonnage, number of ships, he was our most successful submarine captain in the war. This was at a time when the Japanese were winning every single engagement they were involved in: they almost didn't lose a battle for the first two years of the war. We nearly lost Australia! The allies were devoting everything they had to Europe, and the only thing, I mean the *only* thing, slowing the Japanese down were the submarine skippers like Martin. Japan has virtually no natural resources, they depended on sea lanes to feed their people and feed their industry. Martin was making them starve. And he died doing it. But enough people thought he was a war criminal to keep the medal out of his hands."

"Do you think he was a war criminal?"

The captain reflexively shook his head 'no,' but Angi could tell he was thinking about it. "I think…I think war makes you brutal."

There was a heavy pause, then Cindy leaned in toward Angi, catching her slightly off guard. "So," she said, "I hear Muriel Taylor has left town."

Angi shifted uncomfortably. "Yes, I think that's true," she said. Cindy was a virtuoso gossip, Angi knew she couldn't outmaneuver her. She decided just to say as little as possible.

"You two used to be good friends, didn't you?"

"Yes…still are. Still good friends."

"I wonder why she went home?" she said.

"Maybe she just needed to get away," said Angi, trying hard to convey as little information as possible. Part of her wanted to discuss it with Cindy, and that's what Cindy was counting on, she knew. And she resented Cindy for that, for trying to play her so she would have all the available information about all the wives. And even if she and Muriel had drifted apart, she wasn't about to make her friend's heartbreak part of a story that would circle Puget Sound before she got back home.

But if she had been at lunch with Mario alone—she would have liked to tell him. She wanted to know what a man of his experience would think of Mark Taylor's odd behavior. Was it something that happened all the time to officers who'd been at sea for too long? She could certainly understand that, didn't see how anyone could spend years of their lives underwater without going a little crazy. Or was it cause for genuine, immediate alarm?

"Well, I hope she enjoys herself," said Mario, and Angi could hear the disdain in his voice. He knew she'd fled. And Angi could also hear his suspicion that she'd fled into the arms of another man—it was, unfortunately, far from unheard of. Two patrols before, one of the JO's had run his car over their dog shortly before they'd gone to sea. His wife had ended up leaving him for their veterinarian, and, bizarrely, the JO always blamed himself. She could hear then in Soldato's voice an absence of mercy, a rare glimpse for her of the captain that Danny and the other JOs feared so much: hard and unforgiving.

He wiped the corners of his mouth with his napkin. "New topic."

"So...did you buy a crib yet?" asked Cindy.

"Not yet...none of that stuff. My mom is coming out, we'll do it together. I think she wants to help."

"Of course she does. Does she have any other grandbabies?"

"No, this will be her first."

"Oh my...how about Danny's folks?"

"Them too...this is the first grandbaby all the way around."

"How wonderful," said Cindy. "Your mom must be thrilled."

"I think she is...I also think she thinks I'm not ready."

"Well you're not! None of us ever are."

Angi nodded at that.

"Have you scheduled the baptism?"

Angi nodded. "I'm going to wait until Danny gets home."

"Oh," said Cindy, a predictable note of judgment in her voice. Angi had heard it from her mother a dozen times. A baby was supposed to be baptized without delay. And she didn't even know when Danny would be back, couldn't put it on the calendar. But she was doing so much alone. She wasn't about to do that without Danny.

Mario leaned in, sensing the uncomfortable quiet. He put his hand on hers. "I think that's great, Angi. And Danny will be home soon enough to enjoy it."

"Let's hope so," said Angi, once again surprised at Mario's ability to bring her close to sentimental tears.

He was still looking at her with concerned eyes when his phone startled them with five short blasts.

.   .   .

Usually Kincaid couldn't wait to pull his EAB off, the damn thing was uncomfortable, smelled bad, pulled his hair, and was just a general pain in the ass. You couldn't move more than about three feet without taking a deep breath, unplugging, and plugging in somewhere else. It was difficult to understand people who talked to you through the small plastic diaphragm that allowed speech while maintaining the mask's air tight integrity—and impossible to understand those who hadn't learned yet that it didn't work at all when you shouted. The clear plastic mask fogged up when you exerted yourself. No one could wear one for long without getting an unbearable, unreachable itch on the nose. The black rubber of the mask irritated his skin. But Kincaid, like everyone else in the missile compartment, had suddenly fallen in love with his EAB when they confirmed the presence of phosgene. Fucking *phosgene*: nerve gas. One of those things where a single molecule could kill you in seconds. A drop could kill a whole city. Shut down your whole central fucking nervous system. The thought made him reach back and tighten the straps of his mask behind his head again, they were digging into his skin now, but still he worried that a molecule might sneak by. He was ready to wear the EAB the rest of that patrol if necessary.

Kincaid was the man in charge in Machinery Two. He'd sent almost everyone else forward once they'd gotten Howard's body out of there, there was just not much else to do. He still couldn't quite believe what had happened. He'd been at sea with a dead guy once before, on his first patrol back on the USS *Mendel Rivers*, when some kid started throwing up one night, and didn't stop until two days later when he was dead: they never did figure out what was wrong with him. They were somewhere in the Atlantic, somewhere they weren't supposed to be, this was back when submarines still were the tip of the spear. Captain Rorbaugh didn't want to have a burial at sea, and shoot the kid out of a torpedo tube, because they couldn't afford to make that kind of noise. So instead they zipped him in a body bag and stuck him in the freezer. During his two week stint as a mess crank that patrol, Kincaid had to brush up against the thick, olive drab plastic that covered the body as he retrieved twenty pound boxes of tater tots and slabs of frozen hamburger.

"Control requests a status update," said Petty Officer McCormick, his phone talker and one of the two other people left in the compartment. Yaksic was the other, he'd returned and was now periodically checking the air with ampoules, small glass vials that took one-time readings of specific airborne contaminants. Freon was still out of spec, as they could see by the dark blue stain inside the broken ampoule. About a million fucking times the legal limit. They had boxes and boxes of Freon ampoules, could check it once an hour for the rest of the patrol if they needed to. But Phosgene was different, they only had six of those: apparently no one at the Bureau of Ships thought nerve gas was a big concern to a modern submarine at sea, they were probably lucky to have any. They'd used two when they initially confirmed that phosgene was present—mainly because nobody could believe the first one. Kincaid still wondered exactly how Jabo had figured that out from the conn, and how close they'd all come to being facedown on the cold deckplates like Howard, a ghost ship. They'd decided to save the remaining ampoules for after they'd ventilated. They had no other way of testing for phosgene, and they couldn't afford to waste them. But until then, there just wasn't anything else to do in machinery two, so he'd sent everyone else forward, beyond the shut missile compartment watertight hatches, where they might be nominally safer.

"They want a status update?" said Kincaid, trying to contain his frustration. *Me and two other guys are parked in machinery two hoping that there's not any dry rot on these fucking rubber masks that might result in our immediate agonizing deaths,* he thought, *that's our fucking status.*

"The rig," said McCormick. "They're ready to ventilate, just waiting on us."

"Oh, fuck," said Kincaid. He'd sent everyone forward, there was no one to do the rig.

"I got it sir," said Yaksic, grabbing the laminated sheet from the metal holder, and ably moving through the space, unplugging, plugging, checking valves, ducts, and dampers all while reading the sheet. Yaksic had done more than his share of saving people's asses that day, thought Kincaid. In no time he was done.

"Rigged," he said.

Kincaid nodded at McCormick who reported it to control.

"Start the low pressure blower," on the 1MC. Not the diesel, Kincaid was glad to hear, even though the diesel would have moved the air a lot faster off the boat. But a diesel engine burned hot—and they'd learned a valuable lesson about high temps and Freon.

In his feet, Kincaid could feel the rumble of the blower. He checked his watch, watched thirty minutes crawl by.

"Check Freon," he said to Yaksic, who was ready with an ampoule. He cracked it.

"No change, sir." He held it up.

Kincaid did the math in his head—the ventilation half life with the blower should have been about eight minutes, maybe ten minutes max. Which meant after about thirty minutes, the level should have dropped drastically. But it hadn't budged. "What the fuck," he said.

"Maybe it's just that high out of spec—the ampoules are swamped."

"Maybe." He looked at his watch again, leaned against the oxygen generator, and resolved not to check for another thirty minutes.

After an hour, control asked for them again to report the Freon level. Kincaid was actually impressed that they'd been able to restrain themselves that long—he pictured their position on the chart, falling further and further behind the track. But after an hour, the Freon level had still not dropped at all. "What the fuck!" said Kincaid. "Check the rig."

Yaksic grabbed the card and went through the space again. "It's rigged," he said. "You can feel the air moving out of here."

It was true, Kincaid could feel it on his hands, the motion of the air as the blower took its suction on their space. Fresh air from outside should be replacing it, and Kincaid longed to rip off his mask and smell it. But something wasn't working the way it should.

. . .

"Machinery Two reports that Freon levels are not dropping," said the navigator.

"Shit," said Jabo. They'd been up for an hour, transmitted their message about the Freon and Howard's death, gotten a terse reaction from squadron: Jabo pictured Soldato at his desk initialing the message with an angry jab of his pen before it was transmitted. They'd even managed to shoot some trash while they waited, a difficult job for men in EABs. Freon should have been sucked down to nothing after an hour.

"What do you make of that?" said the captain. "Something wrong with the blower?"

"I don't think so—I can hear it. Kincaid has checked the rig twice." Jabo thought it over, again pictured the pool of Freon gathered at the back of the space. The ventilation line up was designed, in large part, to get smoke out of a space. It hit him.

"It's heavy," he said.

"What?"

"Freon's too heavy. What is it, twice as heavy as air?"

Maple appeared at his side, nodding. He got it too. "Four times. Four times heavier than air…"

"So the blower's not moving it," said the captain. "It's just sitting there. Let's get some fans down there, nav."

The navigator called down to Crew's Mess, where everyone was waiting in the masks for the casualty to be over, discussing the death of their shipmate, trading rumors about phosgene.

.   .   .

The supply officer, known affectionately on every boat as Chop, was in charge in Crew's Mess. He was the only officer on the boat not nuclear trained, and sometimes seemed to exist solely to be the butt of jokes from smug nukes. This despite the fact that his responsibilities were among the broadest of any officer on the boat. If halfway through the patrol a carbon brush broke on a 400 Megahertz motor generator and they weren't carrying a proper spare, he would be held responsible. He was also held responsible if pizza crust tasted funny, or if they ran out of Cheerios. His previous assignment had been on an aircraft carrier, where he was one of seventeen supply officers. His sole job had been to ensure the proper distribution of paychecks. Like every man around him, the Chop was worried about Phosgene, trying to fight off real terror about what the hell it might mean. And he was devastated about the loss of a shipmate. But, he felt with some shame, he was also worried about the coolers and freezers around them, the food supply for 154 men that was slowly warming.

"Chop, control requests four men be sent with two red blowers to machinery two."

The supply officer nodded. Christ, he thought, I suppose that means the ventilation isn't working. "Any volunteers?"

One man raised his hand. Hallorann, a striker. This shamed some of the more experienced men, and soon they had three other, slightly more reluctant volunteers.

"Go," said the chop. "And keep those EABs on." It wasn't necessary to remind them.

He watched them struggle with the two big red blowers, getting them through the hatch while wearing EABs was no easy feat. That Hallorann was an impressive kid, he thought. He wondered if he would be interested in striking storekeeper.

.   .   .

Lieutenant Kincaid ordered them into position, pointing one blower into the bilge, and one above it. Hallorann saw what he was attempting to do, stage the blowers so they would boost the heavy Freon high into the compartment. He admired his ingenuity; obviously there was no procedure for what they were attempting to do. And it was difficult; anytime they moved more than about three feet they had to unplug their EABs and find a new manifold. Finally the big blowers were in place and aimed.

"Turn 'em on!" ordered Kincaid. Hallorann found the switch and flipped it as did the other team. The big, powerful blowers came on with a roar. Hallorann could feel the air rushing through the compartment.

Out of the corner of his eye, Hallorann saw a yellow piece of notebook paper blow up from the bilge into which the blowers were pointed. It sailed through the space, and then landed against the curved wall of the hull, where dampness began to soak through it. He tried to reach for it, but it was just a little too far. He saw densely written, neat notes in numbered rows; it just looked like something that should be preserved.

Without giving it too much thought, he unplugged and leaned down to snatch it off the wall. He gave it a quick look; about half of it was still legible.

"Hey nub!" shouted Lieutenant Kincaid. "Get back on that fan!"

Hallorann shoved the page in his pocket and returned to his station. He returned to the fan, plugged in his EAB, and took a deep breath of the oily smelling air.

.   .   .

After an hour of running the red blowers in conjunction with the big low pressure blower, Yaksic took two readings and confirmed that Freon had, at last, drifted into spec. The officers deliberated in the control room, and decided, in light of their very limited ability to test for phosgene, to wait another hour before breaking one of the last two ampoules. When they did, Kincaid reported excitedly to control that the results were negative. The captain ordered them to confirm the reading with the last ampoule. And with that, after three and a half hours at periscope depth, Jabo picked up the 1MC mike.

"Secure from general emergency," he said. "All hands remove EABs."

There was a collective gasp of relief from the crew as they did. The XO rubbed his bare head, which showed red stripes from the rubber straps of the EAB. He turned to the navigator.

"Figure it out, nav. How fast and in which direction." He turned to Jabo. "Officer of the deck—get down and get fast."

"Dive make your depth six hundred feet. Ahead flank."

The helm and the engineroom acknowledged both orders and the ship tipped forward as it drove down. Jabo, like the XO and every other qualified officer on the boat, began to do rough calculations in his head about how far behind they'd fallen and how fast they would have to go to make it up.

Jabo also thought about the all the noise they'd made: the roaring of fans, the clanking of hatches. He pictured sound waves in the sea, travelling for miles, and wondered if anyone was listening. He thought about Sierra Nine.

·   ·   ·

After dinner the navigator unveiled again the great circle chart of the Pacific and showed them their new track. The navigation brief took place with their dinner dishes still on the table, roast beef and gravy: time seemed suddenly compressed, there was a palpable sense of urgency to everything. Jabo noticed that the XO's eyes rarely left the repeater in the corner of the wardroom that displayed their speed. As he finished his last spoonful of potatoes, Jabo felt heavy exhaustion set it. He glanced at his watch: it was four o'clock in the morning. He'd had a cup of coffee before dinner and poured himself the dregs from the pot before the nav began his brief, but caffeine could no longer counteract his lack of sleep.

"Bottom line," said the XO as the navigator concluded his remarks. "Ahead Flank, as fast as we can go, with no more than two trips to PD every day. We'll snatch the broadcast and away we go. I'll be up there with a stopwatch timing you fuckers at PD. Clear?"

The JOs nodded and muttered affirmatively.

"Duggan, let's practice the three-minute rule. How far do we travel in three minutes if we're going ten knots?"

Duggan thought it over just a second. "1,000 yards."

"Exactly right. So how fast do we travel a mile if we're going twenty knots?"

Duggan puzzled over this one a moment longer. "Three minutes."

"That's right. You all get that? We're going to eat up one nautical mile of ocean, two thousand yards, in three minutes, if we're travelling twenty knots. One more question, Duggan. How fast are we travelling right now?"

Duggan looked panicked, strained to remember what the current ship's speed was as they moved at ahead flank.

"I'll give you a hint," said the XO. "The answer is right above your fucking head in big red numbers." He pointed to the repeater, as Duggan twisted awkwardly in his seat to get a look while the wardroom laughed in a release of nervous tension.

"Duggan, is that faster or slower than twenty knots?"

"Faster, sir."

"That's right. So, we're going to travel a mile in *less* than three minutes. Let me show you how fast."

The XO put his beefy left arm on the wardroom table with bang. "You guys ready?" He pushed a button on the side of his black digital watch making it beep. He watched the display, and after a short time, he banged the table again. "There. We just travelled a mile. Went pretty quick, didn't it?"

Again the assembled officers mumbled in agreement.

"This is not what any of us are used to—and we need to be *vigilant*. Look ahead at every chart. Look at the *next* chart. Be aware, at all times, how fast we are moving and how far we are travelling."

"This is going to tax every system on the boat," said the Captain. "As well as the crew. We'll be running fast and deep, and everyone will need to be on their toes. Barring any further disasters...we will still make it to Taiwan in time. The navigator assures me."

They all turned to the nav who nodded humorously in response. Jabo thought he looked awful, like he'd lost weight from his already thin frame. He noticed that the nav's dinner plate, still on the table, was untouched, he hadn't eaten a bite. Jabo didn't envy the nav his job now. But then again...everyone on the crew was going to be tested by the high speed run to Taiwan.

"Ok," said the XO. "You all know what to do now. Get the fuck out of here and get to work."

Jabo stood with the others but the XO grabbed his elbow as he did. Hein and Kincaid looked at him curiously as they passed, wondering, as Jabo did, what the CO and XO wanted to talk to him about. The Nav, rolling up his charts, was the last to leave, and he did so without a word. When the door shut, there was a moment of silence as the XO and captain looked at each other.

"Sit down, Danny."

He did.

"You were investigating the dryer fire, right?" asked the XO.

"Yes sir," said Jabo. "We were going to have an admin hearing after we pulled in."

"Which means you haven't done anything yet, right?" said the XO.

Jabo bristled. "Of course, sir, I have. I can deliver the draft report to you if you'd like to review it."

"Stop being a pussy, Danny, I'm just fucking with you."

The captain spoke. "Danny, since you were already working on the dryer fire, and since, frankly, I really need someone like you to work in this, you'll need to do the report on Howard's death, too. Obviously these two things are related, so we might as well keep you on the case."

"Yes sir."

"I know what you're thinking," said the XO. "That you don't have time to do this."

"Not at all, sir."

"Good. Because obviously, if what just happened to us was an act of sabotage, this is going to bring a lot of attention to this incident, and to your report. I repeat: a lot."

"Understood, sir."

"And we'll want a preliminary report to hand in the minute we tie up in Taiwan."

"Yes sir."

The captain sighed; Jabo could hear in the sound that the official part of their conversation was over. "I still can't believe he did this. He went from making a small fire in the dryer to attempted murder."

"And he did kill himself," said the XO. "Speaking of that, what are we going to do with the body?"

The captain thought it over for a moment. "The port freezer... there's more room in there. Confirm that with the chop. And let's move the body now, while a good portion of the crew is sleeping."

"Are we going to keep all those freezers online? With all that Freon lost?"

"The DCA is investigating, he's hopeful we'll be able to keep at least one of them at temp."

"No burial at sea?"

"No time," said the captain. "We'd have to slow down for that. Tell the chop to put him way in back, cover the body bag with more plastic. It's not the first time I've been at sea with a dead body. The crew will get used to it. And frankly...it could have been so much worse."

"Yes sir."

The XO turned to Jabo. "When's your next watch?" Jabo had to think for a minute, the casualty had gone on so long and screwed him up his internal clock. "Noon tomorrow," he said. "I relieve Hein."

The XO checked his watch. "OK. It's six-thirty now. Go back to machinery two, work on the investigation for a couple of hours; look around, take notes, all that good shit. You'll want to be able to say you went back there within hours of the incident. Then come forward and sleep for two hours, get up, shower, eat lunch, and take the watch. You should be feeling great after that, right?"

"Yes sir."

Jabo stood, and began to walk to the door.

"Danny?" said the captain.

"Yes sir?"

"Don't fuck this up."

"Aye aye sir."

.   .   .

On his way aft, Jabo stopped in Crew's Mess, where the coffee was always fresh due to the huge volume they served up every day, and freshened up his cup. He then went to sick bay, in Missile Compartment Second Level, to see the body.

He was met there by the corpsman. Master Chief Cote was a distinguished-looking old chief with the gray hair and small, scholarly glasses that befit the crew's sole medically trained crewmen. There were no doctors on Trident submarines, but the master chief had thirty years in the service, more time even than the captain. He'd had extensive training for independent duty, and was one of a handful of guys on the boat who'd been in long enough to see Viet Nam, where he'd served as a medic for a Marine rifle platoon. Angi had been horrified when she learned there were no doctors on the boat, but Jabo wasn't just trying to make her feel better when he told her that he would rather put his life in the hands of Master Chief Cote than any doctor he'd ever known.

Master Chief Cote was still in sick bay, filling out paperwork about Howard's body; the Navy had a form for everything. He looked up, unsurprised to see a junior officer arrive in his space.

"Are you doing the investigation, Lieutenant?"

Jabo nodded.

He stepped aside so Jabo could enter. The room was tiny, the size of a broom closet. Howard had been placed in a body bag that was laid out across sick bay's very narrow treatment table.

It was actually not the first time Jabo had seen a military-issue body bag. He and his father had hunted with a man who used them to transport the deer they killed. He raved about the thick watertight plastic and rugged zippers, the thick nylon loops that were perfect for lashing the cargo to the roof of his old Ford Bronco. Jabo could still remember unzipping the bags up in the guy's garage, the thick, wet smell of the deer's fur, the pool of congealing, cold blood that would collect in the bag's lowest crease.

"You want to see him?" said the master chief.

Not really, thought Jabo. But he thought he should. He nodded and leaned back so the master chief could open the bag.

He pulled the zipper down to Howard's neck. He didn't look peaceful, like people always said. He looked stunned. And his eyes were cloudy, Jabo thought probably because they'd dried out.

"Did he die from the Freon or the Phosgene?"

"Not sure," said the master chief. "But I think the Freon—I think he suffocated. I read a little about Phosgene, and apparently it's an agonizing way to die, with violent muscle spasms and seizures and the like. Howard didn't look like that."

Jabo thought he'd probably looked at the body long enough. He didn't know what he should be looking for anyway. He pointed at the bag's zipper and the master chief closed it back up.

"You ever have a dead guy at sea before, master chief?"

He nodded. "Three times, but only once on a submarine. The first two were on carriers, which isn't that unusual. You put five thousand guys on a ship for six months, somebody's going to die... it's almost mathematically unavoidable. The first time was on my first Westpac, on the *Enterprise*, some old warrant officer had a heart attack. Of course we had doctors onboard, a whole room full of them, so I didn't get to do much. Watched them give him CPR, then pronounce him dead. They took him off the boat within an hour on the COD flight. I don't even think most of the crew was aware of it— that's how it is on those big boats. I never heard the guy's name."

"The second time?"

"Another carrier: the *Carl Vinson*. I was a chief by then, and this time was a little more dramatic. It was some poor kid, I think he was a third class electrician, just walking on the flight deck. They weren't even doing flight ops, which is when it is actually dangerous up there, he was probably just grabbing a smoke. I remember it was a beautiful day. Anyhow, he walked by this little forklift that was carrying a big sheet of steel, God only knows what it was for, and the thing hadn't been lashed down properly. The sheet fell off and just pinned the kid to the deck. But it was so heavy, it just crushed him, suffocated him. They couldn't move it, they had like ten guys on it but it was just too heavy. Just like with that chief: he was off the boat before the sun went down."

Jabo thought the chief seemed unaffected by the deaths... he described them in the same mildly regretful way the engineer might talk about a botched scram drill. "What about the one on a submarine?"

With that, the master chief's whole posture changed, and his face darkened. "That was bad. It was on the *Baton Rouge*, my second boat. We were pulling out of Norfolk on a really rough day. Everyone topside was wearing a safety harness and was clipped into the track. Those safety tracks were new then, we had just done the mod during our last overhaul. There was an A-Gang chief topside, one of the most experienced guys on the boat: Senior Chief Sellers. We were friends—his wife taught my wife to play golf. The captain had him up there because it was so rough, he wanted somebody with experience topside.

"We were only about an hour away from the dock, but it gets deep out there fast...not like out here, the continental shelf is close. So we were close to submerging already. I wasn't topside at first, but I had to sign off on the report so I read all about it later. They were really scrambling to get everything buttoned up, rigged for dive, getting everybody below. The ship was just pitching and rolling like crazy, waves were breaking and coming clear up to the sail, water pouring into the control room. And at some point, as he was running around up there helping everyone else, Sellers slipped."

"But he was clipped in, right?"

"That's right. But he was wearing a long line, because he'd been in charge and was running the length of the ship. When he slipped, he fell almost to the water line before the line caught."

"But it held?"

The master chief nodded. "It held him. And it held him above the waterline. Worked just like it was supposed to. He didn't drown."

Jabo felt bad for making him dredge up the bad memory. But the master chief continued.

"He just hung there, right above the water. But the waves would hit him, and he kept slamming against the side of the ship. By then they'd called me up there, and you could hear him yelling. At first, it was just like, 'Shit! Goddamn!' stuff like that, each time he hit the hull. But after a few minutes, he started screaming, in pain, as his bones started breaking. It was getting rougher but now we couldn't submerge, not with the chief hanging there. We were all on the line, trying to haul him up, but every time we got him moving, a big wave would come and knock us down, or we'd lose the grip. By the time we finally pulled him up, he hadn't made a noise for ten minutes. I knew he was dead. The ocean had beaten the shit out of him—broken almost every bone in his body. We put him on a stretcher and then we practically had to pour him into a body bag." There was a long silence as they stared at the brown plastic that hid Howard from view.

"What happened after?"

The master chief sighed. "We stuck him in the cooler until we got to Roda. And after that, the Navy limited those safety lines to three feet in length." He paused, and then took three Polaroid photos from his small desk. "Here…you might need these. I took them before we moved the body so there'd be some record of it."

"Thanks master chief," said Jabo, taking the pictures. "I guess I better get down there."

.   .   .

151

Machinery Two showed few signs of the casualty. It wasn't like the fire, which left blackened walls and a smell of smoke that still clung to that part of the missile compartment. The hazards in this casualty had been invisible, and if there were any residual affects, they were invisible too. All the damage control equipment had been stowed, and the place had been restored well by the crew and the watchstanders who didn't want to be reminded that there were a large number of ways a man might die onboard a submarine.

Machinist Mate Second Class Renfro was on watch, just hanging the oxygen generator logs back on their hook when Jabo walked up.

"You guys port and starboard now?"

Renfro nodded. "Yeah, for now. I guess Padua is getting close to qualifying, but for now it's me and Schmidt, six on and six off." While he'd just begun standing port and starboard, Jabo could see that the prospect of it exhausted him.

"I'm doing the investigation...can I take a look at the logs?"

Renfro nodded and took them off the hook.

The sheet was creased and dirty. Each sheet of logs held twenty-four hours worth of information, four full watches, so the sheet on the clipboard was the same one Howard had used. Jabo could tell they'd hit the deck when Howard did. Looking it over, nothing jumped out as unusual, other than the oxygen generator drifting out of spec. If anything, they were sharper than a normal set of logs, they were written more precisely, each number and word written cleanly in the center of its block, the notes on back more detailed and thoughtful than the norm. Based on the logs only, Howard didn't seem like a guy getting ready to murder the entire crew...he looked like a petty officer trying to impress his chief.

"You notice anything weird?" he asked Renfro.

"Not really," he said. "I can't believe he tried to kill us all."

"We don't know that yet. We may never know. The whole thing is hard for me to understand too."

"No sir, I mean I really don't believe it. I knew Howard, he wasn't a nut case."

"I liked Howard too, but isn't that what everybody says after somebody has gone off the deep end? That's the nature of being crazy, I guess, it's unpredictable."

"You really think Howard was crazy, sir? Then I guess your investigation is pretty much over."

Jabo was stung by that. "You're right. We still don't know exactly what happened, and I'll try my best to find out."

Renfro nodded skeptically. "No sir, it's okay. It's just...I mean, if Howard wanted to kill everyone from back here, there would have better ways to do it than with Freon, for fuck's sake. I mean, did he even know about the nerve gas shit? I sure as fuck didn't. I asked around...nobody else in the division did either."

Jabo nodded...it was a good point. That message had just come out. He was startled to remember that even the captain hadn't seen it.

"And if I was going to try something crazy like that...I'd start right here," he said, slapping the gray metal side of the oxygen generator. "You could flood this space with pure hydrogen in about five minutes. The alarm would be going off in control, but it would be over before anybody could get down here to do anything. Light your cigarette lighter and this thing would blow so hard it would crack the ship in half."

Jabo nodded. It would be a much more efficient way of destroying the ship than dumping a few thousand pounds of Freon and hoping that it would mutate into a deadly gas like it was supposed to. And nothing and no one could prevent the watchstander in machinery two from doing it.

"Bring me a copy of those logs when your watch is over," said Jabo, pointing. "I'll be on the conn."

"Aye, aye sir," said Renfro, still a little surly. Clearly his loyalty to Howard as a shipmate and a member of the same division had trumped the suspicion that he may have tried to sabotage the ship.

But even putting a shipmate's loyalty to one of his peers aside... Renfro had made some valid points.

Jabo climbed the ladder down to lower level: the scene of the crime. He knew that none of the chemical compounds that had so alarmed them, Freon or phosgene, had any odor, but he still inhaled deeply, and smelled only the vague odor of diesel fuel and amine from the scrubbers above. He stepped across the space to the purple-handled Freon valve.

It was one of thousands of valve operators he'd seen thousands of times without ever touching, or even given much thought to. He had been involved in freeze seal maintenance in other areas of the boat. He wasn't sure if that particular valve had ever been operated during his time on *Alabama*. A red DANGER tag hung from the operator now, hung there at the OOD's order after the casualty had abated. It seemed superfluous now, since Jabo was fairly certain that there wasn't an ounce of Freon left in the system.

He pulled the Polaroids that Master Chief Cote had given him from his pocket and looked them over.

He winced at the image of Howard's dead body, rendered harshly in the electric flash. He was sprawled on the deck, his clipboard in front of him, the log sheet that Jabo had just reviewed on the deck behind him. There were three photos in all, of the same scene, taken from different angles. The quality was not great, and the light was poor, but overall the master chief had done an admirable job of preserving images of the scene. Howard seemed to be reaching for the valve handle; his whole body was oriented in that direction. But that didn't make a lot of sense; it had taken a while for all the Freon to dump from the system, Howard wouldn't have collapsed right after turning it. Maybe he'd turned the valve and then had second thoughts, but been overcome before he could save himself.

Jabo backed up and bumped into the treadmill. There was a red tag hanging from it, as well, this one signed by the corpsman. Apparently, the master chief wanted to keep people from exercising down there until they were absolutely positive that there was no atmospheric contamination to worry about....he would find out all the details when he read the captain's night orders on his next watch. He breathed deeply and took in the whole scene. What had happened down there? What had Howard been thinking in those final moments? He took a look at the photos again, flipped through to the tightest close up that the master chief had taken.

In the photograph, Jabo noticed again the log sheet, that record that Howard had so carefully kept. It was lying on the deck beside him. And for the first time, he noticed that another sheet behind it, a piece of yellow notebook paper. Jabo was certain that it was not on the clipboard he had just reviewed with Renfro; he wondered what it might be. The resolution of the picture was too low to offer any clues.

He looked up, realized that he had been staring off into space a little, his mind a blank. It wasn't Freon, he knew, or nerve gas. It was exhaustion. He felt a pang about the accusation in Renfro's words, about how the verdict seemed already to have been made. He vowed to himself to conduct a real investigation, the best he could, but for now…he was tired beyond words. He hadn't slept in a day, and would be on watch in a matter of hours. He checked his watch and verified that he had spent the two hours on the investigation that the XO had directed. He would go forward and get a couple of hours of sleep, and hope he could get through the watch without falling asleep on the conn.

He walked forward through lower level, both because he was too tired to climb a ladder, and to avoid the accusing eyes of MM2 Renfro.

.   .   .

He checked his watch as he neared his stateroom. The XO hadn't been quite right. He would have about an hour and forty-five minutes to sleep before he took the watch. The exhaustion hit him in waves as he anticipated climbing in the rack. It wouldn't be nearly enough, but it would be something, and his body longed for any rest.

He stepped through the door. The overhead lights were off but Kincaid was stepping into his Nikes, ready to go workout.

"Where the fuck you been?" he said. "You need to be getting some sleep, shipmate."

"Investigating. And all the workout gear is secured." He was already out of his poopie suit, down to his plaid boxers and T-shirt. He hung it on the door on the middle hook, his hook, and climbed into the middle rack and pulled the blanket over him. The entire process had taken him about ten seconds.

"Secured? What the fuck! Why is it secured?"

But Jabo was already in his rack with the curtain closed. His thoughts about the tragedy, plus the image of Howard's dead, gray face charged through his mind, fueled by three cups of strong coffee and the residual adrenaline from combating the casualty. As his head hit the pillow, he allowed himself to think about Angi, and felt the sharp pang of how much he missed her, how much he loved her. He thought about their first date, the first time he kissed her, on the steps of McTyeire Hall. He remembered the sound the wind made in the dried leaves of the live oaks that surrounded them, the taste of her lipstick, the surprised way she inhaled a little when he made his move. And then he was asleep.

.   .   .

He never would have awoken from the noise alone when Hallorann entered; the young sailor was deliberately, theatrically quiet as he crept in. Hallorann considered leaving the document without a word, but the significance of it gnawed at him, even if he couldn't attach words to its importance, and it had almost been lost once already. He wanted to convey it personally. And he felt like, for some reason, he should lose no time. He cautiously pulled back the thick red curtain to the middle rack to look at the back of Lieutenant Jabo's sleeping head.

"Sir?" he whispered. He said it again, slightly louder. The only response was slow, even breathing. He reached his hand out, hesitated, and then pushed his shoulder.

The breathing changed rhythm slightly, but it took another sharp push before the lieutenant finally rolled over, and his heavy eyes fluttered awake.

"Sir?"

Jabo licked his lips. "What?"

"I talked to the OOD, Lieutenant Hein...he said you were conducting the investigation. I found this in machinery two...I was on one of the fan teams." He held up the yellow sheet of paper. Jabo raised an eyebrow; even in his sleep he remembered the paper in the photograph.

"What's on it?"

"Not much...I mean I'm not sure. But I thought you should have it."

Jabo stared at him for a moment, and Hallorann was afraid maybe he was still really asleep, talking with his eyes open while his mind slept on. It was a phenomenon he'd become familiar with since his time at sea, where exhaustion and sleep deprivation were taken to levels he'd never known. But then Lieutenant Jabo cleared his throat, and said, "Put it there. On my desk."

Hallorann hesitated, wanted to explain why he thought it was important, how the neat entries made over several days and dated carefully must mean that it was an important document. He was afraid it might get lost, as it nearly had been before, or forgotten, sitting among several piles of documents and books that crowded the lieutenant's desk. He started to say something about the evident importance of the page, but when he turned back from the desk, the lieutenant was already asleep again.

He placed it on the desk as he'd been directed, then pulled the curtain back across Jabo's rack and left. He was due down in the galley in an hour, it was the second day of his two-week long stint in the scullery washing dishes. Must be nice being an officer, he thought as he left: sleeping until nearly eleven o'clock in the morning like that.

.   .   .

The navigator was alone in the stateroom he shared with Ensign Duggan. Normally just a red curtain was pulled across his doorway, as department heads were expected to always be available. But he had closed the seldom-operated sliding door.

Not that he could sleep. He was too conscious of the ship's speed and depth as they raced ahead, almost blind, through the dark ocean. The ship would shudder and groan occasionally, vibrating in resonant frequencies with the massive equipment in the engine room that was operating at its limits. He extended his hand to the hull, just inches from his pillow, and felt the cold steel, the sole barrier between him and the sea. He fought off the panic that always arose when he thought about it.

He wasn't afraid to fall asleep, he just couldn't, his body wouldn't let him. He wasn't afraid of nightmares, he knew the nightmares would come whether he was asleep or awake.

He heard a door shut to stateroom three, across the passageway, someone trying to be quiet. He shut his eyes just in case it was a messenger making the rounds, perhaps with some messages they'd received during the extended trip at PD. It would be okay if he was seen asleep in his rack, but he didn't want anyone to see him awake, brooding in the dark. He'd heard the whispering, didn't need to stoke the rumors about his strange behavior. He unconsciously scratched the wound on his knee. A few minutes passed, no one came to the door, and he reopened his eyes.

The commander was sitting in his chair. The nav recognized him immediately, both from the old khaki dress uniform, the war patrol pin on his chest, and the scars across his face that told of past campaigns. He looked just like the photograph on the back cover of his book. It was Crush Martin.

"Are you proud of yourself?" he said. He was fuming. The only light was the tiny fluorescent fixture above their pull-out sink, so the commander was backlit, his features stark, his mustache and hair pitch black, his skin white. Thin scars ran down his face, like worm-eaten wood, reminders, the nav was sure, of past battles.

"I did what you said…" said the navigator. "A man is dead because of me."

"And you thought that would be enough? Did you think one dead sailor would make them turn the boat around and give up?"

"It could have been more." But he realized how stupid he'd been.

"Never," said the commander. "You could have filled the freezer with bodies, and they would keep moving west, as long as the ship can move. You've barely even slowed them down."

"But I..."

"Do you have any idea what's at stake!" he thundered. Slamming his fist down on the desk. "Your ship, your mission, is going to be the catalyst of the apocalypse! And you turn a Freon valve... and think that will be enough. Idiot."

"Sorry..." whimpered the nav.

"Maybe it's not too late," said the commander. "But you have to start acting with the appropriate level of vigor."

"What should I do?"

"You've got one of the most important jobs on the boat," said the commander. "And it's not because you can turn the handle on a purple valve. There's a reason I chose you, the navigator, for this mission. You're one of the few men who can single-handedly destroy this boat."

"How?" asked the navigator.

But he was already gone.

.   .   .

Jabo slept exactly twenty-five minutes after Hallorann left his stateroom, and when he awoke, he did feel much, much better. He knew it wouldn't last, knew there would come a point early in the watch where no amount of coffee could overcome the sleep deficit he'd accumulated, but for the moment he just felt grateful for the one hundred and five minutes of sleep he'd gotten. And Hallorann's fear had been accurate....he had no recollection of talking to him, or of the yellow sheet of paper that was sitting on his desk, lost among a sea of paper that was awaiting his review. But Jabo felt so good that he walked to the shower whistling, with a towel around his waist, and when he came back to the stateroom, ten minutes later, he was humming. Kincaid was back, sweaty and winded, taking off his running shoes.

"Did you violate those safety tags on the treadmill?" asked Jabo.

"I considered it. Fucking stupid. I ran in missile compartment upper level as best I could. I hate running up there."

"I'll talk to the cruise director."

"Fuck you. I'm glad you got your nap in, slacker."

Jabo laughed at that, started stepping into his poopie, while Kincaid nosed around his desk. He held up the yellow paper and laughed.

"I see that nub found you with this...he was trying to get everybody to look at it, we finally realized you are running the investigation, sent him down to you."

Jabo took the sheet, began to vaguely recall the conversation with Hallorann. More clearly he remembered seeing the yellow paper in the master chief's Polaroids. He looked at his watch. "I need to take the watch," he said. "I'll take a look at it on the conn."

"I have a feeling if you don't, that nub will come after you. He seems like a determined type of guy."

.   .   .

Molly Hein came to Angi's house already in her workout clothes, and then they left together in Angi's car. They were already a little late for the step aerobics class in the gym base that they attended every Tuesday and Thursday when the men were at sea. The instructor was Dee Dee Hysong, the ridiculously fit, ridiculously blonde wife of a lieutenant on *Alaska*.

"We're going to be late," said Angi. "Dee Dee is going to glare at us."

"That's why I like being late," said Molly. "But that's not why she glares at us. It's because you're in better shape than her. She can't tolerate that."

Angi patted her belly. "If that's true, she'll be happy to see this."

"How much longer do you think you can do stuff like this?"

"As long as they let me. Then we can just start going to McDonald's and getting fat together."

"You'll never be fat," said Molly. "You're one of those mutants."

Angi laughed. "Just because you drag me to these classes. You're a good influence on me."

"You're a bad influence on me. I'm going to tell Jay I want to have a baby now."

"God, don't blame me for that…"

"Hey, if I can't get a job, what the hell…I might as well stay barefoot and pregnant." Molly, like her husband, had a degree from MIT. But with the frequent moves and the limited opportunities in a navy town, she'd been unable to get a career started. Angi had studied to be a teacher at Vandy, and was fully licensed to teach kids with learning disabilities—in Tennessee. After arriving in Washington State, she learned that the requirements and licensing were sufficiently different that it would take half their sea tour, and an equally significant chunk of Danny's sea pay, for her to obtain her Washington state license. She sympathized with her friend's frustration.

Angi turned on to Trigger Road, the short drive complete from her house to the gate. Cars were backed up as uniformed marines checked every ID and looked over every auto. A stern gunnery sergeant was supervising the stepped up inspections.

"Heightened security," said Molly. "Must be because of all the China stuff."

"The protestors are here, too," said Angi. There was a small cadre of them just outside the gate, aging hippies in tie-dye, peasant skirts, and white pony tails, handing out flyers with large smiles on their faces. They'd had a long-standing agreement with the base, who allowed them to show up on Tuesday mornings and exercise their freedom of speech just outside the gate while submarine sailors worked to defend that right inside. One of them approached Angi's car, and she started to roll down her window.

"You actually take their flyers?" said Molly.

"Usually. Just seems rude to say no."

"God, you are a such nice person."

Angi took the paper from an older looking man wearing a peace-sign medallion and a crucifix. He nodded thankfully and moved on to the car behind them. She looked it over.

AMERICAN NUKES TO PROVOKE CHINA??!!! There was a black, cartoonish silhouette of a surfaced submarine above the headline, with a nuclear trefoil symbol, as well as the red stars of the Chinese flag.

> Recent statements by the State Department indicate a serious reinterpretation of the nuclear non-proliferation treaty is underway. Officials in the current administration seem to believe that providing Taiwan with nuclear weapons would not be a breech of the treaty which has been honored by the United States (and 189 other nations) since 1970, and is considered a cornerstone of international nuclear peace efforts.
>
> China meanwhile has stated that it will not tolerate a nuclear Taiwan, and that it will consider any attempt to arm Taiwan as an act of war. The Red Army is on alert and the Chinese fleet is operating feverishly.
>
> Are we going to provoke China into starting World War III? Is the United States trying to provoke a nuclear conflict? Are the destabilizing nukes coming from behind these gates?

A car honked. Angi, startled, dropped the flyer into her lap. She realized her heart was pounding. The Marine at the gate was waving her forward, looking annoyed at her for holding up the line.

· · ·

Two cars behind her in that line was Captain Mario Soldato. He saw Angi's Honda, but Angi did not see him, and he prayed silently that the commotion would not cause her to turn around and spot him. Angi was smart, very intuitive, and knew him well; if she saw him, she would see the worry in his eyes and that would make her worry. He turned around and glared at the lieutenant in the minivan who was leaning on his horn; the junior officer, noting the four stripes on Mario's shoulder boards, quickly let up.

Mario had taken a rare afternoon off to spend with Cindy and her sister Sue Ellen, who'd flown in from South Carolina, where her husband, a Marine, had just made colonel. The two sisters were intensely competitive about their husband's careers, and they both were enjoying the fact that their husbands had made O-6, held command, and were now assured not only of decent pensions, but of having served complete, fulfilled careers. Mario took pleasure in the sisters' conversations, who in a very old-fashioned, southern way, regarded their husband's military successes as their own. He'd met them for lunch at The Keg, in Bremerton.

"Tom's boys are in charge of security at the sub base," said Sue Ellen.

"That's an important support role," said Mario.

"Stop it," said Cindy, slapping his hand as he laughed.

"Anyway…" Sue Ellen continued, laughing at the joke. "While one of those boats was deployed, it seems one of the young enlisted wives took up with one of Tom's Marines."

"Oh my."

"They were very serious, and when the boat finally came back, after a six month Westpac, as you can imagine this young sailor was distraught."

"I would think," said Mario.

"So the captain of this boat, Mario, you might know him, Mark Procopius?"

"I do know him…"

Sue Ellen rolled on, not interested in the details. "So this Captain Procopius schedules a meeting with Tom, to tell him about the whole thing, how distraught this sailor is. And you know what Tom tells him?"

"I can only imagine."

"He says, 'Captain, I can understand why you're upset, but I can't be responsible for every Navy wife in Charleston who decides she'd rather be with a United States Marine!'"

Cindy launched into a defense of the attractiveness of submariners when his cell phone rang.

"Soldato."

"Captain, this is Bushbaum. We've got another flash message from 731."

As his Chief of Staff explained, Soldato felt a stab of guilt, not for the first time, about being on shore duty, and for taking a half day away from the pier, as if trouble at sea was somehow his fault. Disaster had again befallen *Alabama*, and this time, someone had died: that's all he knew, all that could be communicated on the unsecure cell phone that he always carried, and even that message was spoken in military jargon that was impenetrable to outsiders. He hung up without saying goodbye, and stood.

"Gotta go," he said.

Cindy turned her head so he could kiss her cheek. She resumed her conversation with her sister before Soldato was gone, unshaken by his sudden departure. She'd been a navy wife too long to ever assume a full meal together was a guarantee.

He sped to the gate where the protestors and added security were slowing him down. He tried hard to control his temper at the two disparate groups that were holding him up, the earnest Marines with their clipboards and inspection mirrors, and the protestors with their glazed eyes, sandals, and smudged pamphlets. He declined to accept one when they came to his window. He actually had a lot in common with the protestors, it occurred to him. Like the protestors, Mario had spent hours worrying about the US, China, and Taiwan. But his concerns at the moment were far more immediate.

He finally made it to the gate and zipped through before the Marine had even lowered his salute. Down Trigger Road and to the pier, he ran up the stairs at squadron headquarters where Commander Bushbaum was standing by his desk with the message. He handed it to him without a word, knowing better than to offer an interpretation before the commodore had read it. Soldato imagined the scene in control as it was typed by the radiomen, vetted by the communicator, and then hurriedly approved by the captain and transmitted. He fought back the urge again to think that none of this would have happened had he still been in charge.

SAFETY FLASH — LARGE AMTS FREON LOST. SOME TRANSFOR-
MATION TO PHOSGENE DUE TO THERMAL CONTACT WITH
SCRUBBERS. ONE DEAD NO INJURIES. SIX HOURS TO VENTI-
LATE INTO SPEC MAKING UP TRACK NOW ESTIMATE ON TIME
ARRIVAL TO PAPA ZULU. INVESTIGATION UNDERWAY IN CON-
JUNCTION WITH PREVIOUS FLASH INCIDENT.

He dropped the message to his desk and rubbed his temples.
Bushbaum took this as a signal that it was time for him to speak.

"I guess the good news is that they still think they can make it
to Taiwan in time."

"I know every man on that crew," Soldato snapped. "Including the dead one." He let the reproach hang in the air.

"Sorry sir...I didn't mean..."

Soldato waved his hand in a way that said...that was a stupid
fucking thing to say, but we've got more important shit to worry
about at the moment. "After six hours at PD fighting the casualty...
in EAB's for Christ sake....they still might make it."

"And it's a good thing," offered Bushbaum cautiously. "The
CNO's office is asking for updates almost hourly. His number two
called me the other day to tell me that a White House speechwriter
was working on something, wanted some facts and figures about
Alabama. He thought POTUS might actually be there in Taiwan
for the weapon transfer." Bushbaum was an absolutely naked ca-
reerist, the reason he'd been able to make 0-5 at the age of thirty.
He couldn't keep the glee out of his voice at being just two degrees
removed from the Commander in Chief.

Soldato looked back down at the message and tried to read
into it what he could. A massive Freon leak, phosgene gas, a dead
sailor. Six hours to replace all the bad air with good: a shit ton of
Freon. Soldato tried to imagine how that much could be dumped,
and failed to come up with a scenario. He imagined large amounts
of food were turning bad inside the coolers of the Alabama. At the
speeds they would be travelling, they wouldn't be able to TDU it
fast enough. They might run out of food. Odor would become an
issue, although it was the least of the issues in his mind.

"Is Navships aware of this Freon-to-Phosgene conversion?"

"They knew there was a theoretical concern."

"More than theoretical now, I guess."

"They're revaluating the advantages of the new refrigerant."

Soldato had to wait a moment again for his anger to subside at that galactic fuck up by Navships, and then looked back down at the message. "Revaluating," he said. "I'll fucking bet. If I had more time, I'd track down that cocksucker EDO who recommended this change."

"Did you also notice, 'In conjunction with the previous incident.'"

"The dryer fire."

"Right. That caught my eye too," said Bushbaum.

It bothered Soldato, too, although he couldn't put his finger on why. Words were like gold in a message like that, you didn't include them unless you absolutely had too. These weren't letters home, they were the first piece of paper in a stack that would grow into a mountain of documentation. They would be studied for months, possible even years, as the bureaucracy went to work and tried to figure out who to blame. Especially with a sailor dead...the incident would employ an army of investigators and desk jockeys for months to come. There was an art to writing messages like that, to include every essential fact and not one thing more.

"Why mention that the two investigations are in "in conjunction?" "

Bushbaum shrugged. "They're being done by the same guy?"

"Probably."

"But why mention that?"

"Maybe they think the two incidents have a common cause."

Bushbaum stepped back. "What in the hell could be the common cause of a dryer fire and a Freon dump?"

Soldato hesitated. "A saboteur."

"Jesus Christ."

"It wouldn't be the first time. You're too young to remember, but when I first got in the navy, during Vietnam, it was a real concern. They called it "Stop our Ship," or SOS. Set fires, threw wrenches into reduction gears, sailors refusing to show up, shit like that."

"On submarines?"

"No, it was mostly those pussies on carriers."

"But you think it might be politically motivated? Because of the Taiwan mission?"

Soldato shook his head. "I doubt it, those orders are secret to the crew, only the officers know."

"You think maybe an officer…"

"No," said Soldato, cutting him off. But the thought chilled him. The boat's equipment had been designed by some of the most brilliant engineers in the world. But none of that mattered without the right men in charge, from the newest enlisted man all the way to the captain, with whom all the responsibility ended up. Admiral Rickover, the patron saint of naval nuclear propulsion, had personally interviewed every officer in the program, knowing that strong men would be the fleet's greatest asset. And if somehow the wrong guy made it into the wardroom of a nuclear submarine…

"I'm glad they didn't put anything about sabotage in the message…we'd have NIS banging down our door right now."

"If that's what it is, they'll need to figure out for themselves what's going on inside the *Alabama*. The NIS can't help them where they are now."

Bushbaum walked to a large map on the wall and took note of the approximate position of the Alabama. "We'll need to figure out how to let the families of the crew know about the death when the boat hits Taiwan. At least we've got a week to figure that out."

"They'll find out before then," said the captain with a sigh. "They always do."

·　　　　·　　　　·

Here's how they found out.

Lieutenant John Knight was Engineering Duty Officer who had recommended the change to the new refrigerant—he was the cocksucker EDO that Captain Soldato had fantasized about finding and beating. He was a Naval Academy graduate who'd dreamed of being a submarine officer himself, but at his pre-commissioning physical, he'd learned to his shock that he was colorblind. Submarine officers need to be able to distinguish the red and the green of port and starboard running lights from the periscope; colorblindness was a disqualifying disability. Knight became an EDO because it was as close as he could get to being on a submarine.

He was in charge of a group of engineers, both civilian and military, who were charged with understanding every facet of the submarine fleet's air conditioning and refrigeration plants. The switch to a new refrigerant, designated R-118, was the result of an exhaustive two year-long study that he and his team had conducted. They'd approved the new Freon because it was more stable in transport, it was more efficient within refrigeration machinery, and yes...it was cheaper. And many different varieties of Freon can, theoretically, break down into other possibly dangerous by-products under various conditions. But the studies they'd done, in conjunction with the manufacturer, had indicated that the amount of R-118 and the amount of heat necessary to cause the transformation into Phosgene were enormous. Like good engineers, they'd decided that the advantages of the change outweighed the potential risks. And, in reading that terse message from the Alabama, Knight realized that they'd made a disastrous miscalculation.

He knew that there would be possibly career-ending consequences for his mistake, but decided quickly that, while he was still in a position to do something about it, he would make sure that no other boat suffered from his error. Rather than try to cover his ass by arguing that R-118 was still safe, or that the men of the *Alabama* must somehow be at fault for the casualty, Knight quickly drafted an emergency safety flash message, explained it to his chain of command, and had it approved and transmitted. By midnight, R-118 was banned from US submarines.

Knight then worked to prepare for a hastily scheduled 0800 meeting with Admiral Patrick Cheever, NAVSEA-08, the man charged with all the engineering on all the navy's nuclear submarines, the heir to Rickover's throne. Banning R-118 had been easy; the details would be hard, and the details were what Knight worked on all night. The meeting was convened precisely on time with Cheever at the head of a table crowded with officers, every one of whom outranked Knight. It was held in a spartan conference room dominated by a scarred table and mismatched chairs; all of Naval Reactors took pride in their no-frills environs. It was yet another vestige of the reign of Admiral Rickover, who bragged that he had designed the *Nautilus*, the world's first nuclear submarine, from an office that was a converted women's restroom.

Despite the array of heavy brass that stared back at him. Knight was so exhausted, and so determined to right any wrong that led to a tragedy, that he was beyond intimidation. He was also certain that however badly he might have fucked up, no one else in the world understood the refrigeration plants of US submarines better than he. He began his brief.

"There are three groups of submarines to consider," he explained. "The first and largest group is those still using the old refrigerant, R-114. They are obviously fine, and just need to cancel any plans they had for switching to R-118." He allowed his audience to view a large list of submarines on the screen, then clicked his mouse and called up the next slide.

"The second group consists of those boats currently at sea that have already switched to R-118. There are only two, both out of Bangor."

"Coincidence?" asked the Admiral. It was the first word he'd spoken.

"No sir. We decided to achieve the modification one squadron at a time, and Trident submarines, with their large refrigeration capacity, were made the top priority. The two boats are the *Alabama* and the *Florida*. I recommend we recall them both immediately."

"The *Alabama* will not be recalled," said the admiral. Everyone waited for him to elaborate, but he did not. As an engineering duty officer, Knight was once again intrigued by the secretive missions of the boats that he devoted his life to, even though they stubbornly refused to allow him, as an engineering duty officer, to know their mysteries.

"Well sir, there's probably very little R-118 left onboard the *Alabama* anyway."

"Doesn't matter," he snapped. "She's staying at sea. The *Florida* we can discuss." With that the most spirited debate of the morning began. Some argued that that while the incident on *Alabama* had been a disaster, it was probably a fluke, and that *Florida* could safely complete her patrol and switch out refrigerants in a normal refit. Others argued that now that disaster had struck, they had no choice but to correct the situation immediately: the position Knight advocated. *Florida* had only been at sea three days, was not yet alert, and with a long patrol ahead of them why take that chance? After ten minutes of arguments and counter-arguments, all heads turned to the admiral.

"Bring her in," he said. There was no uncertainty in his voice, and Knight watched the officers who had advocated leaving *Florida* at sea squirm a little in their seats.

It was an unusual step, recalling a boat like that, and would require logistical mountains to be moved, but suddenly everyone agreed with the admiral that it was necessary and the calls were made to squadron and the machinery began to move to get *Florida* back to Bangor and get its new refrigerant replaced with the old. It was settled. "There is one other boat to consider," said Knight.

"Enlighten us, lieutenant."

"*Alaska*, sir. Also in Bangor. Just completed the modification to R-118 in refit, but she's sitting at the Delta Pier." Knight himself had been on the phone with *Alaska's* engineer just days before discussing the change and how smoothly the operation had gone.

"Well that's easy," said the admiral. "Tell them to switch back."

A message was composed and hurriedly sent to Squadron 17. Lieutenant Dean Hysong was preparing for his last patrol on *Alaska*. He had decided to stay in the Navy, and had orders to the ROTC unit at Creighton, where he hoped to get an MBA on the navy's tab during his two-year shore tour. As the most experienced junior officer in the wardroom, he was the DCA, or Damage Control Assistant, in charge of A-Gang. The refit was in its final days, and he was eager to get home, eager to be with his wife as much as he could. Of course, every man longed to be with his wife in those final days, but Dee Dee was unusually hot, unusually energetic, and unusually demanding in bed. It had been six days since he'd touched her, which was torture. But even worse, he knew soon he'd be gone for one hundred days or more, and every minute he spent on the boat pierside, while his wife waited for him at home, passing the time with crunches and leg lifts, seemed a crime against nature.

But Dean was happy because that night it seemed he might actually get off the boat in time to shower at home, screw his wife, and eat dinner. In that order.

He checked in a final time with the engineer, not quite saying he was getting ready to leave, but verifying that there was nothing preventing him from going home, no urgent problems demanding his attention. He skulked by the XO's stateroom, to control, and actually had one hand on the ladder to freedom when the radioman spotted him. "Lieutenant Hysong?"

"I'm going home."

"You might want to see this," he said, arm extended with a clipboard.

"No. I really don't."

The radioman nodded sympathetically, and Hysong took it from him. He read it with increasing disbelief.

"They can't fucking be serious."

"Priority one, it says. Supposed to start tomorrow. The Freon truck is already on the pier."

Hysong's head was spinning. The message called for a brief, but everyone, including his chief, had already gone home with roughly the same plans he had. But *their* wives weren't freaking aerobics instructors. And they had just completed the incredibly tedious, time-consuming operation of switching out every ounce of refrigerant. Now the navy wanted them to switch back.

"I'm not doing it. Fuck 'em. Retards."

"Says safety issue," said the radioman.

"Fuck safety."

"Look at the bottom," he said.

"Oh fuck, is there something else?" He flipped over to the second page. What he saw there was even weirder.

"Holy shit. They're calling back the *Florida*?"

"That's what it says. They're going to tie up outboard of us and make the same switch."

Dean dropped the message to his side and thought that over. Calling a boat back from patrol was extremely odd...he'd only seen it a couple of times in five years. The whole operation was odd, and reeked of bureaucratic panic. He tried to remember a message they'd gotten a few days earlier, some kind of warning they'd received about R-118. To achieve this kind of rapid motion, to actually turn a boat around at sea and bring it back to the pier, one had to overcome massive amounts of inertia, and it could usually only be achieved by disaster.

Suddenly he was certain that someone had been killed.

And he knew, from the pre-evolution briefs, that only three boats had made the change: *Alaska*, *Florida*, and *Alabama*. And since nothing had happened on *Alaska*, he knew the fatality had to have happened on one of the other two. His gut told him it was the *Florida*. They were bringing her back in, after all, no word about the *Alabama*. And, as much as he hated to admit it, the *Alabama* was the tightest ship in the squadron, always at the top of every ranking. He didn't picture her at the center of this kind of fuck up.

He went topside and walked to the pier to call home, before he'd even shown the message to the engineer or the captain, because he knew that once the word was out he wouldn't have a spare second.

"Hello?" she said. He could hear a lilt in her voice. She thought he was calling to say that he was on his way home.

"I'm stuck here," he said.

"How long?" she said without trying to hide her disappointment or disgust. He sighed. "Probably all night. I'll be lucky if I'm home for dinner tomorrow." "Okay," she said, knowing better than to ask why. "Maybe I'll see you tomorrow."

Hysong worked all night preparing the work plan, and by the morning he was ready to brief all the players. As they scrambled to prepare, everyone was asking the same question: *What the fuck?* Hysong had his theory, that someone had been killed on either *Florida* or *Alabama*, but kept it to himself. After he completed his 0900 briefing in the wardroom, the squadron EDO told them that *Florida* would soon be tying up outboard of them, and would actually get to make the change first—the priority was to get her back to sea as quickly as possible. This gave Hysong a few minutes to catch his breath. He grabbed a cup of coffee and went topside to watch *Florida* pull in.

It was a beautiful, crisp morning, the type of morning that made the coffee taste better, and made him mourn the sunshine and fresh air that he was about to be locked away from for months. *Florida* pulled along their port side head to tail, and was nudged gently into place by the civilian tug the *Mitchell Hebert*. As soon as a gangplank was placed across, Hysong walked over and found Rick Curtis, their DCA. They looked at each other with grim, appraising smiles.

"Hey Rick."

"How are you, Dean?"

"Did you guys kill somebody out there?"

Rick shook his head. "I was just about to ask you the same thing."

.   .   .

The switch on *Florida* took longer than expected, which everyone expected. Then they moved all the hoses over to *Alaska*, where everyone was waiting, eager to get it over with. They were fairly well-practiced at the evolution by this point, and they efficiently evacuated the R-118. There was a moment of tension when they thought the truck might not contain enough R-114 to fill all their systems, and they would have to wait for the nearest truck....in Spokane...to make its way to the pier, probably well after 2200. Had that happened, Dean would have made sure that the Navy saw its second Freon-related death in a week. But they finally got a break and they were able to replace every ounce of the new Freon with the old with what was on the pier, and the entire evolution was complete and signed off by 1900. Dean grabbed his bag, went to the pier and got in his car without even considering asking anyone's permission.

At home, Dee Dee was waiting, still grouchy from being stood up the night before. She looked achingly beautiful, her body toned perfectly from her many hours at the gym. They had two nights left before he went to sea again, and Dean desperately wanted to make things right with her, wanted to explain to her how fucked up the last twenty-four hours had been, how he really, truly, had had no choice. And, as he imagined pulling the thin sweatshirt over her head without even leaving the living room, he wanted to explain it all to her in the shortest possible period of time.

"Hey," she said, hands on her hips, awaiting his justification.

He hesitated for just a moment. "Somebody got killed on the *Alabama*."

The next day was Thursday. A happy and satisfied Dee Dee Hysong told most of the class at the gym what she'd learned before Angi and Molly even showed up, their customary ten minutes late. By the time they took their positions, the entire group was chattering about death aboard the *USS Alabama*.

Jabo checked the position on the chart again, to verify they were making up track. The position was all DR, of course, just an estimate based on speed and heading. They would only be able to get a GPS fix every eight hours or so, during their furtive trips to PD. Any estimate of position between fixes was just a math problem, an educated guess represented by an X on a thin pencil line on a virtually unmarked chart based on course and speed. Whatever errors existed in those measurements were magnified by their high bell. Their location on the planet had become very abstract.

And they were behind. At Ahead Flank, stopping the bare minimum number of times they had to in order to catch a broadcast and a GPS fix, they would arrive at Papa Zulu precisely on time, without a minute to spare. But they would be playing catch up the entire time.

No one on the boat could remember running Ahead Flank for so long. The most strained part of the boat was the engine room, where everything was running at high speed, every back up seawater and coolant pump was on, and nothing could break, or even be secured for routine maintenance. The engineer and his team were managing to keep it together but the strain was showing on both the men and the machinery. Hot bearings alarmed, high pressures caused reliefs to lift, and water levels had to be watched and adjusted continuously.

The pressures in the control room were different and scarier in some ways—they were going fast and deep in an unknown ocean. But other than check course and speed, there was little else the officer of the deck could do except worry about it.

Flather walked into control from radio, a stack of messages in his hand.

"More updates?" said Jabo.

He nodded. He looked exhausted. "All for the chart we're on: JO91747. I'm just barely keeping up with track."

"None for the next chart? It looks like we'll be there in an hour or so."

Flather flipped up the corner of JO91747 to reveal the number of the next chart beneath it: JO90888. He then flipped through the messages in his hand. "Nothing for 0888. Good for us. All on 1747."

"Anything to worry about?"

He shook his head. "Not yet. I won't lie, though—this kind of navigation keeps me awake at night."

Jabo pointed to a faded line that had marked their track...it had been altered slightly, you could see the ghost of the line left by the eraser. "What's this change?"

Flather nodded. "I don't know. The navigator did it last night. Steering us a few degrees south, it looks like."

"But it sounds like there's nothing on the next chart to worry about, right? Was our original track wrong?"

"There must be some reason. Who knows?"

"Shouldn't you know?"

Flather bristled a little at that. "I'm trying to keep these charts up, sir. We're going as fast as we can into an area we've never been. I haven't had time to take a shit, much less ask the navigator to explain everything he's done. I came up here after two hours of sleep and he'd made these changes. If you've got a question, why don't you ask him? I'd like to know the answer too."

"Okay," said Jabo. "Relax. I will ask him." Flather walked over to the table, sat heavily down on the stool, and began marking up the chart.

Jabo took the sound powered phone off the latch and growled the navigator's stateroom; no one answered. He tried the wardroom and officers' study…again no answer. He considered sending the messenger. He had every right to, as officer of the deck, but still there was something mildly untoward about a junior officer summoning the navigator to the conn. He would wait a few minutes; hopefully the navigator would find his way to the control room during the watch.

Jabo turned to the stack of papers on his clipboard, the start of his investigation into Howard's death. He scanned the yellow sheet of notebook paper that Howard had written.

It was wrinkled, and smudged in some places by moisture. But it was by and large readable, thanks to Hallorann, who'd apparently saved it.

It contained a column of information about the day of the laundry fire in boyish yet earnest handwriting. Each entry was dated, Jabo could see, in a way that mimicked the log sheets. There were lots question marks. *Book in Dryer?? Paper towels in dryer???* The document reflected Howard's youth in a way that would have brought a smile to Jabo's face, had Howard not been dead, and had he not been accused of sabotage.

Jabo turned to the Machinery Two logs, the last Howard had kept. These too were neat...extraordinarily neat. Each number was centered in its square, everything was legible, everything was perfect. Jabo turned it over to read the comments section.

These too were neat and squared away, the only unusual thing being perhaps the number of comments—Howard was clearly trying hard to be diligent. Jabo scanned the comments. *Oxygen Generator #2 drifting to high voltage. Navigator Running on treadmill.* Jabo did smile at that. He could review a year's worth of Machinery Two logs and no one would ever have recorded who was working out on what. Howard was trying to take the most complete set of logs ever taken in Machinery Two.

Gurno appeared in front of him with a concerned look on his face.

"What could be wrong? We're not getting any traffic at this speed. You guys should be napping."

"You remember that Freon message you asked me about?" asked Gurno.

"Sure. I wanted you to pull it again for the captain. And for my investigation."

"I can't find it."

"What do you mean?"

Gurno shrugged. "It's not anywhere, not even on any of the hard drives. And I can't find a printed copy anywhere. It's like we never got it."

"I don't get it...I read it. I know we printed it out."

"I know. I don't know what to tell you sir. It's fucked up."

The captain hadn't asked for it since the night of the casualty, it's not like he was being hounded for it. But it did relate directly to what had befallen them...and they just shouldn't be losing fucking messages like that.

"Alright. Go take another look."

"Aye, aye sir," said Gurno. "I don't know what the fuck is going on."

.   .   .

Kincaid appeared to relieve him just as the fatigue was settling in solidly. Jabo was trying to think about the cryptic notes left behind by Howard, the missing message, and their position on the chart, how much time they'd made up during his watch. It was all jumbled together in his mind inside a thick weary fog.

"Duggan qualified EOOW while you were up here," said Kincaid.

"Really? Man, that's pretty fast."

"Yep, I sat on his board. He's smarter than he looks. Going back there to take the watch right now."

"So Morrissey gets the watch off? Is he qualified OOD yet?" He ran through the watchbill in his mind, calculating how an additional watchstander in the wardroom might somehow add a few hours of sleep to his week.

"Not yet."

"But if Morrissey gets his OOD board scheduled..."

"That's right. Then it helps us," said Kincaid. "So go down there and sign whatever's left on his card."

"Not right now," said Jabo. "I'm fucking exhausted."

Kincaid stepped up to the conn and scanned the night orders. He scowled.

"What's the matter?" asked Jabo.

"Why can't we untag the fucking treadmill yet?"

Jabo laughed. "I think you're the only one that still gives a shit."

"Must be," said Kincaid. "My own private gym. Boats gonna be full of fat fucks when we pull in."

Jabo took lanyard heavy with keys from around his neck and handed it to Kincaid.

"I relieve you," said Kincaid.

"I stand relieved," said Jabo.

"This is Lieutenant Kincaid; I have the deck and the conn."

The control room watchstanders acknowledged in turn.

.   .   .

Jabo intended on going directly to his rack; he dreaded even taking the time to undress. At his stateroom door, however, still bothered vaguely by the events of his last watch, he walked down the narrow passageway to the navigator's stateroom.

He got to the stateroom and the sliding door was shut...odd.

He knocked, and knocked again. "Nav?' He pulled the unlocked door open.

The lights were on and the stateroom was, as always, neat and organized. His desktop was closed as were all his cabinets. The bed was made with the kind of anxious rigor that was the mark of most Academy-trained officers. The only thing out of order on it was the old book in the center of the rack: *Rig for Dive,* by Crush Martin. He stepped in and flipped it over; saw the black and white photo of Martin, a stern looking man with scars on his face and neck not completely hidden by the old-fashioned khaki dress uniform. He had commander's shoulder boards, but other than that the only insignia on his uniform were his gold dolphins and a war patrol pin. Jabo flipped through it and saw, to his surprise, that the pages and margins were filled with dense notes in the nav's tiny handwriting. Every page had passages highlighted, and on some pages every word had been highlighted. The notes seemed to bear little relation to the page, or to Martin's story at all. On an early page detailing Martin's childhood in rural Florida, Jabo saw where the nav had written the formula for the reactor average temperature calculation in three different colors of ink. It bothered Jabo: the formula was classified. Not exactly a state secret, but an odd lapse in discipline from a man as buttoned-up as the navigator.

He hesitated, then opened the top cabinet above the nav's desk, where he knew he kept hardcopies of every broadcast. And there they were, neatly organized in white, three-inch binders across the shelf, each with a range of dates printed in the navigator's neat script across the spine. Jabo pulled the most recent one down, paged through it looking for the Freon message. He remembered the approximate date, remembered some of the other things in the broadcast, but couldn't be certain where it would be exactly. It would take hours to page through them all to find it, if it was even in there. Jabo hoped that the navigator had pulled it for some reason, maybe because of the incident. Otherwise…it would be yet another set of hours Jabo would have to find, to pour through the binders one page at a time to look for the misplaced message.

Jabo saw, as he removed the binder, a metal clipboard flat against the back of the cabinet: *hidden?* It was one of the thin clipboards used to move a single classified message around the boat, two thin sheets of metal joined by a hinge. He pulled it down.

No classification page marked the front of it. Which would normally mean it was empty. But when Jabo opened it, there were several sheets of paper. He knew in an instant it was the Freon message.

"Having a look around, Lieutenant?"

Jabo almost dropped the board; it was the navigator, standing at the door to his stateroom. "Jesus, Nav, you scared the shit out of me."

"Guilty conscience?" He had a weird look on his face, twitchy and uncomfortable.

"No, Nav, not at all. Just looking for this message…" Jabo realized suddenly that he was in the wrong, that he had no business digging through the nav's stateroom like that. He saw the navigator glance toward his other hand, which held *Rig for Dive*. He tossed it back on the rack.

"You're the communicator, shouldn't you have access to all this in radio?"

"There's a message missing…"

"How come no one's told me about it?"

"I guess I'm telling you now. And it's not missing anymore." He held up the clipboard.

There was a sudden shift between them. Jabo realized how small a man the navigator was. Jabo had been defensive at first, caught doing something he shouldn't. But the nav, who'd looked absolutely haunted for days, suddenly looked off balance, almost frightened.

The navigator gathered himself, trying to recapture the initiative. "Lieutenant Jabo, I really don't appreciate you tearing through my stateroom. And I don't appreciate the way you've decided to tell me about this lapse in radio. I think I'd like you to meet me in the captain's stateroom in about ten minutes, after I've had chance to brief him about your work. Your attitude."

"Fine," said Jabo. He welcomed the chance; wanted to put all the pieces of the puzzle in front of the captain and see what he could make out of it. The navigator's face twitched again, and then he turned around, walking toward the captain's stateroom.

Jabo stood there, the thin clipboard still in his hand. He checked his watch, intending to the give the nav exactly his requested ten minutes. He tried to think of a legitimate reason the nav might have that message, by itself, hidden in his stateroom, while no one else in communications could find a copy. There were possibilities; perhaps he had been tasked with his own investigation. Perhaps the Nav had pulled the message on the night of the incident, and just never returned it.

But that kind of fuck up seemed unlikely in the nav's ruthlessly ordered, organized world. Jabo had heard that at the academy, visitors weren't allowed to see a midshipman's dormitory room. Instead, they had a "model" room complete with neatly made racks and ownerless uniforms hung in the wardrobe. That's what the nav's stateroom seemed like, right down to his polished oxfords awaiting the return to port sticking out from his bed, right next to a pair of unblemished Nike running shoes that looked right out of the box.

A slight buzz went through Jabo's mind. He checked his watch; he still had eight minutes before he was supposed to meet with the navigator and the captain. He left the stateroom, clipboard still in his hand, and began walking aft.

· — · · ·

The navigator stormed out of his stateroom, disappointed that he couldn't actually drag Jabo before the captain. Jabo was long overdue for a humbling, and the nav was more than willing to deliver it. He knew the captain and the XO loved the guy, but there's no way even they would abide him digging through his stateroom, looking at his personal belongings. Jabo should be disciplined; he could have insisted upon it. It was flagrant disrespect, insubordination. But there was no time.

As he rounded the corner from the staterooms, he saw a flash of khaki going down into Machinery One. It was something that got your attention at this point in patrol; everyone, officer, chief, and enlisted, were all wearing identical blue poopies. It didn't surprise him; he was overdue for a briefing with the dark commander. He glanced around to see if anyone else had seen him. The only other person around was a young sailor reading the plan of the day, trying to avoid eye contact. The nav hurried down the ladder.

·   ·   ·

The commander was waiting for him in machinery one, sitting on a stool at the foot of the diesel engine. He had his legs crossed in a strange way; the nav thought maybe his posture was the result of an injury, some earlier encounter with the enemy. He was smoking an odd, wrinkled looking cigarette, one the nav thought was perhaps hand-rolled, or a product of wartime austerity.

"Is your plan in motion?" he asked.

"Yes sir," said the navigator. "It's too late to do anything now."

"You seem upset by that. Are you having second thoughts?"

"No," said the nav. "This has to be done."

"That's right. Sometimes we have to do things we don't want to do. Things other people may condemn. But they still have to be done."

"Yes sir."

"So, your plan is adequate this time? No more half-ass measures?"

"No sir. It's adequate. The ship won't survive."

"You're sure?"

"Positive," said the navigator. "It will all be over soon. In minutes."

The commander nodded and smiled at that. He shut his eyes and took a deep drag from his cheap-looking cigarette, the tip glowing bright red. "*No one* knows?" he asked without opening his eyes.

"It's too late to do anything about it anyway," said the Nav.

The commander eyes flew open and he looked at him sharply. "Does anyone know?"

"No one knows."

"I think you're mistaken."

"No one knows!"

"One person knows. And we know from past experience that he is weak. You need to get rid of him before that weakness betrays us, and ruins the plan."

The navigator was at first confused. But then he realized that the commander was talking about him.

. . .

Hallorann sat on the edge of his rack and looked through his qualification book for the millionth time. Like most new men, when a page was full, with every signature block signed, he laminated it with a sheet of plastic, a necessity for a book that was carried next to your body for hour after sweaty hour. It was also a measure of progress, and Hallorann's book only had two un-laminated pages remaining. He had everything about the book memorized, every signature, every question he'd answered to get the signature. He knew which signatures he'd really earned, the areas and systems on the boat that he really understood: sonar and the main ballast system were his best. And he knew which ones were harder for him to understand: the reactor, which still seemed like some kind of black magic to him, a perpetual motion machine that really worked.

But most of all, he knew which signatures he had left to get. He'd made amazing, rapid progress, and it had been noticed. But that also meant that his questioners were less apt to give him a pass on anything. He was supposed to be hot shit, and they all wanted to see it for themselves. And one of the biggest blocks that was left was the diesel.

His confidence was high as he approached the ladder that would take him down into the torpedo room and Machinery One, home of both the diesel and the battery. As he rounded the corner, however, the navigator was hustling toward the same ladder, a grim look on his face. Hallorann hesitated and let the navigator pass, turning to pretend to read the posted Plan of the Day.

He'd hoped to wander down there and find some beneficent A Ganger, bored and looking for something to do, like perhaps spending twenty or thirty minutes talking to Hallorann and signing his qualification book. He knew it was a long shot, especially with A Gang being short handed and always busy. His second choice, if there was no one down there, would be to spend a few minutes alone with the machine, walking through the procedures, getting that much more prepared for his qualification.

But he had no desire to be down there alone with the navigator. The crew liked to make fun of the eccentricities of the other officers, like Hein's dweebishness, Jabo's goofy country charm, and Kincaid's constant reminders to everyone that he had been enlisted once, too. But the feelings about the nav were different, an almost superstitious kind of discomfort. He was weird, and nobody wanted even to talk about him, other than an occasional word of pity for those enlisted men like Flather who worked directly for him. Which is why Hallorann hesitated, deciding to wait a few minutes to see if the nav might come back up quickly before he descended into Machinery One.

After a few minutes he began to feel uncomfortable loitering in the heart of Officers' Country. He was standing near the CO's and XO's staterooms, the Officers' Study, and the wardroom. Plus, he was ready, eager to get down the ladder, to the diesel and that much closer to his dolphins. He had no reason to be afraid of the nav...did he? He hesitated one more moment in front of the officer's bulletin board, pretending again to read the plan of the day and the watchbill. Then he turned and climbed down the ladder.

There was a watchstander in the torpedo room, laughing at something on his computer screen, waiting for his watch to end. Hallorann took a few steps forward into Machinery One.

He saw the nav's feet first. The soles of his back oxfords dangled a few inches off the deck. Hallorann's eyes went up. The navigator had hung himself from an overhead pipe with his khaki belt. The navigator seemed to have oriented the belt with deliberate precision, centering the *Alabama* belt buckle right below his Adam's apple. His face was turning bright purple and his eyes were bulging, looking directly at him. Then the nav blinked and emitted a small croak, and Hallorann knew that, for the moment, he was still alive.

. . .

Duggan got permission from Lieutenant (jg) Brian Morgan, his best friend on board, to enter maneuvering. He'd just completed perhaps the most thorough pre-watch tour in submarine history. He lifted the chain and went inside, aware that for the first time, he was doing so alone, without Morrissey watching over him.

"Gosh!" said Morgan. "I can't believe it! You're actually going to start contributing around here." Morgan was a Mormon, and the fact that he could get through a submarine patrol avoiding both caffeine and profanity was one of the most impressive displays of religious devotion Duggan had ever witnessed.

Duggan nodded and smiled. "I guess so." He'd spent hundreds of hours in maneuvering on the boat. He'd stood every enlisted watchstation and performed every job in the engine room, from turbidity tests in lower level to analyzing samples of radioactive reactor coolant in the small chemistry lab. And before that, he'd done the exact same thing on a working, land-based reactor in Charleston, South Carolina, as part of his training. And before that...the meat grinder of nuclear power school. But it felt undeniably different, getting ready to take the watch over an operating nuclear reactor on a warship at sea. Nothing could match the terror of actually being the man in charge.

He took note of the maneuvering watchsection, all three men with their backs to him as they dutifully concentrated on their indications: EM1 Patterson at his far right on the electrical plant, ET1 Barnes in the center as reactor operator, and MM2 Tremain on the left, the throttleman. Out in the spaces, he'd seen during his tour, MMC Fissel was the Engineering Watch Supervisor. It was a very experienced, senior group of enlisted men that he was ostensibly supervising on his first watch—Duggan was sure that was not an accident. The XO had probably orchestrated it that way when he scheduled his board, putting the newest EOOW with the saltiest enlisted team. Duggan wasn't insulted; he was deeply grateful. He started scanning the logs from the previous six, uneventful hours.

"How was your board?" Morgan asked. "Who sat it?"

"The eng, the XO, and Lieutenant Kincaid."

The reactor operator, Barnes, turned around slightly. "I heard he used to be enlisted, is that true?" They all laughed.

"Kincaid was the hardest," he said. "He made me go through the complete electrical system, one bus at a time."

"Every bus?"

"Everything…even the 400 hertz stuff. Really drilled me on it, made me draw it all out. I think that's when they decided to qualify me, because I actually knew all that shit."

"Now you can start working on OOD," said Morgan. "And then…your dolphins. You are definitely on track. Congratulations."

"Thanks," said Duggan, a little embarrassed at the praise.

He looked up at the three panels, a final check before taking the watch from Morgan. Everything was pegged…they were still at ahead flank and you could almost sense the engine room, and the reactor, begging for mercy. There were a few yellow warning lights scattered across the panels, bearings that were hot, water levels that were low. One red light caught his attention. "The alarm?"

"Engine room upper level ambient. It's a hundred and ten degrees up there, hotter than heck."

"From the main engines?"

"The main engines and those high pressure drains. All that steam is really heating things up, the refrigeration units can't keep up. Especially since we're down to two, with all that Freon we lost."

"And water?"

"Everything is going into the reserve feed tanks. We're probably going to have to suspend showers on your watch. Hope you took one."

"I didn't."

"Well let me get mine in before you shut the valve."

Duggan looked behind Morgan, at the primary system status board, wondering if there was anything else he should ask.

"You're ready," said Morgan. He said it as a friend, not as someone just trying to get out of the box and to dinner.

"You think so?" Duggan laughed. "The watch qual book says I am, so I guess I am."

"You know something is going to happen right?"

"I've heard." It was an old superstition, one he'd heard many times in the days leading up to his board.

"It always does. Something always happens on your first qualified watch."

"What happened on yours?"

"I remember," said Barnes, without turning around. "That was my first watch too. Thought we had carry over. Almost shut the whole thing down."

"That's right!" said Morgan. "I forgot you were in here with me. They'd done SGWL maintenance on the previous watch." He referred to the system that controlled steam generator water levels, pronouncing it as 'squiggle.'

"They fried one of the flip flops," said Barnett. "But we didn't know because it was high range. Didn't pick up till we increased power on our watch."

"That's right. So we get over fifty-percent reactor power, and in here, it just looks like level is going up. In both generators."

"Doesn't shoot up...just creeps up," said Barnett. "Just like it really would in a casualty."

"But we didn't have any of the collateral indications," said Morgan. "No noise in the engine room, nothing. But all I know is what I'm seeing here. I'm afraid water is getting ready to carry over, go right out there and shred both main engines, both turbine generators." It was a frightening prospect—any moisture travelling into the thin, precisely engineered turbine blades at their high speeds would destroy them, obliterating both propulsion and electricity. Morgan continued.

"Tremain was the throttleman...he had his hands on the cutouts." He pointed to the big hydraulic valve handles that should shut off all steam to the engine room. "We'd still lose power, still lose propulsion, but we'd save the turbines."

"Jesus," said Duggan.

"Right, I know...it would cause a scram, too, don't forget, automatically. And we were ready to do it. I was ready to give the order. I was two hours into my first watch."

"Then Chief Flora comes haulin' ass in here from instrument alley," says Barnett. "Saying, 'don't do it! Don't do it! We fried the flip flop!'"

"He'd been reviewing the maintenance records and noticed a discrepancy...ran back to the engine room just as we were calling it away, put it all together and stopped us just in time," said Morgan.

"I still think you should have called it away," says Barnes. "If you'd been following the procedure...you had the indications. You had no way of knowing. What if Flora had just lost his mind? What if he'd decided to try to kill us all?"

"I guess Flora was right," said Morgan, grinning. "And so was I. So...I wonder what will happen on your watch?"

"We'll see," said Duggan. "Hopefully nothing." He took a deep breath. "Lieutenant Morgan, I am ready to relieve you."

"I'm ready to be relieved. Reactor is at 100% power, normal full power line up, reactor plant is in forced circulation, all main coolant pumps on fast. Keep an eye on the main engine bearings, and make sure someone takes McCormick some ice water in upper level, so he doesn't pass out or puke."

"Will do. I relieve you."

"I stand relieved!" Morgan slapped him on the back and started to walk out.

"Ensign Duggan is the Engineering Officer of the watch," he said. He wrote the time and same words on the EOOW's log, his first entry as a qualified watch officer.

"Throttleman, aye."

"Reactor operator, aye."

"Electrical operator, aye."

Morgan spoke from the other side of the chain. "Good luck, pal."

"Thanks," said Duggan. He watched him walk away, and a few seconds later heard the clank of the engine room watertight door. Morgan was gone, and Duggan felt the full weight and loneliness of being the sole officer in the engine room of a United States nuclear submarine. He reached below his small desk, where copies of all the reactor plant manuals and casualty procedures, thousands of pages of documentation, were kept. He pulled out one of the thicker books, opened it, and began to review the procedures for steam generator water level casualties.

.   .   .

As Jabo walked aft he was aware of the throbbing in the deck plates beneath his feet—it was the feeling of the boat moving very fast, a harmonic that ran through the very hull caused by both the friction of the cold sea against the ship and by every piece of machinery on the boat running at maximum speed. He'd never been on the boat when they ran so fast for so long. Or, for that matter, so deep for so long, the depth dictated by the submerged operating envelope. The boat was designed to operate at that speed indefinitely, of course, but it was just so unusual, after a few days it was unnerving, a feeling that the boat was frothing like an overworked horse, begging to catch her breath.

As he walked, he thought again about the nav, and all that had happened that patrol. That business about him stabbing himself in the leg; the talking to himself in the officer's study, all the general weirdness. And now…a missing message hidden in his desk.

Jabo was glad he'd kept the folder with him, lest the message disappear again before he got a chance to talk to the captain. The word 'evidence' floated through his mind, and he thought again about another odd place the nav's name had come up: on Howard's yellow sheet of paper, where the sailor had been trying to compile evidence (that word again) to exonerate himself.

Jabo arrived in Machinery Two, nodded at Renfro, who was exhausted and trying to stay awake by the oxygen generators.

"You doin' alright, Renfro?"

"Fuck no, sir. You ever been port and starboard this long? It kinda sucks."

He pointed to the deck. "Anybody down there?"

Renfro nodded. "No, all that exercise shit is still tagged out. Not that anybody has the energy or the time to work out right now anyway."

Jabo climbed down the ladder into the lower level.

The treadmill was silent, a red DANGER tag hanging from its switch. Jabo walked over to it, read the tag. Signed by the corpsman, which was unusual, within hours of Howard's death and the Freon casualty. He checked his watch; the navigator wanted to meet him in the captain's stateroom in about two minutes. Jabo's confidence was building, and he didn't want to get their meeting started by arriving late.

He hesitated at the treadmill, and then on impulse flipped the switch to ON, in violation of the danger tag. All the lights on the console came on, and then the readout began to scroll. WORKOUT COMPLETE....10.0 MILES....WORKOUT COMPLETE...

He stepped off the treadmill and thought it over. Kincaid was right...he was the only person on the boat that would put those kind of miles on the treadmill in one workout. Certainly the navigator hadn't devoted that kind of time to running in his pristine running shoes. So Kincaid *had* been the last person to run before the Freon casualty and the treadmill got tagged out. And yet...the navigator had been down there, in his workout gear, right before the Freon casualty. His presence down there had seemed notable enough for Howard to write down in the logs. And now it seemed the navigator hadn't even exercised while he was there. Which begged the question…what had he been doing in Machinery Two?

Jabo suddenly felt the clipboard in his hands again, and he opened it up to the Freon message. He noticed for the first time that there was another message on the page behind it. He read the subject line: NOTICE TO MARINERS, and got about halfway though the body where a chart number was highlighted: J090888. Jabo remembered the faded pencil line of their track on the chart, and the slight adjustment the navigator had made for no apparent reason.

He lunged toward the 4MC against the starboard bulkhead, lifted the handset and shouted into it.

"Rig for collision!" he shouted. "Kincaid, get shallow now!"

He ran forward, as fast as he could, his feet pounding heavily on the lower level deck plates. He now understood why the navigator had wanted him to wait ten minutes.

.   .   .

Duggan was stooped over, returning the casualty procedures to their place beneath his desk, when the amplified voice of Jabo came across the 4MC speaker behind him.

"RIG FOR COLLISION! KINCAID, GET SHALLOW NOW!"

Duggan jumped to his feet, all the watchstanders sat straight in their chairs, their eyes alert, scanning their panels. He turned slightly to his right, to an analog depth gage. He felt a slight up angle in his feet, and the ship's depth, at that speed, responded quickly. The needle began to move counter-clockwise as the ship drove upwards. Duggan waited for something to happen.

The ship collided with an underwater mountain, and everything went dark.

BOOK THREE

DISASTER
AT SEA

The seamount that *Alabama* struck was shaped like a tree stump, a flat-topped ocean floor feature called a *guyot*. Made out of dark brown volcanic basalt that had hardened into place a million years before, it was slightly over 10,000 feet high, but it was atop and in the center of a much larger, much rounder feature that rose from the sea floor. It had all only recently been identified by oceanographers, mapped in precise detail by the oceanographic research vessel *White Holly* three weeks before the collision. *White Holly* had meticulously mapped the guyot and transmitted the results to the NOAA, which in turn transmitted the information to the mariners of the world so they might update their charts. With the exception of the precisely aimed beams of sound from the *White Holly's* fathometers, no part of the mount had ever been touched by man until the *Alabama* crashed into it, eighteen thousand tons of steel travelling faster than twenty knots.

Thanks to Jabo's 4MC announcement, and Kincaid's quick reaction to it, the ship had achieved a slight up angle and some slight upward momentum, which reduced fractionally the total amount of force transmitted through the hull. The ship struck the seamount with its front, port side.

The first thing damaged was the forwardmost part of the ship: the fiberglass dome that protected the sonar sphere. Dome and sphere were ripped from the hull.

Next, the three front main ballast tanks hit. These tanks were always exposed to sea pressure, designed to be either all the way empty, when the ship was surfaced, or all the way full of seawater, when the boat was submerged. As the collision crushed them, it didn't flood the *Alabama*, but it did greatly affect the ship's ability to come to the surface, as they could no longer expel water from them and completely fill them with air, to make the ship buoyant. But the tanks did save the ship in another way. By absorbing so much of the shock, they functioned like the crumple zones on a car, absorbing energy even as they were destroyed, so that when the ship's pressure hull finally came in contact with the hard basalt, it was not breeched, and the "people tank" remained largely in tact. The ship came to a complete, sudden halt.

Most of the immediate damage to the ship was done by that sudden deceleration. Since the ship's equipment was designed to withstand the shock of battle, the pumps, motors, and electrical panels remained safe. A breaker on the propulsion lube oil system did trip, momentarily causing the throttles to shut. Two pitometers, eighteen inch rods that struck from the bottom of the ship and measured speed through the water, were sheered off, which problematically caused every digital indicator inside *Alabama* to show that the ship was still travelling at Ahead Flank even has it sat motionless near the ocean bottom. But other than that, at the moment of impact, the machinery of the *Alabama* held up remarkably, miraculously, well.

The human beings of the *Alabama* suffered more damage. In general, men who were sitting down or in their racks withstood the collision with few injuries. Men who were walking through the ship were less fortunate, at the mercy of where they were on the boat, and, most importantly, what piece of equipment was directly in front of them as they were propelled forward into it by the ship's sudden stop. Hallorann, in Machinery One, was saved from crashing into the diesel engine by the navigator, as he collided with his swinging body and held on.

Chief Palko, the ship's leading electrician, fractured his skull as he was thrown against the bulkhead between the missile compartment and the forward compartment. He'd been going forward to the scullery with a toolbox in hand to take a look at one of the ship's two dishwashers, which had stopped running during the night. After the collision, he lay groaning, unconscious, bleeding from his nose and ears.

Two crewmen were killed within seconds of the impact. Missile Technician Third Class Simpson had been standing atop the ladder from Missile Compartment Third Level to Lower Level when the collision occurred. Out of every eighteen hour period at sea, Simpson roamed the missile compartment for six, a billy club on his belt and a clipboard in his hand, watching over all twenty-four missiles much like a zookeeper watches his animals, monitoring their temperature, their humidity, and their general well-being. He was preparing to climb down into missile compartment lower level when the ship hit. He was thrown forward, then fell down the ladder. His chin struck the deck plate just forward of the ladder, snapping his head back as he fell and breaking his neck. He was dead before he hit the deckplates.

The other death was Petty Officer Juani, the torpedoman on watch whom Hallorann had seen laughing at his computer screen immediately before discovering the dying navigator. Earlier that watch he'd done some minor maintenance on one of the idle torpedo trays, re-attaching a nylon roller that had come loose during the last time they "indexed" the torpedoes, or moved them around the space. While he had placed the large tool box back in its proper position, he had failed to lash it in place with the nylon straps that were there for that purpose. When the ship hit the seamount, the tool box shot forward, aimed at Juani's skull with an assassin's precision. His entire head was flattened, and he was dead without ever realizing what had happened.

Almost everyone not hurt critically was shaken or dazed. As quickly as they could, they picked themselves up, and without waiting for an alarm or an announcement, moved toward their stations to fight to save the ship.

·   ·   ·

The hull itself was badly deformed where it struck the seamount, but remained intact, a testament to the overcaution of the submarine's designers and the strength of HY80 steel. A large breech through the actual wall of the hull would have been impossible to staunch, and the forward compartment, at that depth, would have filled completely with seawater in minutes until the ship could never rise again. In the language of submarine design, the ship didn't have enough "reserve buoyancy" to overcome a completely flooded forward compartment, even with an emergency blow of all main ballast tanks, even if all the main ballast tanks had survived the collision.

But along the port side of the ship, one of the ship's four torpedo tubes was deformed, its perfectly circular opening pushed into an oval, an oval that the round brass breech door no longer sealed. The sea pressure was so great at that depth that the water entered the hull through that crescent-shaped gap with an almost explosive force, a roar that sounded more like an oncoming freight train than flowing liquid. Seaman Hallorann, still clutching the navigator's body a few feet away, heard it and assumed at first that it was a high pressure air leak, because that was the only sound he'd heard in his life that could compare. He let go of the navigator's body, got to his feet, and stumbled into the torpedo room to fight the flooding.

·   ·   ·

Jabo flew forward when the ship hit, completely destroying a stationary bicycle that was mounted to the deck in front of him, and briefly losing consciousness. When he awoke, he felt the steep, odd angle of the stopped ship, and he heard people running above him, at the berthing level. He was groggy, and thoroughly entangled in the remains of the bike, but as he got to his feet, he determined that the worst thing wrong with him was a badly torn uniform. He wondered if he'd missed an announcement while knocked out. He realized with a start that he must know more about what had happened to the *Alabama* than any man onboard. Any man, that is, other than the navigator. *The navigator*, he realized again, *the navigator did this*. He'd tried to kill them all. He'd also set the fire in the laundry, and killed Howard with the Freon. Now, with the whole crew fighting for their lives, who knew what else he might be capable of. He had to tell someone. His ears popped painfully as the flooding caused a pressure change; he swallowed to clear them.

He stood up in the lower level between the two rows of missiles. He was okay. Whatever was wrong with the ship, he was going to fight.

He ran forward through the passageway between the two rows of missiles. He felt strong and in control, grateful to be of sound mind and body after the collision. He was an officer of the United States Navy's submarine force, and he wanted to get quickly to where there was the most danger, to fight it in the way he was trained. And, if along the way, he found the navigator, he was going to beat the shit out of him.

At the end of the compartment, he came to Petty Officer Simpson's body at the bottom of the ladder. His head was at almost a right angle to his body; there was no question he was dead. Jabo again felt a surging rage toward the navigator.

He considered grabbing the nearest 4MC and alerting control about the body, but quickly decided not to. Simpson was dead, there was nothing anyone could do about that, and he was sure that control was being overwhelmed with information. He didn't want his report to distract Kincaid from his real priority: saving the ship. With a twinge of guilt, he climbed over the sailor's dead body and shot up the ladder.

The hatch to the forward compartment was right at the top of the ladder. Just as Jabo started to climb through it, one hand on the top sealing ring, the watchstander from Missile Control Central, on the other side of the hatch, heard the rush of water in the forward compartment. Anticipating the order to rig for collision and flooding, he jumped from his chair, ran into the passageway, and slammed the three-hundred pound steel hatch shut, breaking every finger on Jabo's left hand.

. . .

When Kincaid heard his friend and roommate yelling on the 4MC, he was startled. But he followed his recommendation.

"Dive make your depth one-six-zero feet!" he said. The Diving Officer immediately gave the orders to the helm and lee helm, and they both pulled back on their controls. The ship rose, giving Kincaid just a moment to wonder what the fuck Jabo was doing. Then they hit.

Kincaid was thrown forward into the Dive's chair. The Dive was actually wearing his seat belt, one of those small miracles of the day that might have prevented immediate and total catastrophe. He was thrown forward and jackknifed across the nylon strap, but not propelled headfirst into the ship's control panel, not knocked out when the ship's survival depended on his quick actions.

Kincaid got to his feet and jumped back onto the conn. The lights in control flickered but stayed on. The chief of the watch climbed back onto his stool and hurriedly cut out the dozen or so wailing alarms that dotted his panel. Not everyone else had gotten up; a number of men were sprawled across the control room, bleeding and unconscious. Paper was everywhere; while the ship's equipment had been designed to withstand such an impact, the ship's innumerable three-ring binders had never been shock tested, and the control room floor was awash in paper. Paper and blood.

There was a bang followed by a roar below his feet, in the torpedo room.

While Jabo had feared that Kincaid, the Officer of the Deck, would be inundated with frantic reports, the opposite was true. He had almost no information, just indications: the bilge alarms in the torpedo room, the horrifying sound of the ship's hull scraping the earth, the roar of the flooding below decks. He knew intuitively they had collided with something, but the repeaters in control all said they were still going flank speed. In a drill, the communications were carefully choreographed, and the exercise always began with a 4MC announcement. Had Petty Officer Juani in the torpedo room lived, he might have made such an announcement, telling control about the flooding in the torpedo room. But he was dead, and Hallorann was fighting his way into the space past a frigid blast of water.

Kincaid waited what seemed like an eternity for someone to say something informative on the 4MC, to give him something he could announce, pass along, sound the alarm, get the crew moving. But he'd been around long enough to witness real casualties at sea, and he realized that a cogent announcement might not come any time soon. More importantly, he realized that whatever was wrong, he was the Officer of the Deck, and he wasn't doing any good by standing there with his thumb up his ass waiting for someone to tell him that something was wrong. He muttered, "fuck it," and grabbed the 1MC.

"Flooding in the forward compartment!" he announced. "Rig ship for flooding and general emergency."

He hung up the mike, his heart racing and sweat running down the back of his neck. As calmly as he could, he turned to the chief of the watch, one of several watchstanders in control who were staring at him, waiting to see what would happen next.

"Chief of the watch," he said. "Sound the alarm. Ahead Full."

· · ·

In lesser casualties, one of the major purposes of the ship's clanging alarm was to wake up all the off-watch crewmen to get every hand devoted to fighting the casualty. That was unnecessary in this case; the only men of the ship's 154 man crew who weren't awake were unconscious with head injuries. But the clanging alarm did serve the purpose of triggering an automatic response from the well-trained crew, getting systems aligned in the safest possible configuration, and getting every man moving toward the position where he could do the most good. The highest ranking and second highest ranking men on the boat crossed paths without a word to each other leaving their staterooms, the captain on his way to control, the XO on his way toward the sound of rushing water.

· · ·

Duggan opened eyes and heard the frantic reports of all three of his watchstanders. No one in maneuvering had noticed that he was knocked out.

"Sir, the electric plant is in a half power line up," reported Patterson.

"Throttles are still shut," said Tremain.

The EWS growled a report into maneuvering, but Duggan was processing it all slowly, his vision hazy. He couldn't keep up.

The engine room watchstanders continued to call in reports. In everyone's tone was this request: *someone please tell us what the fuck is going on.* Except for Duggan, the men in maneuvering were all on their feet, facing their panels, cutting out alarms. About one quarter of the electrical control panel was dark; one of the turbine generators had for some reason tripped off. Patterson, without an order, deftly shifted the electric plant into a half power line up, where everything was powered by a single turbine generator. The lights for all the electrical busses again glowed blue. Duggan looked down at the EOOW's small desk, which was covered in blood. He touched his forehead, felt a large gash. He'd slipped when the boat grounded, slammed his head into the desk, right onto the metal bracket that held the 7MC microphone. Blood streamed down the sides of the desk onto the deck.

Reports continued pouring in, the impact had knocked dozens of things off kilter. Blood ran into his eyes, he wiped it off with the back of hand, felt the slick smear of it against his face. As his eyes focused Duggan saw yellow lights all over maneuvering, warning lights, and a few red alarms: one for the knocked out turbine generator, one for the pressurizer level detector, and one for salinity in the feed system. Every time a watchstander announced one and cut out the alarm, another one would come in. It was almost overwhelming, especially coupled with the chorus of concerned, urgent announcements being made by his team in maneuvering, as they tried to sort out their own problems. And the splitting pain in his skull.

But at the very center of the center panel, reactor power held steady at 50 percent: a lower bell must have been ordered and answered during his unconsciousness. And the electrical plant, while slightly degraded in its half-power line up, was functioning, with all busses energized. The lights were burning and the screw was turning. And Duggan, on his first day as a qualified watchstander, knew that was important enough to pass along.

"Quiet!" he said, his first words in maneuvering since the casualty. The watchstanders silenced immediately, expecting guidance, or orders to prosecute the casualties that beset the engine room. Instead, Duggan grabbed the bloody 7MC microphone in front of him, a direct, amplified link to the control room and the officer of the deck.

"Control, maneuvering....the reactor is critical. The electrical plant is in a half power line up. Ready to answer all bells."

.   .   .

Jabo stood at the hatch for an agonizing second, screaming, while the missile tech struggled to open it. Finally it flew open.

The pain in his hand was blinding, unbearable, but it was the sight of his hand that almost made him pass out: his fingers were flattened and dangling uselessly from the first knuckle on. The flattening had made his fingers unnaturally large and floppy and all the blood had been pressed from them; it looked like he was wearing an oversized white glove. Jabo looked away and fought to stay conscious.

"Jesus Christ, I'm sorry sir," said the missile tech. He had glimpsed Jabo's mangled hand and was looking away, too, pale and in shock.

"Don't worry about it," said Jabo. Hot tears of pain ran down his face. He wanted to move toward the sound of the flooding, but the pain in his hand kept him frozen in place. Another missile tech ran out of MCC with a first aid kit and a roll of gauze. He looked down at Jabo's flattened hand.

"Oh fuck," he said. His hands dropped.

"Wrap it up," said Jabo through gritted teeth. He knew gauze wouldn't stop the pain, but at least it would make his useless fingers stop flopping around. And it would keep people from staring at the fucking things. "You got any Motrin in that thing?"

The missile tech dug a small white bottle out of the bag, and shook out two pills, looked at his hand, and shook out two more, and handed them to Jabo. He swallowed all four without water. They wrapped his hand, taped it, and Jabo ran forward.

⋅ ⋅ ⋅

The XO and Jabo got to the torpedo room at the same time. They stared at each other. Jabo started to tell the XO what he knew about the navigator, but the roar from the flooding was too loud. The XO pointed and they moved aft into Machinery One, right by the diesel, where they could hear each other, barely, over the noise.

"Holy shit!" said the XO, as they entered.

"The navigator did all this!" shouted Jabo. He involuntarily raised his bandaged hand.

"How?"

"He drove us toward a seamount!" Jabo realized he'd dropped the NTM message, probably when the hatch shut on his hand. "He set the fire and killed Howard!"

The XO rapidly processed that information and concluded it was important, but, at the moment, not urgent. "Get a phone talker in here," he said. "It will be too loud in the torpedo room. Let's go." He started marching toward the casualty.

"But XO!" Jabo actually grabbed his shoulder. "Don't we need to find the navigator? Stop him from doing anything else?"

The XO paused and raised an eyebrow. He pointed over Jabo's shoulder. Jabo turned and found himself at eye level with the waist of the navigator's dead body, right where his belt buckle would have been had it not been digging into the soft flesh of his neck. "Jesus Christ!" he said, startled so bad he almost fell down as he recoiled from the corpse.

"Shit, sorry about that Jabo," said the XO. "I thought you saw him."

⋅ ⋅ ⋅

"All stop!" ordered Kincaid just as the captain arrived control. Kincaid shot a look to him as he appeared, because his was not the conventional order to give in a flooding casualty, not what a drill monitor would look for. But the captain nodded; it was the right call. With their severe down angle, forward motion would only make the ship go deeper. And they were already very deep.

"Shit, we're not slowing down," said Kincaid.

The captain looked where Kincaid was looking, the red digital numbers of the bearing repeater where speed wasn't budging from Ahead Flank.

"We're not moving," he said.

"What...?"

"We're motionless," said the captain. "The pitometers are probably sheered off." It had happened to him once before, when he took the *Tecumseh* through the Panama Canal on his JO tour.

"Fuck," said Kincaid. Loss of forward motion was a catastrophe in almost any casualty.

The captain took just a second to look out over the control room and take it all in: the alarms, the odd down angle of the ship, the wailing of the alarms, the reports of injuries that were starting to trickle in, and, above all else, the roar of rushing water below their feet. Within seconds he knew that, before it was all over, they would perform an emergency blow.

But he also knew that the emergency blow was not a "get out of jail free" card, not a reset button that would put them up on the roof, basking in the sunshine, allowing them to start writing the incident reports and cleaning up the mess. Performing an emergency blow was the damage control equivalent of launching all their ballistic missiles. You had better make sure you do it right, because the consequences are pretty fucking dramatic. And you only get to do it once.

"Back two-thirds," ordered Kincaid, and maneuvering quickly answered. It was another non-conventional reaction that was laden with common sense. If a forward bell would drive the ship deeper, then a backing bell should pull it up. The captain could feel the rumble in his feet as the screw began turning backwards. The BRI still indicated a huge forward speed; the digital indicator was officially useless to them now. He stepped down to look at the bubble in the glass that indicated the ship's angle; as he watched it went from thirty-one degrees to thirty-three. It was what he feared.

"Take it off," he said. "It's pulling the angle more." The water that had entered the forward compartment was acting like an anchor, pulling the front of the ship down. Pulling the rear of the ship up with a backing bell only exaggerated the angle.

"All stop!" said Kincaid, and the bell was quickly answered. "Captain, the ship is rigged for flooding and general emergency." Kincaid was collected, remarkably so, thought the captain, and he was glad that an experienced hand was on watch when the shit hit the fan. "Depth is continuing to increase," said Kincaid, and the captain's eyes followed his to the bearing repeater above the conn: while the speed indication appeared fucked, depth was accurate. He was certain that while they weren't moving forward at all, they were deep, and getting deeper.

"All the auxiliary tanks are emptied," said the chief of the watch. He'd been furiously pumping them with the trim pumps, emptying the tanks in an attempt to make the ship lighter and rise. But a submarine is more like an airplane than it is a hot air balloon; its motion through the water, more than any other factor, makes it rise or fall, as water flows across it's control surfaces like air across a wing. And at the moment, in their motionlessness, their submarine was just an 18,000 ton object drifting slowly downward, slowly tracing the downward slope on the other side of the guyot that had nearly killed them.

"Sounding!" said the captain. The quartermaster jumped toward the console.

"Sixty fathoms beneath the keel," he reported. Whatever they'd hit was sloping away beneath them. Which was good news, because it meant they wouldn't bottom out again. And bad news: because there was nothing to stop their descent.

"We could flood the aft tanks," said Kincaid. "Bring the angle down..."

"No," said the captain. In this case, Kincaid's common sense response wasn't the right one. "It would bring the angle down, but it would reduce our reserve buoyancy that much more...we can't afford it." There were calculations they could run to determine exactly what reserve buoyancy they had at this depth, with the tanks at these levels, but the captain knew intuitively that they were too close to the edge of that envelope to bring any water onboard that they didn't have to. He was almost certain they'd lost the forward MBTs, which massively reduced their potential buoyancy. And with every second, with water pouring into the front of the boat, the situation got worse.

"Captain..." Kincaid was looking toward the emergency blow valves above the COW panel, the chicken switches.

"Not yet," said the captain. "Not with this angle. We'll end up with our tail out of the water, unable to move, water still coming in forward and pulling us down. At this depth...the blow might not even get us all the way upstairs. We need to stop the flooding. And we need to get this angle off."

"All the aux tanks are empty," said the COW again.

"Use the trim pump to move water aft," said the captain. The diving officer gave the order.

The forward trim pump took a suction on the forward variable ballast tanks and moved that water the length of the ship, to the aft tanks. This was water that was already on board, not new water, so it had no net effect on the ship's buoyancy. But it moved the ship's center of buoyancy aft. The rear of the ship slowly began to descend and the angle of the ship decreased.

"Is that working?" said the Captain.

The diving officer scanned his indications, finishing with a look at the bubble indicator that was the old fashioned, but most accurate way to look at the ship's angle. He stared at that for a full minute.

"Angle is coming down," he said. "Slowly."

The captain glanced at Kincaid. In a normal situation, the trim pump moving water from all the way forward to all the way aft like that, for that long, would have an immediate and noticeable affect on ship's trim. But now...it indicated that the trim pump could barely keep up with the flooding in the torpedo room. And as the flooding continued and the ship remained nearly motionless, it continued to descend, backwards, its nose pointing at gradual slope, following it down.

"We have to slow down the flooding," said the captain, to the entire control room. "What the fuck is going on down there?"

.   .   .

There was only noise. Not a wall of noise, but a solid impenetrable mass of noise. Stepping into the torpedo room was like walking into a furnace with flames of pure, roaring sound.

Only after overcoming that sound did Jabo notice the sheer amount of water in the space: dark, frigid water that was roaring in from the port side, deflected by one of the torpedoes in storage, crashing against the port bulkhead. The water had long since filled up the bilge and was up over the deckplates, sloshing around his feet. He saw Juoni's body laying face down in the water, another death. And he saw another enlisted man, alone, the canvas bag of a DC kit across his shoulder, lugging a submersible pump.

"Any one try this yet?" yelled the XO. He had his hands on the flood control switches at the back of the space. They controlled hydraulic valves that shut every opening to the sea in the space. He threw them forward; nothing happened.

Jabo ran over to him. "I didn't hear it, but it's so loud…"

The XO shook his head. "Nothing happened…I was watching the panel…" he pointed to the torpedo room control panel. A number of valves were represented by green "Os" indicating they were open. The flood control system should have shut everything tight.

"Problem with hydraulics?" shouted Jabo.

The XO shook his head. "Problem with something."

Two men jumped down the ladder. They looked around briefly, wide eyed, stunned as Jabo had been by the violence of the noise. The XO grabbed each by the shoulder to get their attention. "Set up a hand pump!" he shouted, pointing to the flood control station. "See what that can do."

They nodded and started back up the ladder to go the Crew's Mess to get the necessary equipment. "While you're up there, get an officer down here to be phone talker."

They nodded again.

"Who's that?" said the XO, noticing for the first time the lone enlisted man in the space who had set down the submersible pump and was attempting to rig it by himself. He was soaking wet, but his head was down, completely focused on the task.

"Not sure," said Jabo. "I think it might be that new kid."

"Help him out."

Jabo waded toward him.

·   ·   ·

"Sir, ship is at 900 feet," said the diving officer.

"Aye," said the captain. Reports were steadily coming into control, all the spaces reporting their rigs, and from the EOOW, who reported he was ready to answer any bell that they ordered. All over the control room, alarms sounded from virtually every system on the boat. But their focus had gone entirely to the number that was most fundamental measure of a submarine's peril: depth.

"Nine-fifty," said the Dive.

"Aye," said the captain again. He was running a dozen calculations in his head. To completely emergency blow now, he was certain, to expend all their high pressure air, would be a catastrophic error. With all the water they'd taken aboard, it might not even get them to the top. And even if it did, the ass end of the ship would be sticking out, the screw turning hopelessly in the air. The flooding would continue, and without propulsion to aid them, they would certainly sink again. If they were lucky they'd have enough time to transmit an SOS so a salvage ship could find their wreckage. He computed the ship's reserve buoyancy in his head, the capacity of the emergency high pressure air banks, a rough estimate of the rate of flooding based on the rate at which it competed with the trim pump.

"Ship is at test depth, sir," said the dive. No one reacted, but everyone stared at the depth indicator to watch something they'd never seen before. They drifted down another foot, and the ship had exceeded its test depth.

"Captain…" said Kincaid.

"Blow the forward tanks for three seconds," interrupted the captain. "That's it…not another second."

"Emergency blow the forward tanks, three seconds."

"Emergency blow the forward tanks three seconds, aye sir," said the chief of the watch. He stood and put his hands on forward switch only. It was an unusual posture; they were trained to completely blow the tanks dry if they ever needed too. To blow only one tank for a limited time was like trying to use half your parachute. The COW hesitated, then threw the single valve forward.

High pressure air flowed roared through the valve, rushing into the forward main ballast tanks and the valves that sat atop them. Those valves turned, and for three seconds they admitted the ship's highest pressure air, the air that had nearly ruptured Hallorann's ear drums on his first day in the engine room. Released into the forward tanks, the air expanded. While the tanks were destroyed at the bottom, enough of the tank remained intact at the top that the air expanded and pooled there, forcing seawater out through the bottom. After three seconds at that sea pressure, a bubble of air roughly the size of a car developed in each of the front three main ballast tanks. It expelled from the ship an equivalent volume of water, and they almost instantly became buoyant again. The action also shifted the center of buoyancy aft, which pushed the front of the ship up.

After three seconds, the COW pulled back the valve. The indicator lights for all three tanks turned amber again.

"Angle is coming up!" said the Dive, confirming what the captain felt in his feet.

Beneath them, thousands of gallons of seawater that had flooded into the torpedo room rolled aft. One positive effect of this was that it further shifted the ship's center of buoyancy, accentuating the angle that the captain wanted to generate. But it also covered everything in its path in a rolling wall of cold, salty seawater. A great many of the things it touched had electricity coursing through them. Some of them, like the battery well, were designed to be watertight. Many of the machines, however, were designed only to be "splash proof," and could not be submerged long without consequences.

"We're still going down," said the Kincaid, quietly, straining to mask the worry in his voice. The angle was coming up but the ship was still sinking.

"Give it time," said the captain. He'd pictured it in his mind like one of those computer animations the shipyard engineers used, a graph of the ship's depth versus time as air flowed into the front tanks, lifting the front of the ship up, the ship's overall buoyancy turning positive. But there was downward momentum to overcome, and the captain knew it would take a few long seconds for the ship to rise. He'd tried to calculate the bare minimum amount of air he could expend and achieve positive buoyancy, and he hoped he was right. He had two bold, horizontal lines in the diagram he was constructing in his mind. The higher one was test depth, which they'd already exceeded. Beneath that line was crush depth, which if they exceeded they would never again rise above. But between those lines was a third line, a third important depth limit. And the Captain knew that before their momentum changed, they would cross it.

"Still deeper," said the Dive. "But the rate is slowing..."

"We caught it," said the captain. "We're going to come up."

Suddenly, a new alarm rang through control, one no one had heard before, a primitive buzzing sound that came from the corner of control by the main ladder. On each side of control came a dull pop, one that made Kincaid jump. Something bumped against both sides of the hull. All but the captain were startled.

"What the fuck was that?" asked Kincaid.

"The BST buoys," said the captain. "We're going to be famous."

. . .

Once the ship exceeded its test depth by a predetermined percentage, the explosive bolts that held the BST buoys to the outside of the hull detonated, and the buoys were released. Like so many key systems on the boat, there were two of them, redundant and identical, and both functioned flawlessly. Highly buoyant, they shot upward, untethered to the ship, until after twenty-one seconds they popped to the surface. A mechanical accelerometer sensed their stoppage, and the transmitters of both buoys began broadcasting a powerful, repetitive distress signal along a frequency that had been reserved by the Navy for just that purpose. The recorded message consisted of an SOS, a sequence of numbers that identified the *Alabama*, and the message SUBSUNK.

Three radio rooms placed on three different continents were manned around the clock by radiomen whose only job was to await a signal that, much like the message ordering the launch of nuclear missiles, they all hoped would never come. Like the buoys themselves, the listening posts were designed with redundancy in mind: one was at the Marine Corps base in Okinawa, Japan. The second was in Holy Loch, Scotland. And the third was deep within the United State's Strategic Command, in Omaha, Nebraska. All three listening posts began alarming simultaneously, even the one in Holy Loch, which was half a world away. Quickly the message was decoded and handed to a duty officer at each station, who in turn notified his commanding officer, who in turn notified the Chief of Naval Operations. The CNO made a call to the president's chief of staff, and the president of the United States was then awoken with the news that a United States Submarine was in distress. From the time the buoys were launched until the president was awoken took a total of sixteen minutes.

· · ·

Throughout the history of the submarine fleet, there has always been a degree of fatalism inherent in the various theories of submarine rescue. *Alabama*, like all ships in her class, was fitted with three Logistics Escape Trunks, or LETs, designed to mate with a Deep Submergence Rescue Vehicle and allow the egress of crewmen. Assuming total disaster and loss of power, each LET had affixed to it a steel plate describing a series of hammer signals men in and outside the trunk could use to communicate with each other. It read:

ONE TAP MEANS TANK IS FLOODED

TWO TAPS MEANS TANKS IS PRESSURIZED

THREE TAPS MEANS TANKS IS DRAINED

On the plate outside of each trunk of Alabama, someone had long ago scratched "ZERO TAPS MEANS I'M DEAD."

For several decades the submarine force relied on a fleet of submarine rescue ships, each with the hull designator ASR. These vessels were of World War II vintage, and were in effect modified salvage ships who could hover over a sunken boat and release divers. Submarine rescue theory of that era was startlingly crude, and revolved around "free ascent"—the process of having men egress a sunken boat and swim to the surface, arms crossed, and exhaling in concentrated, forced gasps to minimize the effects of decompression and the formation of lethal nitrogen bubbles in the blood. Every old submarine base had as its central landmark a tall, cylindrical "dive tower" where recruits could practice this procedure, a rite of passage for generations of submariners. It was officially estimated, and universally doubted, that a man might actually survive free ascent from a depth of up to 300 feet.

The Navy lost two nuclear-powered submarines in the 1960s. First was *Thresher*, lost at sea in 1963, followed by *Scorpion*, lost in 1968. This led the Navy to seriously reevaluate its rescue capabilities, given the depths at which modern nuclear submarines operated, and the DSRV, or Deep Submergence Rescue Vehicle, was born. The Navy built two of these ships, *Mystic* (commissioned in 1970) and *Avalon* (1971), and positioned them both at the North Island Naval Air Station in San Diego. They were, in effect, deep-diving miniature submarines that could fit inside the belly of an Air Force C-5 cargo plane, to be flown within hours of a submarine disaster to its last reported location. Once on the scene, they had to operate with a mother vessel, either an ASR, or another submarine. They were not perfect, but their capabilities vastly exceeded that of the old ASRs operating by themselves. The DSRVs could operate at depths up to 5,000 feet, and rescue up to 24 men at a time.

The DSRV program lasted until *Mystic* was decommissioned in 2008. The program was officially replaced by the SRDRS program, Submarine Rescue Diving and Recompression System. The very title of the program addressed one of the DSRV program's greatest weakness: the fact that another vessel was needed to rescue submariners at pressure. The main vehicle of the SRDRS program, named *Falcon*, was self-contained, and not reliant on another vessel. But in some ways the program was a step backwards. *Falcon* could only conduct rescue operations in water up to 2,000 feet. And it could only rescue 16 men at a time. Finally, the old DSRV program was abolished before the cornerstone of the SRDRS program was even completed: the decompression system. For years, during the Cold War, some had believed deep water submarine rescue to be so unlikely that they deemed the DSRV program a cover operation, and claimed that *Mystic* and *Avalon* were actually spy ships. With the last hope of a sunken submarine being the *Falcon* and its half-complete support systems, it seemed the Navy had almost given up on the concept as well.

But with the message launched from *Alabama's* BST buoys, *Falcon* was hurriedly loaded aboard the USNS *Navajo*, a seagoing tug, and raced westward, toward the location of *Alabama*. The water at their destination was far deeper than 2,000 feet, they already knew, and they would be approximately twenty-four hours to the scene. Getting *Falcon* to the site of the bleating BST buoys seemed almost a hopeless gesture. But the Navy had to do something, and deploying *Falcon* was all they could do.

·　　　·　　　·

Captain Soldato was the fifth person notified about the BST buoys, forty-six minutes after they were launched, at 5:30 in the morning. He'd been dreaming of his grandson when the phone rang, dreaming about the first time they'd fished together, off a pier in Groton Long Point, Connecticut. His grandson was tiny then, small even for the six year old that he was, and was fishing with his line barely off the pier. But he'd hauled in a massive Tautog, a fat, glistening black fish that weighed at least eight pounds. His grandson had literally jumped up and down with excitement when they landed the gasping fish on the pier. The dream was free from any psychedelic or odd associations like dreams often have: the tautog didn't start talking, or flying. It was more like an exact replay of an exceedingly pleasant moment, a home movie that his memory had wished to replay.

He was so groggy that the Group Nine duty officer had to ask him twice to switch to a secure phone. As Soldato stumbled out of the bedroom, Cindy stirred and frowned, alert on some level that bad news had arrived.

In his study, he picked up the antiquated-looking secure phone that the Navy had provided him and connected with the duty officer. They both turned plastic keys simultaneously, switching the phone to secure mode.

"Captain, we have flash traffic from a BST buoy in the western pacific."

Soldato was now fully awake. "Which boat?" he asked. But he already knew.

"Seven-thirty-one. The Admiral is calling an emergency meeting in the secure conference room in thirty minutes."

Soldato hung up without saying another word and donned his uniform silently to avoid waking Cindy, who had fallen back asleep.

·   ·   ·

Angi was running. It had rained during the night, cooling the air to a perfect running temperature. It was still dark, but she planned to run fourteen miles, which would take her a good two hours, and she had timed her start so she could enjoy the sunrise as she ran. She was already nostalgic about running, knowing she'd have to give it up soon. She'd come to the sport late, never ran in high school, but took it up with a vengeance in her junior year at Vanderbilt, after completing her first 5K. Her boyfriend at the time had talked her into it, and she decided she very much liked the feeling of running by him, and those sorority girls wearing make up for a race, and, even more, those posturing fraternity boys, who gasped for breath as she glided by. She'd run seven marathons in her life, a dozen half marathons, and more 5Ks than she could count. Now it would be taken away from her. She could get one of those jogging strollers, she supposed, after the baby was born…but sometime between now and then she would just have to stop for a while. In the meantime, she would enjoy each run like it was her last.

She ran her usual route, out of her neighborhood onto Trigger Road, feeling good in her legs, with only a slight twinge in the right knee that occasionally gave her problems. She was fast and strong, enjoying the first part of the run down to the Trigger gate that was all slightly downhill, the perfect warm up. The run to the gate was about a mile and a half, just about the amount of time it took for her to begin sweating mildly, breathe properly, and to feel the soreness in her feet and hips disappear. She was alert for any sign that her pregnancy was affecting her running—or that her running was affecting her pregnancy—but so far, so good. She just felt fast. She cruised down the hill toward the gate, her stride lengthening.

There were a few cars at the gate, some government vehicles, some civilian contractors showing up early. Only two gates were open, so even though it was early, the cars were backed up, their brake lights casting long, red reflections on the damp asphalt. She approached the back of a minivan and recognized it immediately; the Soldato's. What would bring him to base so early? She wondered. There was no telling when your world consisted of eight submarines and all that could go wrong with them.

She ran past it, and confirmed that Soldato was driving, but he was worriedly fumbling with something in his passenger seat, maybe getting out his military ID for the gate guard, and he didn't see her. She ran about another one hundred yards to the gate and turned around, ready now to really get into the meat of her run. She was facing Soldato now.

As she neared him, he saw her, then recognized her. She lifted her hand to wave, but the look on his face stopped her cold. He looked like a man who was staring absolute calamity in the face, and when their eyes locked, she knew beyond any doubt that it involved Danny.

He drove through the gate and left her behind, standing on an empty road outside a submarine base, on the side of the gate where no one knew anything.

.   .   .

In Maneuvering, Duggan pulled a cloth flash hood from an EAB, twisted it a few times, and tied it around his forehead, banzai style. He pushed on the center of it, felt the blood soaking through, hoped it would at least keep the blood out of his eyes so he could do his fucking job.

He heard the twin bangs of the BST buoys as they launched, not knowing what it was: they all jumped at the sound. He knew he lacked perspective, was the least experienced guy in the maneuvering, but was certain their crisis was dire. He knew it from his training, and he knew it from the tense fervor with which the three enlisted men in maneuvering were now performing their jobs. When the odd order for the three-second emergency blow came across the 1MC, Duggan felt his heart sink. It seemed to him an improvisation, tinged with desperation.

The depth gage in maneuvering was just inches from his head. It looked like an antique, a large analog dial. But like everything else in maneuvering, Duggan had studied the gage, and he'd always taken comfort in the fact that while crude-looking, that depth gage was a completely reliable pressure gage that was attached, by means of a long, thin pipe, directly to the ocean that surrounded them. In a world of electronic and digital intermediation, his depth gage represented an undeniable, hardwired reality.

The big ship reacted almost instantly to the emergency blow; Duggan could feel the angle in his feet. They were starting to point up. But, he could see on his depth gage, the ship's depth didn't immediately respond. They continued to drift down, albeit at a slower rate. Then their descent seemed to stop, and they hovered for a moment. And then, almost imperceptibly, they began to rise. Duggan realized that he'd been holding his breath; he exhaled loudly.

"Going up?" said Barnes.

"Yes."

"Thank God."

Duggan sat back down in his chair and thought to himself: whatever happens now, we're moving up. Things are improving.

A blaring alarm on the electrical panel yanked him back into the crisis. Patterson cut out the alarm and scanned his panel. "Erratic voltage," he said, and Duggan could see it. All the AC voltage meters were drifting around. Electrical voltage was one of the most static indicators in maneuvering, seeing the needles move around made the panel seem funhouse bizarre. Patterson reached to the center of his panel, on instinct: the ground detector. He turned a switch and took a reading. "Fuck," he said.

Duggan didn't wait for Patterson to announce it to him, he could see it himself. He keyed the 7MC mike to control. The ground detector was an exponential meter that could measure the resistance of a specified electrical bus to ground in Ohms; the normal reading was 8, the symbol for infinity. On the panel now the readout was in the thousands of Ohms, and dropping. He knew what had happened, and while he couldn't have done anything about it, he cursed himself for not anticipating it: the floodwater had grounded some piece (or pieces) of equipment.

"Lowering grounds on the port AC electrical bus," he announced into the 7MC. "Commencing ground isolation." He released the microphone key and spoke to Patterson. "Start dropping busses."

The roaming electrician appeared at the entrance to maneuvering to assist, a checklist on his clipboard.

"Dropping the port non-vital bus," said Patterson, without waiting for an order. He turned a black switch on his panel, and the blue light for the bus went dark. But the Ohmmeter continued to drop. He flipped the switch back on.

"Port DC bus," he said. He was moving fast, as the grounds continued to drop. With every switch he threw, equipment was de-energized, potentially affecting the casualty control efforts. But there was no question that they should do it. If that ground got to zero, it meant a complete short: an electrical fire. The old submarine saying was: if you don't find the ground…the ground will find you.

"It's got to be on the port vital bus," said Patterson. They'd tried everything else, so by process of elimination, it had to be. But the equipment on that bus was, by definition, vital. The ground isolation had to proceed slightly more deliberately lest they make a bad situation worse.

Duggan grabbed the 7MC again. "Commencing isolation on the port vital bus."

The roaming electrician flipped to a new check list. "Number two main feed pump."

"No," said Duggan. "Start with whatever is in the forward compartment. That's where the floodwater is."

He scanned the list. "Ten loads in all forward on that bus. First on the list is forward ventilation."

"Start there," said Duggan.

"Too late!" said Patterson. The needle on the ground detector was swinging counter clockwise, plunging like a punctured balloon. They all stared at it. Just a moment passed before once again they heard the adrenalin-inducing crackle of the 4MC speaker.

Fire in the forward compartment!

Jabo was working right next to Hallorann, trying to supervise the frantic efforts of about six men crammed into a very small space in the front of the torpedo room. The work consisted of two efforts: removing the water that had poured into the space, and stopping the flooding.

Hallorann was working with two others to remove water. They'd already sunk a submersible pump into the torpedo room bilge and hooked it up to the trim header. It had been an exhausting task. The submersible pump was heavy and everything had to be done in a soaking, frigid torrent of sea water. Hallorann had only recently learned to operate the pump, working on his quals, but he'd taken control of the operation, attacking the flooding, shoving the pump into the deepest part of the bilge. His hands were so cold that at one point he dropped the spanner wrench into the flooded bilge; without hesitating he went completely underwater to retrieve it. He came up shivering and soaking, with the wrench in hand, and they completed the connection. When they turned the pump on, he felt a small sense of triumph when the outlet hose went rigid; they were getting water out of there and it felt good. By then, the second submersible pump had arrived from the Crew's Mess. The crewmen went to work hooking it up, the effort and the cold water sapping them of strength.

Just a few feet away from him Jabo watched and worried. He wanted to help but his left hand was completely useless. The submersible pump would make a small difference in the overall rate of flooding. Their great depth worked against them in two ways: the massive sea pressure made the rate of flooding huge. And it slowed the rate at which they could pump water overboard. The water was well above the deck plates now, sloshing at their ankles, and Jabo realized that the ocean wasn't trying to infiltrate their little world, like a parasitic invader. Instead, *they* were the invaders, the foreign body, and now the ocean was trying to consume them, the way a white blood cell surrounds and kills a bacterium. The second pump would help some, a decrease in depth would help a lot, and slowing the rate of flooding would help even more.

To that end, an array of damage control kits had been brought to the scene. Some consisted of wooden plugs designed to be hammered into place, designed for punctured pipes. Once in the hole, the wood would swell and seal it, and hammering a wooden plug into a gushing hole was a skill every submariner mastered.

Unfortunately, the flooding they faced wasn't a round hole that could so easily be sealed. As far as Jabo could tell, the torpedo tube breech door had been deformed to form a hole the shape of a thin crescent. They'd tried to hammer wooden plugs into it, but it did little good.

The XO appeared at his arm. "What about the outer doors?" He had to shout.

"They're fucked up!" he said. The XO nodded. He couldn't hear him, the sound was too loud. They moved to the back of the space, Jabo still holding a conical DC plug in his hand.

"I'm assuming it's fucked up," said Jabo. "It must be or water wouldn't get in. Whatever we hit fucked it up."

The XO looked at the panel, and Jabo followed his eyes.

"I know—it indicates that all the outer doors are shut. The indicators must be fucked up too."

"How is it doing in there, at the breech?"

Jabo waved his arms in frustration. "I'm getting nowhere with these plugs." He threw the plug down. It bobbed on the surface of the water.

The XO stared at it, lost in thought for the moment. "Maybe the outer door is just fouled," he said. "Jammed it in the dirt or something. Can we cycle it?"

Jabo shook his head. "The interlocks won't let us because the breech door doesn't indicate shut."

"Hand pump it," said the XO. "If it's fouled we should exercise it, all the way open, all the way shut, maybe clear what ever is in there. Fuck the interlocks."

"But what if...what if it makes the flooding worse? Opening that outer door all the way..."

"If that makes any difference, we'll know as soon as we start cracking it open. And frankly, Jabo..." he looked around to see if anyone else was in earshot. He smirked at the DC plug that was bobbing in the water. "Frankly Jabo, I'm about fucking out of ideas."

"Okay, let's do it," said Jabo. He looked over at Hallorann and yelled. "You're an A-Ganger, right?"

Hallorann looked up from the second submersible pump which he'd just completed hooking up. He pushed the START button and raised his fist in exhausted satisfaction as it started. "Striker, sir. I'm an A Gang striker."

"Close enough," said the XO. "Get lined up to hand pump this door outer door. Pump it all the way open, then all the way shut. Do it as fast as you can."

"Yes sir," said Hallorann. He was already moving towards the rear of the torpedo room, where the hand pump equipment was staged.

"I'm going to go to control and brief the captain," said the XO, and he too started moving aft. Jabo moved forward, back to the gushing water.

As they moved, a warm, acrid smell suddenly cut through the damp coldness of the sea. Jabo stopped and the XO froze half way up the ladder. Then, from an unseen corner of machinery one, there was a electric blue flash. The XO dropped to the deck, grabbed the 4MC, and called away the fire.

·　　　·　　　·

The XO got out F-10, the nearest fire hose. Once he had it out of the rack, he pulled an EAB from a locker under the diesel control panel and tightened the straps around his head. Smoke was already thick in the compartment. He looked up the ladder; no one was coming down yet and he couldn't operate the hose by himself. Everyone was fighting something, the crew was at its limits.

He turned around, Jabo was at the door to the Machinery One, putting on his own EAB. The dead body of the navigator swung between them. Christ, this is getting awful, he thought. He waved Jabo over. "Get on the front of that hose!" he said, pointing.

Jabo trotted over and picked up the hose in a funny way, stuck the nozzle in his left armpit and put his right hand on the bail. He turned around and nodded at the XO who had his hand on the wheel ready to pressurize the hose. The XO unplugged his EAB and walked over.

"What the fuck are you doing Jabo?"

Jabo held up his hand. The bandages were soggy and had come undone, his mangled fingers dangling.

"Jesus Christ, that's disgusting."

"Missile compartment hatch, by MCC," said Jabo, "slammed it shut on my hand."

"Does it hurt?"

"Like a motherfucker," said Jabo. He looked him over; his eyes were slightly glassy. The XO thought he might be going into shock from the pain.

The XO glanced over his shoulder, two other men were coming down the ladder, both in EABs. He couldn't tell who they were, or even what rank they were. He saw by their reactions that one of them saw the navigator's body, the other didn't.

He shouted at them. "You two get on this hose...one on the wheel the other one get on this fucking nozzle!" He turned back to Jabo. "Go to Crew's Mess, see the doc. You are of limited usefulness to me. At least get something for the pain."

"XO, I'm fine..."

"Do what I fucking tell you, Jabo, go get fixed up. Your fingers are going to fall off and clog the trim pump."

·   ·   ·

Jabo climbed the ladder one-handed and walked the short distance to Crew's Mess. Master Chief Cote had turned it into a makeshift trauma center, with men laid out on each of the six small tables, IV bottles hanging from the pipes that ran overhead. Men with lesser injuries were seated in chairs, slumped over with the profound fatigue brought on by fear and pain. The bins of the small steam table, normally filled with mashed potatoes and green beans, were overflowing with medical supplies, bandages, tape, and gauze. A nylon case was rolled out, an array of shiny scalpels glinting in the fluorescent light. Beside it the ice cream machine had somehow been almost ripped in half; melted white soft-serve ice cream leaked into a bucket beneath it. Cote was putting a splint on the broken leg of a groaning petty officer. He looked up at Jabo.

"Where were you sir?"

"Torpedo Room. And Machinery One."

"Don't they need you down there?"

Jabo held up his hand, but tried not to look at it himself as his two fingers dangled loosely at a weird angles. "XO sent me up here." He felt a little stupid presenting the master chief an injured hand; the room was filled with broken bones and what looked, to Jabo's untrained eye, to be serious head injuries. But Cote put down the small scissors he was using and walked over to take a look. Jabo noted that the front part of the master chief's poopie suit had been stained dark with the blood of his shipmates.

"Take care of these other guys first, master chief."

"These guys aren't going anywhere, Lieutenant. If it's alright with you, I'd like to have as many people fighting this fucking casualty as I can. Maybe I can get you back in the fight."

"Alright," said Jabo. Cote took his hand.

"What happened?"

"Missile Compartment hatch got slammed on it."

The master chief touched each one of his fingers in turn. "Feel that?"

"Not a thing."

He squeezed another, and Jabo winced in pain.

"These two," said the master chief, pointing to his middle finger and ring finger. "They're pretty fucked up. The other ones look okay, although your pinky maybe broken too."

"Can you tape them up or something?"

"They're so mangled...and if you're going back down there, the bandage will get soaked through instantly...."

"What do you think?"

Cote looked him in the eye. "We might have a better chance of saving them if I cut them off. Make it as clean as I can, get them on ice. Plus, that will probably make you more effective on the scene."

"Do it," said Jabo.

"You're sure?"

"Yep," said Jabo. "Cut them off and stick'em in ice."

"Alright," he said, "You're the one with a college degree." He walked over to the ice cream machine and grabbed his scalpels and a syringe that Jabo hadn't notice before.

"Novocain," he said. It's all I've got. Well, I've got morphine too, but you won't do us much good if you're in la la land. Give me your hand."

Jabo stuck it out and the master chief moved fast, sticking the needle in the middle of the back of Jabo's hand, and depressing the plunger. There was a momentary sharp sting, bad enough to penetrate even the pain that was pulsing through him, but quickly a wave of relief swept through, so strong that he almost gasped. "Oh fuck that feels better," he said. He hadn't realized how bad he was still hurting until the drug made it go away. Jabo felt nothing when he removed the needle.

"Okay, tough guy, you still sure about this?" He'd selected a scalpel from the middle of the pack.

"Do it, master chief."

Cote hesitated. "At least sit down. I don't want you passing out and falling into the blade or anything."

All the seats were taken by men hurting too badly for Jabo to ask them to move, so he sat on the deck, his back against the starboard bulkhead, and the master chief got on his knees in front of him. "Look away while I do this," he said, and Jabo gladly complied. He couldn't feel anything in his hand or fingers, but he felt the master chief's grip on his elbow grow stronger as he cut through the fingers. He felt him tugging, turning his arm slightly, trying to saw through the broken bone. He was reminded, nauseatingly, of his father carving a chicken.

"Okay, almost done," he said. Jabo was still looking away, but he felt gauze being wrapped around his hand, from about the wrist down, and then he heard tape being ripped off a roll.

"Can I look now?"

"Sure," said the master chief.

The wrapping job was tight, neat and compact...it paid to have the job done by a man with thirty years experience. His three remaining fingers stuck straight out, and the gap in the middle was completely covered with clean white gauze. He looked like he was making the "devil" sign at a rock concert. He noticed a zip-lock bag of crushed ice in the master chief's hand, some of it turning pink.

"Those my fingers?"

"Yes sir. We'll keep them on ice, maybe get them surgically re-attached when we pull in."

"Don't lose that bag," said Jabo, getting to his feet.

"I'll put your name on it," said the master chief, already returning to the table and the sailor with the broken leg.

.   .   .

Hallorann had just grabbed the hand pump kit and was returning to the front of the torpedo room when he felt the bloom of heat on his back, as the motor generator exploded into a flash of heat and light. He turned briefly, squinting to see the XO disappear into the light, He fought the urge to follow, but he felt the weight of the canvas bag in his hand, knew that he'd already been given his orders.

He found his way to the front of the torpedo room, seawater now up to his knees, and acrid electrical smoke rapidly filling what was left of the space. The EAB fed him clean air but the smoke was growing impenetrable, a wall that he couldn't see through. All the space's battle lanterns had been turned on, and they shot beams of light through the smoke but did nothing to make the situation easier to understand.

Hallorann found the EAB manifold adjacent to the port torpedo tubes by touch, and plugged in. He had seen the hand pump rig in action exactly one time, and he'd never used it himself. He started pulling pieces out of the canvas bag. He would have liked to lay them out on the deck, but the deck was covered in water and he wasn't about to lose some critical fitting in the deluge.

As quickly as he could, he hooked up the hoses and the pump. The parts were labeled but it was too dark to see them and the mask of his EAB was covered in mist from the flooding. He found the connections on the torpedo tube by hand, hooked up a hose to each. Behind him he could hear the stomping of booted feet, hose teams rushing to the fire, the crackle of water on fire.

He was not completely alone in the torpedo room. Two men still struggled to keep the submersible pump running. But no one appeared to be in charge. He had his orders, anyway, from the XO. The water was up to his knees now, he knew he couldn't wait for a confirmation.

He removed the hand pump from the bag. It looked like a more rugged version of one of those large staplers used to fasten together hundreds of sheets of paper. There was a written procedure, he knew, but he'd never find it in the chaos, so he hooked it up by sight and feel, lining up what he knew were the inlets and outlets, lining up the pump to open the outer door.

A torpedoman showed up at his shoulder. "Hey! You're lined up to open…"

"I know!" said Hallorann. "That's the order. We're going to pump it open, then pump it shut. They think it might be fouled."

The torpedoman looked over his rig, verified it correct, and then threw open the two valves that aligned hydraulic fluid to the hand pump. As the hoses went slightly rigid, Hallorann began furiously pumping.

He watched alertly as he began to see if opening the outer door increased the rate of flooding. It didn't appear to, based on the noise level, but the space was so full of water now it was hard to tell.

"How long?" said Hallorann to the torpedoman.

"A while longer til' it's fully open. Here." They switched off while Hallorann caught his breath.

Twice more they switched. As the torpedoman was pumping, Hallorann saw a green circle light up on the torpedo control console. "It's fully open!" he said.

The torpedoman quickly shut the two isolation valves and switched the positions of the hoses on the pump. He reopened the valves and began pumping. The green circle disappeared, as they were now pumping the door shut. His arms felt like rubber, but it was easier to get energized about closing the hole that was allowing water into the ship. He and the torpedoman switched off more frequently. When he wasn't pumping, he stared aft, trying to get an idea of how the firefighting was progressing, but it was impossible to tell. There were still a great number of men in the space, that was all he could tell for certain, based on the noise, and the number of feet he could see illuminated by a single battle lantern as they descended the ladder.

The torpedoman stood up and Hallorann replaced him, pumping until his arm felt like it would break. He started to notice, to his excitement, that the noise of rushing water was starting to decrease. The water was up to his waist now. But the sound got higher in pitch and lower in volume as he pumped, like they were pinching off the flow. Finally, the roar stopped.

"It's shut!" said the torpedoman, pointing to an amber line on to the torpedo console. "It fucking worked...we cleared it, and now its shut!"

The space was filled with a huge, dangerous amount of water, water that sloshed with the slightest motion of the crippled ship. But after twenty-three minutes, they'd plugged the hole.

Hallorann slogged forward and picked up the 4MC, which was just inches above the water.

"This is Seaman Hallorann in the torpedo room," he said. "The flooding is stopped."

· · ·

"Captain, the flooding is stopped," said Kincaid, even though everyone in control had heard the report.

The captain said nothing, but continued running it all through his mind, still trying to calculate if the time had come to perform the complete emergency blow. He was convinced now that the front main ballast tanks had been nearly destroyed in the collision, meaning the blow would only get them about half the effective buoyancy that it might if the ship were intact.

Secondly, the flooding had stopped, and they were moving water off the boat. Getting shallow would make it easier to do this—the reduced sea pressure at a shallower depth would make the all the pumps that much more effective.

But the fire—that changed everything. They wouldn't be able to ventilate until the fire was stopped and overhauled. Any sudden influx of fresh air could inflame the fire, or cause hot spots to reignite, like blowing on a campfire.

As much as it pained the captain to stay at this depth, in this damaged condition, they wouldn't emergency blow. Not for the moment.

"Captain?" said Kincaid.

"Continue prosecuting that fire," said the captain. "And get water off the boat." He looked around control. "Has anybody seen the navigator?"

·   ·   ·

Jabo ran forward, squeezed down the ladder to Machinery One past two fire hoses that were heading for the same destination. Almost out of breath, he plugged his EAB into the manifold at the bottom of the ladder. He took in the scene.

The fire raged. Flames licked up the aft bulkhead, orange and blue, and the compartment was filling with thick black smoke. Six men on two hoses crowded the space, aiming water at the base of the flame. The beams of the battle lanterns criss-crossed the darkness randomly, cutting swaths through the smoke. Several crossed in front of the dead pale face of the navigator, the only human face visible in the compartment, as everyone else's was covered by an EAB. His was covered in water that ran in dirty, sooty tracks down his cheeks. His neck had stretched since Jabo first saw him, it looked almost like he was leaning over to get a better look at the men who were fighting the damage he'd caused. The hose teams had organized themselves, one on each side of the hanging body. Jabo's feet were freezing, his shoes soaked through. The rest of him cooked, the space was becoming a furnace. Jabo took a deep breath, unplugged, and moved forward, found the XO.

He tapped him hard on the shoulder. The XO looked at him, eyes fierce.

"Good!" he said. "Take over. Can you?"

Jabo nodded, holding up his bandaged hand.

"Lieutenant Jabo is the man in charge!" the XO announced. He unplugged and moved to control.

The hose teams moved in closer. Jabo could not see what was actually on fire, but he assumed that the electricity that had originally fed the fire was gone: hopefully Maneuvering had secured that machine immediately. But the original heat from that ground had been enough to set ablaze all the wiring and insulation inside the motor generator, and some of the insulation on the surrounding walls. A chunk of lagging fell off a pipe over their heads, almost at their feet, trailed by a shower of orange sparks. The hose team next to him quickly doused it with water. The nozzle man stomped on it, breaking it up into ash and embers.

The hose teams were not tiring, Jabo saw, they were fighting the fire with a fury.

"Stop!" said Jabo, tapping each nozzleman in the small of his back with his closed fist. They all threw the bails forward, and the gushing water stopped.

They waited a few minutes, hoping that the fire had stopped. But like a good campfire, a tendril of smoke came from what was left of the machine, the smoke turned dark, there was a pop, a flash, and then more flames.

Without waiting for Jabo's order, both nozzle men threw open their hoses and doused the fire again. Jabo counted to five, then hit their backs again.

They waited again. This time, there was nothing. The room was now filled with a combination of thick smoke and steam, the water that had vaporized after hitting the flames; it was almost impossible to see anything. The battle lanterns could no longer penetrate the haze, each was just now a dull, smeared glow, like a tired sun behind fog. Jabo moved forward cautiously, felt his way forward with his bad hand. If he was going to get burned, shocked, or sliced, he wanted it to be the hand that was already fucked up. He knelt down, feeling everything, looking over the front part of the space.

He turned to the phone talker who was kneeling slightly behind the hose teams. The men stared at him wide-eyed, pointing their hoses at him like he was the condemned man in front of a firing squad. "To control," he said. "The fire is stopped. Send in an overhaul team."

He turned to the nearest nozzleman. "You're the reflash watch."

He nodded, breathless, too exhausted to acknowledge the order with words.

Jabo looked again at the dangling body of the navigator, then unplugged his EAB and walked to the ladder.

.   .   .

The XO stomped into control, covered in water and the stench of the fire. He stopped at the top of the ladder, plugged in his EAB, and took a few breaths, ready to report to the captain. Just as he was about to speak came the announcement that the fire has stopped.

He started to talk again but before he could, the captain held his hand up to silence him. Had he not been wearing his EAB, the XO would have known he was concentrating, looking at the CODC console in front of him.

The XO moved behind him: the screen was filled with columns of green numbers. The lower you looked, the more exotic the data became, derivatives of derivatives. First came depth, speed, then pitch, roll, acceleration on each axis, the rate of acceleration on each axis. They were almost motionless forward, the XO saw, but they were moving slightly upward. He could see from the history on the screen that this was a recent change: they were now positively buoyant. Books would be written, the XO knew, about why the captain hadn't emergency blown immediately. Time would tell whether or not this was looked at as a wise decision or a disastrous one. The captain waited one more second, looking at the very bottom of the screen, where the rate of change of acceleration was increasing. They were accelerating, ever so slightly, in the upward direction. Then he saw something else, an asymptote they been approaching in the calculus of their motion through the sea. The captain stood up straight.

"Chief of the watch, emergency blow."

"Emergency blow, aye sir." The chief of the watch stood and this time threw open both chicken switches, the giant valve handles that channeled high pressure air into the main ballast tanks. It made a huge noise, and frost covered the valve handles as the giant pressure change reduced the temperature of the air that passed through. Almost immediately, the ship took a steep down angle, which was intuitively alarming for the experienced men in control: generally a downward angle meant you were travelling deeper. But in this case it was just because the forward main ballast tanks were nearly destroyed, and more air was filling the aft tanks, pulling that end of the ship higher.

The captain looked at the console again. They were zooming upward. And the rate was increasing. Once they started moving upward, they had another factor in their favor. The ship became more buoyant at shallower depths. As sea pressure decreased, the ship expanded, making it displace more water, and more buoyant.

"Five hundred feet, sir," said the diving offer.

"Very well," said the captain."

"Four hundred...three hundred...two hundred...one hundred..."

There was a sound as the ship broke through the surface of the ocean, the sound of water breaking against the side of the hull. It crashed back down, then settled out.

"Raising number two periscope," said Kincaid. He quickly spun around. "No close contacts!" he said.

There was a murmur of relief in control.

The captain turned to the XO. "Are you here to tell me what the hell is going on?"

"The navigator is hanging from a pipe in machinery one by his belt. Jabo tells me he did all this."

The captain nodded, tried to digest what the XO had said. "Any reason you can think of we shouldn't ventilate the ship?"

The XO turned to Lieutenant Maple, who was on the phones with Machinery One. "Hot spots?"

"They reported no hot spots while we were on our way up."

The captain turned to Kincaid. "Prepare to ventilate with the low pressure blower—we'll get the diesel up and running when we can, if we can. Who knows what the damage is down there."

"Prepare to ventilate with the low pressure blower, aye sir."

An ET leaned around from the small ESM console behind the conn. "Sir, I have a military freq broadcasting near us. Very near."

"Jesus Christ," said the XO. What next. A military frequency? He immediately thought of the Chinese.

"Bearing?" asked Kincaid, still rotating around on the scope. "I don't see anybody."

"It's loud and clear!" said the ET, his code book in hand. "SUBSUNK!"

"It's us," sighed the captain. "The BST buoys. We're the sunken submarine."

.   .   .

Jabo was still in machinery one when Master Chief Cote showed up holding his Polaroid in one hand and a large knife in the other, something Jabo suspected he'd been taking to sea since Vietnam. He carefully took photos from every angle of the navigator's lifeless body. Then they pulled a stool over from the diesel control panel, and Jabo held it steady as Cote climbed up, and slashed through the belt that held the navigator. The dead man landed on pointed toes, like a gymnast, and then fell straight over on his face with a splash. There was no hurry to get him out of there, and moving the body was a pain in the ass in EABs, but Jabo and the master chief did it anyway, both of them, without saying it, feeling it important to get him out of there. They got two men on the upper side of the ladder to help pull him up, and then wrestled him into the freezer, where they sat him next to the heavy green bag that held Howard, the first man he'd killed.

.   .   .

It took four hours to get all the water off the boat, with both trim pumps and the submersible pumps working in concert, very efficiently at the shallow depth. Wipe down teams went in with bags stuffed with rags afterward, still encumbered by their EABs, wiping up whatever trace of water that remained. As they did so, maneuvering kept close track of electrical grounds, which slowly climbed into the normal range as the ship dried out.

·　　　·　　　·

It took six hours to ventilate the ship to the point where EABs could be removed. When the word was passed, every man pulled his mask off and breathed in the fresh Pacific air that had displaced the smoke, fear, and steam that had filled their ship for so long. The men looked at each other, having not seen each others' faces in many hours. Their eyes met briefly, knowingly. They allowed themselves to acknowledge what they had all just gone through, then looked away, eager to move on, eager to keep busy with the endless activity needed to restore the ship to normal.

·　　　·　　　·

Shortly after EABs were removed, Jabo climbed the ladder in the middle of the control room, ready to shift the watch topside, to the bridge. There had been a lively debate about this in control. The XO thought they should keep the ship buttoned up, keep the watch in control, afraid that if the ship went down again with the bridge open, for any reason, they would not recover. The captain, on the other hand, wanted real human eyes topside as long as they were travelling under their own power, and was confident, after six hours, that the ship was securely on the surface. As was typical in these types of debates...the captain won.

Jabo would be the first on the bridge. He climbed until he could reach the opening ring of the lower hatch, spun it all the way counter-clockwise. Then he climbed another step, so he could push his shoulder against the hatch. A slight difference in pressure had developed between the ship and the world, and it took all of Jabo's considerable strength to move the hatch against it. As it opened a crack, warm air rushed in, as if the giant ship were taking a deep breath.

The interior of the bridge trunk was lit by a single yellow bulb. It smelled good, like the sea, the smell of being close to home, because that was generally the only time the ship was surfaced, at the very beginning and the very end of patrol. He scurried up the next ladder, to the upper hatch. He spun the ring and opened it, revealing a circle of blindingly bright daylight above him. He climbed up a third ladder, toward the light.

As he climbed, something glistening in the dark cavity behind the rungs caught his eye.

He reached through with his damaged, left hand. He felt something slimy against the small bare patch of un-bandaged skin on his palm. He pulled the flashlight off his belt, curious, and looked again.

It was a small octopus, its head about the size of a grapefruit. It legs were writhing, trying to escape in a panic. It had found its way into the bridge trunk somehow, and was stranded when they surfaced. Jesus Christ, thought Jabo, startled, he'd never seen that before. It was a patrol of firsts. He carefully reached through the rungs and grabbed it, palming it like a basketball, and scooped it toward him. He held it against his stomach as he climbed the ladder the rest of the way, feeling its legs beating helplessly against his stomach. The thing was soft but strong, like one big muscle.

He climbed the rest of the way to the bridge. Getting up first was always a moment he savored. Jabo had no problem working in close quarters with minimal privacy for months at a time, it was one of the reasons he was a good submariner. But he always did treasure those first seconds on the bridge, when the OOD and all his responsibility still resided in control while he enjoyed the best view of any man on the submarine, surrounded by fresh air, water, and daylight. He was alone except for the octopus.

"Hello!" said Jabo, looking it over. It was fascinating, he could have stared at it for hours. Another time, he might have sent it below in a bucket, let the crew take a look at it, everybody would find it interesting. On some patrols, it might rank as one of the most interesting things to happen, a legendary episode, the time they caught an octopus and made it their mascot for a few weeks.

Jabo hefted it with his good hand, holding it in front of his face like Yorick's skull. Its eight legs groped around his wrist and arm. Jabo leaned over as far as he could, and then he heaved the animal, shot put style. It landed in the water with a splash. Its legs spread outward like the petals of a flower, perfectly symmetrical, then closed powerfully. It shot forward and down, disappearing into the safety of deep water.

· · ·

Within thirty minutes, they shifted the watch topside, and Jabo was the officer of the deck. He had company, Seaman Connelly as lookout. Connelly had a large bloody bandage on the side of his head, and a swatch of his hair had been ripped off.

"How'd you do that?" said Jabo.

"Not real sure, sir," he said. "After the collision, I guess. The doc saw me after we removed EABs and slapped this bandage on my head." He reached up and brushed it with the tips of his fingers. "How about you?" he pointed at Jabo's hand.

"Hatch slammed on it." He held his hand up.

"Fuck, sir, are those fingers gone?"

"Yep. Two of them."

"Holy shit," said Connelly. He stared at it a moment before putting his binoculars back to his face.

"XO to the bridge," came an amplified announcement from the bridge box at their knees, and moments later they heard quick footsteps on the ladder.

The XO scaled the ladder and was soon standing beside them. He took a look around, especially at the bow. "Can't really see any damage from up here," he said.

"Look at the port bow wave," said Jabo. "You can see it's a little asymmetrical."

The XO peered at the water for a few minutes. "You're right. I can see that." The bow wave on that side of the ship was frothier, compared to the smooth green swell on the starboard side. But other than that, all the ship's damage was invisible, below the surface. "I can't fucking wait to see it in drydock."

"Is that where we are heading?" said Jabo.

"Still sorting everything out. But I'm pretty sure we're not delivering anything to Taiwan." He shot a look back at Connelly to make sure he wasn't paying attention, or at least pretending not to pay attention. "Wouldn't make good TV to make a delivery like that from a broken ship. Know what I mean?"

Jabo felt a pang as the XO said the words: *broken ship*. But that's what they were. "So where are we going?"

"For now, where going to stay up here, within our assigned operating area. I expect a revision soon. Probably to the nearest submarine drydock, which, by my estimate, is Pearl."

Jabo nodded. They were travelling less than eight knots. It would take them two weeks on the surface to get to Pearl.

"But listen," said the XO. "Let's get some immediate priorities set, officer of the deck. We need to feed this crew, and we need to rest this crew."

"Can we feed them now?"

"The chop is working on it. The doc says there are just nine men bad enough he wants to keep them in bed. So we've cleared out bunkroom eight, that's where we're going to put them all. After that, he's going to clear out of Crew's Mess, and the chop says he can have sandwiches and soup ready in an hour. After that, hopefully, we can start getting some guys some sleep. We've already shifted back to a normal watch section, with a few modifications. We'll change the watch in four hours, start cycling guys through."

Jabo nodded. It felt good to be thinking about normal shit: food, sleep, watchbills. He contemplated for a moment which he wanted to do more: eat or sleep. He decided overwhelmingly he'd rather sleep.

"How 'bout you?" said the XO. "How are you, Jabo?"

"I'm good."

The XO reached for his bandaged hand and held it up. "Look at that. What are you missing, two of them? Can't the doc super glue them back on or something?"

Connelly laughed at that and so did Jabo. "I don't know," said Jabo. "The doc's got them somewhere in a bag of ice, says we might be able to re-attach them."

"Make sure he gets you the right ones. I wouldn't want you touching Angi with someone else's fingers."

A scratchy announcement came from the box again. "Officer of the Deck, ESM, we have a military band radar at 045 relative." Connelly swung that way and Jabo raised his glasses. He couldn't see anything yet.

The XO found another set of glasses in the bridge bag and looked in the same direction. "Nothing there yet."

Another voice on the box: "Officer of the Deck, radio, we are being hailed on band nine, can't quite make it out yet, they are very far out. But they are using our NATO call sign."

"Well, at least it's one of ours," said XO.

"And they know who we are?" said Jabo. He was confused. He put down his glasses and the XO was nodding grimly, glasses still raised, waiting to see it.

Radio again: "Sir they've identified themselves: it's a tug from the military sealift command, the USNS *Navajo*."

"The *Navajo*?" said Jabo. "What the fuck is the *Navajo*?"

The XO sighed then finally put down the glasses and looked at his watch. "Our rescuers."

      ·   ·   ·

The captain stayed in control until the watch was shifted and he was absolutely certain the situation was stable. Even then he found it difficult to leave until the XO went up the ladder. He made his way to Bunkroom Eight.

The doc had done an incredible job throughout, just as the captain expected. These old master chief corpsmen were a god-send, and they were getting harder and harder to find, no boat ever wanted to let theirs go. They were like the old klaxon diving alarms, passed from boat to boat, never allowed to retire or go to shore. Guys like Cote, who'd actually patched up Marines under fire in Vietnam....they were all years past their twenty-year point.

Even the ones like Cote who loved it all—the navy couldn't keep them at sea forever.

The bunkroom was quiet. The nine most injured men on the boat all seemed to be sleeping soundly, and the captain wondered if they had all been sedated or were at least doped up on pain killers. Three of the bunks had IV bags suspended from them. Cote was sitting on a small stool in the middle, writing on a clipboard that he was looking at through his tiny reading glass. Something that looked a lot like a fishing tackle box was on the deck at his feet, full of rolls of gauze, tape, and shiny stainless steel scissors. The scene was a portrait of utter competence.

"Doc."

"Captain, hello…" said Cote. He started to get up.

"Don't," said the captain, raising a hand. "But do you have a second to tell me what's going on?"

Cote put down the clipboard and stood up anyway, eager to tell the captain about the status of his most injured men.

"These three are probably the most serious," said Cote, pointing to the forward three racks.

"Who are they?

"Palko has a fractured skull…he's not moving. Rogers and Ferrero have concussions."

Jesus, thought the captain, two a-gangers and the E-div chief.

"How bad?"

"Hard to say," said the master chief. "That's why I want to keep an eye on them. But all three were knocked out, I don't know for how long. The good news is, that's the worst injuries we've got."

There was a pause between them where they both thought the same thing: *except for the bodies in the freezer.*

"What else?" said the captain.

The master chief pointed toward the three outboard bunks. "Here we've got two pretty severe bleeding cuts, that I stitched up, and they should be fine. I just want to keep them still for a while and make sure—since we really don't know how much blood they lost. And the bottom rack there is Frazier with a complex fracture. He got thrown into the ice cream machine at the moment of the collision. Broke his ulna clean through and absolutely destroyed the ice cream maker."

The captain pulled back the curtain with a finger, and Petty Officer Frazier looked back up at him, apparently the only sick man of the nine awake. "Hello Frazier."

"Hello, Captain," he said with a smile and the slightly elongated vowels of a man on heavy pain medication.

"How are you feeling?"

"Pretty good now," he said. "The doc fixed me up with some of the good stuff." He laughed a little as he said it.

The captain looked up at the doc. "How is that holding out? Do we have enough pain medication?"

Cote closed the dark curtain in front of Frazier's rack, and Frazier didn't protest. "I'm being careful with it," said Cote. "For a lot of reasons. We've got tons of aspirin and ibuprofen...we'll never run out of that shit. I'm already low on the more powerful stuff like Vicodin and Percocet. So I'm rationing that out. But the worst ones here..." he pointed discretely at Frazier's rack. "I've got morphine."

"Ok, good," said the captain. "Who else?"

"Over here are the three worst burns," said the master chief. "They're all bandaged up but need to stay still. They are probably done until we pull in and get them to a hospital."

The captain nodded. It was horrible...but better than he'd feared. It didn't look like they would have any more deaths.

"Any others? Any walking wounded around here with an injury bad enough I should know about it?"

"The worst is probably Lieutenant Jabo," he said. "Lost two fingers and went right back to the fire."

"I heard about it," said the captain.

"Captain, I know it's not my place...but if I had any say in it, that young officer should really get some kind of citation for what he did today."

The captain looked at Cote, and for a moment, the difference in their ranks fell away, and they were just the two oldest, most experienced men on the boat, two men with over fifty years at sea between them. And they both knew what the score was.

"Well," said the captain. "That's something you'll probably have to discuss with my replacement."

·   ·   ·

Data about *Alabama* trickled in to Soldato's office, as he sat helplessly behind the desk that he despised, the plaques of the ships he loved on the wall behind him.

First came the word the ship was not sunk, via a transmission of the ship itself, a flash message saying virtually nothing other than that most important facts: the ship had suffered a severe casualty: collision, flooding, and fire, but was now on the surface and apparently moving under her own power. It was a message that raised more questions than it answered, but it was with absolute profound relief that Soldato read it. Not just relief for the ship, and for the men he knew onboard, but profound relief for his country: the United States had not lost a submarine.

Ten minutes later came a follow-on message that set his mood back: three men dead. Two enlisted, one officer. He thought of Angi Jabo at the gate again, and vowed that somehow, if the dead officer was Jabo, he would be the one to tell her. He thought about what it would feel like to drive to her house, ringing that door bell... then forced himself to put that thought away. Telling Angi about her husband's death might very well be the last thing he ever did in a Navy uniform. The message, of course, contained no names, and Soldato would have no way of finding out more details until the ship came in. But he knew that the dead man was probably a junior officer...they were the first to the scene of a casualty. And the best ones, like Jabo, were usually the first ones to get there.

Information of a more banal nature dripped in. Group Nine got involved to handle the press that they would inevitably have to deal with when word got out: only Group Nine had dedicated PR staff, a group of three officers who set up a press "command center" at the Group Nine building. Anything involving the words "nuclear" and "collision" would have to be explained endlessly, and the anti-nuke groups were always ready to pounce on news like this. Thank God he didn't have to screw with that, and he probably never would, since dealing with twenty-five year old journalists was deemed a crucial enough activity that only an Admiral was capable of handling it.

A message came in from *Alabama* with a warning about the collision, an uncharted seamount. Soldato referenced the chart he had in his office. He couldn't find anything on that vast expanse of ocean that the ship might have run into. Group Nine wrote orders for *Alabama* to turn around and go the floating drydock in Pearl, entirely on the surface. Soldato approved the orders and they went to the Group Nine radio room to be transmitted. The Taiwanese wouldn't be getting their nuclear warheads, at least, not from the *Alabama*.

He'd been at his desk for almost eight hours when Commander Bushbaum knocked and stuck his head in the door. "Sir, the *Navajo* is in visual contact with *Alabama*."

Despite the fact that he'd been reading radio transmissions from the boat for hours, that made him feel good, a shot of optimism, the thought that of real human eyes seeing the ship on the ocean. "What do they see?"

Bushbaum shrugged. "Nothing out of the ordinary, but probably most of the damage is below the waterline. These guys are skimmers anyway, not sure they would know what they were looking at if something was wrong."

"True," said the Captain. He wished he was out there, on the bow of the *Navajo*, speeding toward his old boat with salt spray soaking through his uniform.

"The two OODs are communicating with each other on bridge-to-bridge, sounds like the *Alabama* is making about eight knots."

Soldato looked up at that "They're talking on VHF?"

"Yes," said Bushbaum, a little startled by the strength of Soldato's reaction. "They're no longer on alert, and they're using call signs anyway, so it's acceptable."

"Can we hear them?"

"Yes," said Bushbaum. "It's being patched through in Group Nine's radio room….I was just down there."

Soldato stood and darted past Bushbaum, who followed him. They took the drab Navy van in front of the pier up to Group Nine, whose headquarters looked as nondescript as a small insurance agency, or a public library built sometime in the late seventies. Only the prickly array of exotic radio antennas atop the roof gave away the fact that interesting things might occur inside.

Soldato flashed his ID at the guard with Bushbaum right behind him and with an electronic buzz at the inner door they were allowed inside. They descended down a narrow staircase into the part of the building that was reinforced and "survivable," built to withstand a nuclear blast for at least a moment, so they could transmit to the boats of Group Nine the orders to launch their missiles and fight a nuclear war. The space was small, windowless, and packed with electronics. Perhaps not intentionally, it was exceedingly reminiscent of being on a submarine. The duty radioman nodded briefly as the two men entered. Soldato was surprised that he knew him: RM1 Hanson, he'd been a striker onboard *Skipjack*. He was one of those guys you knew would do alright, and he was a natural for the Group Nine billet: a kid confident enough in his abilities that he wouldn't mind admirals and captains constantly looking over his shoulder.

"You've got 731 on bridge-to-bridge?" said Soldato.

"Yes sir," said Hanson. He was wearing a working uniform and sat in front of an actual operational radio console, and it made Soldato's spirits soar again, just to be in the room with someone who was actually accomplishing something, doing real work. "We're not listening to it now, because we have all these priority one messages we're sending back and forth, modifying patrol orders and alerting the other boats…"

"I understand," said Soldato. "But can you patch it in for me? I need to hear it."

"They're really not saying much now, sir," said Hanson. "Once the two OOD's made contact, they didn't have much to say to each other. And we can't talk to them, we're just patched through."

"I understand," said Soldato again.

Hanson shrugged, and looked down at his messages, which were becoming increasingly lengthy and administrative. As a radioman, he liked hearing the scratchy voices of men's voices being carried on the airwaves too…so if the commodore wanted to hear it, who was he to say no?

He stood and leaned toward a controller that was over his main computer monitor, and flipped a toggle switch. Immediately the white noise of static came through a speaker behind them. He adjusted another switch, and the static quieted slightly, replaced by an occasional crackle that told them they were tuned to a radio signal. Soldato turned and found the speaker by his shoulder, turned a knob to raise the volume.

"That's it," said Hansen. "They're not saying anything right now."

They waited, until finally a voice came through.

Sturgeon, this is steelhead, do you copy?

"Sturgeon is *Alabama*," said Hanson. He pointed to the frayed book of NATO call signs on his desk. "Steelhead is the *Navajo*."

After a pause…*Sturgeon, this is steelhead, do you copy?*

Soldato held his breath awaiting a response. Even though he too was eager to hear something from the submarine, he scowled at the impatient tone of the second request from that skimmer officer on *Navajo*: my God, do you know what they've been through? What they must still be combating on their end? Give him a fucking second.

Finally, a response. *Steelhead this is sturgeon, go ahead.* But the sound was garbled, hard to hear, and trailed off.

Sturgeon, this is steelhead, are you changing course?

There was a long pause, and then the officer of the deck of the *Alabama* replied: *Steelhead this is sturgeon, we are turning to port to heading zero-seven-zero, request you stay on station, over.*

This time, the voice of the officer of the deck came in remarkably clear, despite the many miles that separated them. And there was no mistaking in it a mild Tennessee twang.

"Thank you Hanson," said Soldato, turning toward the steps. Bushbaum reflexively turned to follow him, a look of confusion still on his face. "You wait here," said Soldato. "Meet me in the van in ten minutes."

"Aye aye, sir," said Bushbaum, looking a little stung, a hint of reproach behind his eyes. He didn't know what Soldato was doing, but it was something he didn't want his Chief of Staff to hear.

And Soldato didn't give a shit.

He strode out of Group Nine into the van, sat in the passenger seat, and pulled his cell phone from his pocket. He dialed a number that he had stored.

"Hello?" Angi picked up before the first ring was over, her voice weak with worry. He could hear a news station in the background. She was waiting for CNN to tell her what the Navy wouldn't.

"Angi, this is Mario. I can't tell you anything else, but...Danny is fine."

.   .   .

The wounded submarine limped eastward on the surface, crippled but operating under her own power. For a time the Navy had two sea-going tugs standing by, but towing was a humiliation the proud boat was able to avoid.

The XO took over the navigator's duties, and spent almost all his time in Control. While the navigator had been crushed by his responsibilities, the XO was energized. With a sharpened pencil tucked behind his ear, he studied the chart like a general looking for weaknesses in an enemy position. Between fixes and DRs, he updated the charts, coached the JOs on the conn, and told dirty stories about the glory days of Subic Bay and Olongapo.

.   .   .

Jabo was the last one into the Officers' Study, having just left the watch. The captain and Chief Flora were there waiting to begin the qualification board.

As dictated by tradition, Hallorann had supplied the room with snacks and beverages; the coffee pot was full, and a pitcher of coke sat in the middle of the table. A mixing bowl full of Hershey's Kisses was being passed around. Jabo was handed Hallorann's battered yellow qualification book to review for completeness. He flipped through it, saw signatures from the men he knew so well in every blank. He stopped at one page and felt a pang seeing the signature JUONI, TM1, one of their dead.

Hallorann stood at the front, in a neatly pressed poopie suit, dry erase marker in hand. As Jabo took his seat, the captain said, "Ok, chief, why don't you start us off?"

Flora cleared his throat. "Diagram our ship's sonar system."

Jabo fought back a chuckle. It was a very hard question... and Hallorann, when he saw that a nuke chief was on his board, had probably boned up on all the engine room stuff. But if he got through this...

Hallorann paused, and then turned to the board. He drew a crude approximation of the spherical array, and then the towed array. He took a red marker and drew acoustic beams emanating from it. When the drawing was complete, he turned and began to explain it to them.

Jabo's mind wandered as he spoke; he could tell immediately that Hallorann knew the system passably well. Better than that—he seemed to actually understand what he was saying, and wasn't just repeating back by rote something that he'd read. Jabo, and everyone else on the boat, already knew Hallorann was smart. They also knew that he worked his ass off. The only thing he had left to prove during the board was that he could function under pressure. And this, too, was something Jabo already knew, he'd seen Hallorann perform under much greater pressure than this, in the heat of a fire and the cold of nearly freezing ocean water pouring in under such pressure that the noise alone was a hazard.

"Any follow up questions?" said the captain when Hallorann paused. "Lieutenant Jabo?"

"What's the status of the spherical array right now?" said Jabo. Hallorann hesitated. "It's out of commission, sir."

They all chuckled at that. "That's one way to put it," said Jabo.

"Ok," said the captain. "Lieutenant, I believe it's your turn to ask young Hallorann a question."

Jabo paused. He was really pulling for the kid, wanted to ask him something hard enough that it would impress the captain, but not so hard that he would stumble and drop the ball. He thought about all that Hallorann might know, the things he'd learned at sea.

"Hallorann, can you explain how the torpedo room flood control works?"

Hallorann turned, erased the board, and started drawing a line diagram of the system.

.   .   .

Twenty-four hours before Alabama was due to pull in to Pearl Harbor, a tug pulled alongside to make a brief exchange. From the tug came three boxes of critical spare parts, a bright orange bag of mail, and some fresh food that the chop, in a small act of heroism, had somehow managed to requisition: fresh lettuce, tomatoes, apples, oranges, and real milk. The last container of milk was followed by a lieutenant commander in dress whites. Jabo waited for him at the bottom of the forward LET as the XO had requested him to do; he was Lieutenant Commander Carr of the Naval Investigative Service.

"Lieutenant Jabo, sir," he said, feeling sloppy in his poopie suit.

He extended his hand. "Lieutenant Commander Carr. Nice to meet you lieutenant."

Jabo led him to the navigator's stateroom.

He looked it over. Flipped through the copy of *Rig for Dive* that was still on his rack. The messages he'd hidden. Nodded his head thoughtfully. He seemed more down to earth than the few other NIS agents Jabo had met before; he suspected based on his age and that air of confidence that he was prior enlisted. He also suspected that the NIS had probably sent one of their top men to get the initial groundwork done. He was a good listener, barely saying a word as Jabo told the whole story, from the leg stabbing before their departure to seeing the Nav's dead body in Machinery One. He found himself recalling scenes he'd almost forgotten, like the time he'd heard the Nav talking to himself in the Officers' Study. Jabo wondered if he was getting too comfortable, and forced himself to stop.

"Well," said the commander. "I'm just here to do the preliminaries. There's never been a case like this—sabotage on a nuclear submarine. So the final report will be signed by someone several pay grades above me."

"But what do you think?" said Jabo. He found himself wanting answers.

"I think...based on my initial investigation...that you're navigator was fucking nuts."

"And that's it?"

"Lieutenant, you've been in the Navy long enough to know what's coming next. Something this major...there will have to be consequences. Maybe someone could have seen this coming. Maybe there were enough signs..." He jabbed his finger into his leg with a stabbing motion.

There was a rap at the door...the yeoman. Danny wondered how long he'd been standing there. He had a courtier's aptitude for eavesdropping.

"Any outgoing mail, lieutenant?"

Danny shook his head.

"Are you sure? The bag is getting ready to go across and the captain specifically told me to ask you."

Danny thought for a moment, wondering what that could mean. He'd already written a short note to Angi and put it in the bag, but that's nothing the Captain would take an interest in. Then he remembered, the letter that had passed between them on their first day at sea.

"No," he said. "No letter from me."

The yeoman nodded and walked back to his office to seal the outgoing mail bag.

"Lieutenant, let's go take a look at the body," said Carr. "And then maybe you can help me find a cup of coffee."

"Aye sir," said Jabo, backing out of the stateroom.

. . .

Angi flew to Hawaii with a group of the other wives to meet the boat. During their layover in Los Angeles, she bought a newspaper where for the first time, she saw a story about the events onboard the *USS Alabama*: the vaguest possible description of an incident at sea, the Navy's vaguest possible confirmation of fatalities, and a boilerplate description of a ballistic missile submarine. Captain Shields was mentioned by name, his official photograph positioned over a stock photo of a submarine, a Los Angeles class submarine that Angi could tell was misidentified as a Trident. The dead men were not named, but their families had been notified, and Angi thought it probably wouldn't be long before the world knew. While waiting to board in LA, a first: a grandmotherly passenger recognized that she was pregnant, and put her hand on Angi's belly.

During the long flight, Angi read through the rest of the paper, including an article on page four about the cooling off of tensions between Taiwan and China. The prime minister of Taiwan had made some conciliatory remarks toward the mainland leadership, and shortly after the Chinese had made a remarkable apology and agreed to pay damages to the shipping companies and the families of the dead crewmen of *Ever Able*. That article finished with a series of numbers about the staggering importance of China in the world economy.

The *Alabama* was scheduled to go into the floating drydock in the shipyard but would pull in first to the pier at Ford Island, a tiny dot of land in the middle of Pearl Harbor. By the time they got there, the tropical sun was low. The weather was, of course, beautiful. Just off the pier was the twisted, rusty wreckage of the USS *Utah*, sunk on December 7, 1941. Angi was surprised to learn that in addition to the famous *Arizona* memorial, just on the other side of Ford Island, there were uncelebrated reminders of the Japanese sneak attack everywhere in Pearl Harbor. Ford Island, in particular, isolated from the rest of Oahu, seemed frozen in time, as if they might at any moment hear the buzz of descending Japanese Zeros. The place was so fundamentally beautiful, Angi could see how a sneak attack had succeeded. It would be easy to be lulled by a place like this, deceived into a sense that nothing could ever go wrong.

She stood waiting at the small *Utah* memorial with a group of four other wives, including the captain's wife and Cindy Soldato, and read and re-read the plaque a dozen times while they waited:

NEAR THIS SPOT, AT BERTH FOX 11
ON THE MORNING OF 7 DECEMBER 1941,
THE USS UTAH WAS STRUCK ON THE PORTSIDE
WITH WHAT IS BELIEVED TO HAVE BEEN
THREE AERIAL TORPEDOES AND WAS SUNK.
SHE WAS SUBSEQUENTLY ROLLED OVER
TO CLEAR THE CHANNEL BUT WAS
LEFT ON THE BOTTOM.

At first they were the only people there. As a group, they tried to fight off the fear that the ship's plans had been changed, perhaps they were pulling into a different berth, or directly into the drydock. None of them expected the Navy to tell them anything if such a change were ordered.

Within an hour, though, two salty looking bosun's mates arrived on the scene, and began pulling serious looking ropes from a line locker on the pier, a sight that set Angi's heart soaring. One of them had a black radio clipped to his belt, and Angi

listened closely to the crackling communications on it, alert for any mention that would mean anything to her; the name of the ship, Danny's voice, anything of the kind.

She heard a whistle from sea before she saw anything.

"There they are," said Cindy, pointing.

Angi could see them then, a single dot on the horizon that soon grew. She saw that there were tugs on either side of the submarine, their jaunty profiles contrasting with the round, black mysteriousness of the submarine's hull.

A jeep suddenly pulled up behind them on the pier, one captain driving another captain. The driver was Mario Soldato. Angi didn't know the other one, but she thought she might have seen him around base, at some function or another. He wore gold dolphins and a command pin. She presumed he was Shields' relief. Or, perhaps, Soldato's relief. While the *Alabama* had survived catastrophe, Angi knew that many careers would not.

"Can you see them?" said Mario.

Angi nodded and Cindy stepped to her side. They got out of the jeep and walked to the *Utah* memorial with them to get a better view. Both captains, Angi saw, had binoculars.

After taking a look and focusing his, Soldato handed them to Angi. "Take a look?"

She lifted them to her eyes, taking a moment to find the *Alabama* in the view. Danny was on the bridge.

He was serious, but happy, she could see. He was pointing toward them with a massively bandaged hand. She wondered if he'd already spotted them, and recognized her the same way she had instantly recognized him. Without lowering her binoculars, she lifted her left hand and waved.

His smile broadening, he lifted his bandaged hand and waved back.

Angi put the binoculars down. With her free hand, she verified again that in her pocket was the ultrasound photo of their unborn baby girl.

THE END